D0204997

Quiet Ops

Look for other exciting bounty hunter books from

Bob Burton

&

L. J. Martin

Crimson Hit
Bullet Blues

Both available on Amazon
& other fine booksellers

Edited by Ronald K. Clausen

Thanks, Ron

Copyright 2012 Bob Burton & L. J. Martin

Wolfpack Publishing
PMB 414
1001 E. Broadway #2
Missoula, Montana 59825

All rights reserved. No part of this book may be reproduced by any means without the prior written consent of the publisher, other than brief quotes for reviews.

Prologue

I can feel the heat creep up the back of my neck and my jaw's knotting; bad signs as, at best, it usually ends with at least a busted knuckle. At worst the damage is far more serious…but, with luck, to others.

I don't know if it's the three grand Dolce and Gabbana tailored suit, the Patek Philippe gold watch with the lapis face, or the ten dollar shine on the Gucci loafers that seems to attract apian throwbacks whenever I wander into a less-than-sophisticated bar—this one should more correctly be referred to as a red-neck roadhouse—but it happens too often, particularly to a guy who tries to keep a low profile.

The two leather-jacketed ham-handed country boys five empty stools to my right have made a half-dozen smartass remarks, knowing I can overhear them. I'm truly trying to ignore them and have a quiet conversation with Marcus, the Cuban bartender, who's schooling me on a Harley riding customer of his who looks like a Hell's Angel, but only on the weekends. He's one of the new breed of dot-com guys about to knock down a cool billion from an IPO, presuming it flies in this tough market.

Marcus, who's one of the best at his trade, has chastised these two rednecks more than once about popping off, and has just threatened to eighty-six them. They don't seem impressed.

I'm fairly sure these two Neanderthals are just feeling their half dozen or more boilermakers, and wanting a little fun with the city boy in the slick suit, but one never knows what a boy in baggy jeans has in his pocket and caution should never be flung to the wind without good cause.

Marcus continues as the two no-necks get a little louder, "Anyway, my man, about Poindexter,...he's slapping uglies with this nine point five face and bod, with this perfect set of thirty six d's, and she'll take him to the dog pound if he doesn't wise up. I've known this trampster, Ronnell, for twenty years, my mon, since she was six and like an outbreak of crab nits in your mustache, she's bad, bad news. Ronnell has dug more California gold than the forty niners and is already wearing five carets of what looks to be VVS1 or better...you know I hustled diamonds for a while? Anyway, our boy's talking Las Vegas and that so-called preacher in the Elvis suit and sideburns." He smiles knowingly before continuing.

"Now, you want the good news? She's already married to this cat from San Francisco, who's the puppeteer for the whole gig. Barnaby Oldstrum is the guy's name and Barney baby's got a rap sheet longer than a donkey dick and all for hustles from phony driveway treatments to forging grandma's social security checks. He's a nickel and dime act but thinks he's got a mammoth score coming from love struck, hard-body-hypnotized Poindexter.

"I imagine the gig will be Barney stepping up and showing off pictures of them in fragrant dilecto—"

"It's flagantre dilecto," I correct him.

He's unfazed and continues. "...then the marriage license, while she screams 'I thought the divorce went through' and him saying 'I didn't file the papers cause I still love you darlin',' then wanting to be paid off to set her free. It's an old scam." He shines a glass, trying to rub out the calcium streaks, while he prods. "...Is that worth anything, Brad my lad?"

My business is other people's problems, rich people problems, and one of my prime sources to knowing who has problems is barmen. The average bartender hears more problems in a month than most folks hear in a lifetime, some of it addressed face to face to them as patrons cry in their beer, other problems they merely overhear. And many have parabolic mikes for ears. Of course, my favorites are bartenders in the highest class joints in the country, as the high class joints cater to fat wallets, the country club set who can afford my services. Once in a great while I wander into a low class joint, like the one where I perch now on a bar stool with a split in its utilitarian green vinyl with cheap cotton stuffing pushing out the smile. And I've been beckoned to this one by someone who I know is familiar with the clientele fiting my customer profile.

I never, never go into a saloon looking like an escapee from Goldman Sachs, but this time I was on my way home from an appointment at Bacara, the most ostentatious hotel on California's central coast, just north of Santa Barbara, when I got a call from Marcus, formerly a barman at the Biltmore, which is why he had my number.

Marcus knows that the right lead can gain him an easy five franklins and if one pays off with a job, another forty-five. Five grand for passing a little hearsay isn't bad in anyone's bailiwick.

Proving my instincts about not wearing Italian silk into a saloon, the two throwbacks dismount their stools and head our way. They think I'm not paying attention, but I'm tracking them in the fly-spotted back-bar mirror, between the bottles of cheap whiskey.

"Brad, don't fuck up my furniture," Marcus rasps under his breath; like most barmen he can anticipate a rumble just from the vibes in the room.

"Do you really think I want to stretch this suit out of shape, much less get scumbag blood on it?" I say it quietly, keeping the eyes on the reflection of the no-necks who've paused behind me.

"You guys beat a trail," Marcus says, but is ignored.

"Hey, slick," one of them mumbles. Condensation drips from only two words.

"Can I buy you guys a beer?" I ask, purposefully raising my voice from base to tenor to a hint of soprano, imitating the skippy interior designer who's redoing our offices. I'm not turning, still watching them in the mirror. Marcus gives me a curious look. He's yet to see this act.

While I proceed a little like my recreational preference is toe dancing and raise my right hand up and flip it back an forth, "Anything you fellows want, maybe a mixed drink," I offer. Knowing their eyes will follow the flip-flop hand, I slip my left hand under my coat and to the holster on my hip, but don't pull the 9mm…rather the ink-pen-thin tube of mace. Modern science is a wonder and the last thing I want to do is mess the suit, and the second to last is to bust a knuckle, so a hook-em-up bar brawl is out of the question.

"I don't want no fucking beer from this fag fuck, do you, Toby?"

"Don't screw with my customers, Frank," Marcus growls. "I'd hate to eighty-six you guys."

The one he'd called Toby ignores him and reaches by my right shoulder, and hooks a hand over my right wrist, the wrist with the Patek—and I go limp, limp-wristed being expected—letting him turn the wrist so he can see the watch. Normally I don't allow any asshole to lay his hands on me, but I can see these two are way too confident for their own good as they think I'm light in my loafers.

"I'll give you twenty bucks for this phony gold piece of shit," he says.

I've dicked with them enough, as they're way too close for comfort and reach my right hand over my left shoulder and give Toby a quick shot of the mace, center punched in his pock-marked face.

He squeals like a turpentined cat and reels back. Before Frank knows what's happened to his buddy, and is still standing wide-eyed and stupid, I spin on the barstool and give him a shot as well. Wide eyed is not good with mace on it's way.

Mace gives the purveyor plenty of time to act while the subjects of his wrath are trying to get the pain out of eye sockets and airways.

"Goddamn it, Brad," Marcus says, but stays behind the bar and doesn't go for the bat I know he keeps there.   In fact, his tone is bemused.   But not befuddled.   He's thinking of the possibility of fifty Franklins in his future.

I carefully remove the Italian hand-stitched jacket and drape it on a convenient bar stool, then take two steps to where Frank is still on his feet but has both hands covering his eyes; he's now looking and sounding more like a howler monkey than an ape, and he's doing a fancy little Texas two step while he tries to rid himself of the pain-in-a-spray-can.

As much as I'd like to re-decorate his nose, but deciding I have no interest in messing up my gun hand, so like an NFL punter going for sixty yards I bury the Gucci loafer about four inches up into his crotch.   All those years I spent in dojo's are not challenged by this low kick.   As he goes down he drops both hands to grab his gonads, if he can find them as I imagine I've put then back where they were when he was eight before both his balls and voice dropped.   His face is fading to a drab shade of green under eyes now rolled back in the sockets, so, knowing the symptoms, I drop back a couple of steps, hopefully out of projectile vomit range.

Toby is down on one knee, to his credit not crying like a two year old, but he's gasping for breath like he's just finished the Boston Marathon.   The one knee stance leaves him a little vulnerable, so I drive the other loafer—wouldn't do to have it jealous of its mate—deep into his unguarded genitalia.   I'm an ambidextrous nut crusher.   He's not as polite as Frank and is fire-hose barfing boiler makers as he knots into a fetal position.

I walk back over to eye Marcus over the bar. He's shaking his head like the plastic doll on the dashboard of his cherry nineteen fifty-seven red and white Chevy Bel Aire.

Digging my wallet out I drop five Franklins and a Grant on the bar, five hundred fifty smacks. "This joint is not the Biltmore, is it?" I give him a shrug and get a shake of the head in return, then add, "The fifty's for the extra clean up. I'll let you know how the Poindexter thing plays."

"Always a pleasure, my mon. Thanks for sparing the furniture." Marcus is shaking his head, but smiling tightly, as I grab my coat and head out to my Mercedes. Just a presumption, but as I pass the two Harleys parked in front the place, I give the one on my side a shove with the sole of my still shining Gucci, and it goes over, taking the one next to it into a pile of chrome and now scratched orange and yellow flame stripes. A childish act, but I'm feeling a little churlish as the suit could have been soiled or stained with Neanderthal blood, never to be pristine again.

I get only a slight pain of remorse, knowing I could have played it smarter, but I really didn't want the suit to suffer from my reticence. However, I well know that seldom does any act of violence go without repercussions. I sigh deeply, and shake it off.

Now to see if I can make a buck. So far today I'm five hun and fifty in, so it's make up time.

Chapter One

Days seem to alternate between one being the bug or being the windshield.

Today, life is good. My rent is paid, my people are paid, my glass is definitely half full. Now for the coming month. Every month is a new challenge.

My office is on the top of a two story Spanish replica a couple of doors down from Café del Sol, my favorite watering hole on the edge of Montecito. From my veranda, dripping with bougainvillea and lined with hen and chickens, gardenas, and rimmed with flame trees, I can see a patch of the peaceful Pacific, a redundancy, in the distance, and with my Nikon spotting scope watch the sail and power yachts at play as they leave the Santa Barbara harbor and display, some of them disdainfully, for the peons in the twenty million dollar ocean front estates. I'm way out of my class here, but so far none of them have been smart enough to find me out, or if they have, don't care.

The good news is the place comes with four parking spots, and I utilize four vehicles. My Mercedes, good for working high class neighborhoods and clients; a Harley Sportster which fits in lots of places, including small places; a van, with eye-bolt tie-downs for hauling skips in chains to the lock up; and a wheat colored, slightly dented, four door, ten year old Chevy Blazer, an innocuous ride that doesn't stand out yet hides a polished, relieved and balanced new 350 Chevy short block crate engine that is 375 horsepower out of the box, and with the work I've had done, including power injection, is well over 400. Good enough for screaming fast road-work, and a real surprise to anyone who tries to follow when you don't want them to do so. I've pegged it at 155 on a desert straight-away.

Being a little archaic I still employ the use of a landline and answering machine...and a call is waiting. Monique, one of my associates and a junior partner in Quiet Ops, runs our East coast office in West Palm Beach. Unless it's pressing, we don't call each other on our cells as a ring or even a vibration could interrupt business or worse get someone hurt badly, and email seems a little untrustworthy these days with half the population of the Ukraine reading one's communiqués.

I poke up the call, and smile when I hear the voice. "Hey, Bulldog, I'm onto what could be a major conquest. You've probably heard of the Stanton twins, Britney and Bobbie...they've made the 'I'm a slut' gossip rags along with Paris a time or half dozen." She pauses a moment, awaiting a reaction, but when it doesn't come continues. "Well, they've taken a hike with Jo Jo Bling, the rapper. Word around the beach is that he ruffied them, then shot them up...and God knows what else...while they were out and got them hooked on the needle and now, two or three weeks later, they're in residence in his Malibu compound. You know the scumbag as I recall?"

"I know the slimy bastard," I offer.

"On hearing the news I had a long conversation with dad…hundred mil plus, maybe a half bil…Grenwald G. Stanton and he's distraught, needless to say. I told him a quarter mil would guarantee their safe return to Boca Raton, and he's on the verge but wants a conversation with you before he lays down the hundred retainer. Give him a call."

"Can do."

"By the way I had to snitch a cocktail waitresses costume and invade his club to get to the boy…I made fifty bucks in tips in fifteen minutes so I may change career paths."

I don't laugh as she's worth ten times that.

She continues, "His cell numbers are like in a lock box in Fort Knox, but I sprung them."

She gives me G.G.'s personal cell number.

But before I make the call I go to my bank of file cabinets and pull a folder on Mohammad Jamal, who was originally known as Jimmy O. Jefferson. Knickname Jo Jo. That was before he did a tour in Huntsville, got decorated with one-color tats and converted to the seventy virgin reward in the great beyond, then learned to rap. I had a gig that involved one of his bodyguards, so I am fairly up on the boy and what I do know I do not admire. When I worked in Jo Jo's neighborhood I felt like there was a red laser dot constantly dancing from my forehead to my chest and back to between the eyes.

G.G. picks up on the second ring and I introduce myself.

"I hear you're the best, Mr. Bennedict," he says, his voice hopeful.

"I'm diligent, Mr. Stanton, and I normally satisfy my clients."

"I'm not your normal client, Mr. Bennedict. I insist on satisfaction."

"Like I said, Mr. Stanton, I'm diligent."

He pauses for a moment, and his voice hardens to flint. "Would you bet your life on it, Mr. Bennedict? A quarter million is a lot of money."

I've heard this before, and I'm less than impressed, but I wait until the hair on the back of my neck stands down before I answer, and I answer slowly and emphatically. "I do the best I can, Mr. Stanton, and I have the best people on my payroll and as my associates. If that's not good enough for you, I suggest you go elsewhere. I understand you're stressed, so I'll ignore what might be taken as a threat."

There's a long silence before he takes a deep breath then speaks. "I apologize, Mr. Bennedict. I'm very distraught about my daughters...uh...situation...and my wife is catatonic. We must get the girls back home...safely."

"Then I'll ignore that last comment, but Mr. Stanton...."

"Yes, please."

"Okay, so let's start over."

"As I said, Mr. Bennedict, I apologize. Can you get my daughters back?"

"You must know that I've dealt with lot of scumbags, and with these particular scumbags before, although it was with one of Jo Jo's bodyguards not the man himself. And I prevailed in that effort."

"Can you get my daughters back?"

"How old are they?"

"They are twenty-two. Roberta...Bobbie to her friends...is ten minutes older than her sister."

"You understand that taking them against their will is kidnapping, even upon their parent's request? This will have to be a lure operation."

"Lure?"

"Yes, we'll have to lure them away...no force involved."

"I don't care how you do it, Mr. Bennedict. I'll pay your price and have a cashier's check ready this afternoon or tomorrow or the next day... for the hundred thousand retainer, but we want them back."

We talk for a few minutes, making like friendly and bonding a bit more, him asking about my background, me being humble enough not to run past scorecards including those who bought the farm at the hands of Quiet Ops, all very bad people of course, as it might scare him off, and him now trying to impress me with how much he cares for his daughters. Finally I get to the grilling, which I know won't set well with him.

I didn't relate all that Quiet Ops has been involved in, as leaving body bags in your wake doesn't set well with many.

Chapter Two

I can still hear Mrs. Stanton sobbing in the background.

"Mr. Stanton, there are some questions I have to ask if I'm to do this project, questions for both you and your wife."

"Fire away, Mr. Bennedict."

"For both of you, Mr. Stanton. Do you have a speaker phone?"

"I'll bring her over," he says, and I hear the phone slightly click over as he puts his cell on speaker and sits it down somewhere. "Tricia," I hear him call out. Then he's back.

"I understand you have a report that your daughters were drugged and are now being held under duress and the influence of drugs."

"True."

"And I understand your daughters are attractive young women?"

"More than merely attractive. As I'm sure you know, they are New York model beautiful."

"Are you there, Mrs. Stanton?"

"Yes," she says, and I try and judge her tone, and she does sound distraught. "Please, call me Tricia."

"In the future, Mrs. Stanton. Now, is there any other reason, other than their physical beauty, that this rapper could have an interest in your daughters."

"Isn't that enough?" G.G. says.

"How about the money?" his wife, Tricia, offers.

"Money?" I ask.

"Yes, Mr. Bennedict, the money," his wife continues. "The girls each receive twenty five thousand a month from a trust their grandfather set up for them."

"Well," he says, "I guess that could be motivation."

I think, 'yeah, Sherlock', but don't say it. "So, can you cut this flow of money off?"

"No," she says, "it's a trust fund, and went from five thousand a month to twenty five when they turned twenty one, a year and a half ago. We have no control over it. My father was an old fool in that regard."

We're all silent for a moment, then I offer, "I appreciate the fact your daughters may be beautiful, but fifty thousand a month is a lot of motivation."

It's G.G. who now offers, "No matter the motivation, just get the girls back."

"My associate, Monique St. Marmont, and you have spoken. She'll be in touch with you tomorrow sometime and will have a lot more questions regarding the girls and their friends and associates, and whatever else she feels appropriate. You'll give her your help and trust?"

There's silence on the other end.

"Mr. & Mrs. Stanton, I apologize if I sound too strong and pointed, but this is a serious matter and if we're to succeed, for the sake of your daughters, we must have your full and frank cooperation."

"Of course, yes," they both say, then G.G. asks, "Is there a way for us to talk that's more...let's say...confidential?"

"Monique will fill you in on our procedure. Now's not the time to talk about it. Have her check ready if possible as I'd like to get on this ASAP."

"I'll try—" G.G. says, but is interrupted.

"He'll have it by eleven tomorrow," his wife says, her tone demanding.

"Of course," he adds, "I can do that." Then he reverts to tough mode, which he does unconvincingly, "I expect success, Mr. Bennedict."

"We are the best at what we do. If it's in anyone's power, you'll get success. My email is bulldog at quiet ops dot com, please send me an email outlining our agreement. I agree to my firm's best efforts, you agree to the retainer and a total of two hundred fifty thousand upon my delivery to you of your two daughters...alive, I can't guarantee their condition beyond that." I can hear Mrs. Stanton break into sobs in the background.

"I'll have my attorney—"

"Don't do that, Mr. Stanton. I don't want a twenty page email full of whereas's. You write it simply in your own words and send it from your personal email account, then print it, sign it with a witness...your wife is fine...and mail me two signed copies. Presuming it's per our conversation here today, I'll sign and return one. I'll go to work immediately upon receipt of the email. But, Mr. Stanton, keep the emails to the business side of things. Monique will tell you how to contact me with any other details."

With his verbal agreement to proceed we hang up and I dial Monique. Monique's maiden name was Schwartz, and her married name was Goldstein, and when she divorced she took a great grandmother's name, St. Marmont, with the 't' silent, so it's Marmo…and I must admit it works fine with the expatriate Nor'easter set, the Gucci set as they're known by the locals, who fill the multi-million dollar estates of Florida's gold coast.

She answers, "Operations."

I don't bother with the niceties. "We got a deal with Stanton. Good work, Stretch. They expect to hear from you tomorrow morning. Take him a throwaway phone and give him this number…hold on." I go to my desk and retrieve the next throwaway phone among dozens in the drawer, and give her it's number, and she knows that the number I'm giving her is one digit high—2 is actually a 1, etc.—on each I call out. A simple code, but it seems to work. "Pick up the retainer. He says…or should I say his wife insisted, that he has it in hand by eleven A.M. tomorrow. Great work, kid." She's a couple of years older than me at forty-six, but I can't help thinking of her as my little sister. I've nicknamed her Stretch as she's willowy tall, and as she hates to be called Red, even though she's one of those beautiful auburn haired ladies with what's so unusual with a redhead, a smooth blemish-free complexion—she could model for Coppertone in the complexion department and for Victoria's Secret with the rest of the package. We were an item at one time, until she decided she wanted to go in the quiet op biz.

I hated hiring her, as I don't mess my own nest.

"Thanks," she replies to the 'great work.' Her tone is casual but I know she values the compliment.

"Is Cocoa around? He's not on a bender is he?"

"Nope, at least he wasn't this morning. He's on the wagon, or so he says. He was going to Jazzersize."

I can't contain myself with that bit of info, and laugh out loud. "Now, that's got to be a sight to see. Three hundred fifty pounds of Somoan fire dancer...I hope they have concrete floors."

"I'll round him up. You want him?"

"Next flight you can get him on. Tell him not to try to check any weapons. I've got all his favorites here."

"You must think this a serious gig. You want me to come out?"

"Not yet, I want you to work this from your end. I got a feeling we're going to have some trouble getting straight stuff from the Stanton's. I'm getting bad vibes."

"Okay, Bulldog, but I need some adrenalin to cleanse my arteries, so don't leave me out of the action."

"Would I?"

"Do I have to tell you the wood eye joke again?"

"Call me after you work the Stantons over."

"Ten four."

I spend the rest of the afternoon and half the evening letting Google et al do my leg work, learning what I can about Jo Jo and adding an inch of thickness to his file, then going to work on Alvin Poindexter. Al Poindexter is the dot com guy who's fallen for whom Marcus the bartender refers to as a "trampster." However, upon seeing her pics, a few of which find her scantily clad, I can understand the ol' boy's infatuation.

Marcus referred to her as a nine point five, and from first glance I'd say he was not exaggerating, and there are no tens. Between Google, Facebook, Linkedin and Twitter, I find that Poindexter's never been married; is now forty four years old; and may have never had a date that could be called serious, the ones and zeros of computer programming have been his only love.

Poindexter's in way over his head with the twenty four year old blonde bomber with the larcenous, lascivious, licentious husband. But it's the toughest kind of gig in that he'll have to be approached with kid gloves...however, I'm just the kid who knows how, particularly since he's looking for a huge score from an upcoming public offering. And the SEC can be as nosey as a blue tic hound and can sniff out the slightest scandal when dogging an applicant for a public offering.

My crib is the gardener's cottage at the rear of General Tobin S. McClanahan's fifteen acre estate on East Valley Road on the uphill side of Montecito. Tobin retired a five star general in the Air Force and went on to the board of directors of a number of defense contractors, so the fifteen mil he laid out for the place didn't strain his net worth, and even the gardener's pad is far more space than I need. I run the chapparral and sand stone hills behind the estate before returning and doing a few reps with the weights he keeps in one bay of his five car garage, then twenty full out laps in the pool, then hit the shower just as the throwaway cell rings. It must be a few minutes after eight California time and after eleven Florida time.

It's, of course, G.G. Stanton as he's the only human other than Monique to have this number.

"Mr. Stanton," I answer, confident of the caller.

"Are you sure this line is secure?"

"Yes, sir, both of these phones are throwaways." The fact is, I'm not sure any conversation is secure any more, as I have a hunch the military can pick one up from a satellite...if they can see the writing on a golf ball?

Stanton is emphatic, "I want you to kill that son of a bitch."

Chapter Three

I guess I was wrong about scaring Stanton off by telling him how many have bought the farm at the hands of Quiet Ops. He now seems like a guy who'd like to know, I take a deep breath before answering. "Mr. ~~Benedict~~, Quiet Ops is not a murder-for-hire company. We're a legitimate security firm."

"I'll pay you another quarter million if you kill that motherfucker."

"You could sign over half of West Palm Beach to me—"

"A million. I'll pay you a million…total of course."

"You've got the wrong party, Mr. Stanton. I'll have Monique return the retainer to you if you have the impression you were buying something other than the return of your daughters."

"No…no…I want the girls back. We have a deal, but—"

"No buts, Mr. Stanton. I can't hear of this again, understand?"

"Of course—"

"And I can't hear of you hiring someone else for what you propose. I can't have some half-ass Miami hit man getting in our way…understand?"

There's too long a silence before he speaks, and his tone is not convincing. "You have my word, Mr. Bennedict. I'll stay out of it. Now I have to go back to meet with your girl—"

"She's my associate, Mr. Stanton, and a very competent one."

"Of course."

We disconnect.   That was an interesting conversation, to say the least. Had it not been a quarter of a mil deal, and did I not totally understand from whence he comes, I would have broken off all bargains with Stanton then and there...but a quarter mil will pay a lot of bills, and we all have bills, and his anger and outrage is well founded. So I decide to forget it ever happened; I just hope Stanton forgets it. I also have my personal reasons to stay involved.

Pulling on a pair of well worn Levi's, a faded sweat shirt, and my hiking boots, I climb on my Harley Sportster for a quick morning roar down the waterfront.

I go to the office, just to make a quick pass through, running into Lance LeRoy, my illustrious decorator, in pink Polo shirt, chartreuse and pink plaid shorts, and pink Reeboks, who, since he owes me big time for saving his sweet ass from a pair of homophobe Neanderthals one evening, is redecorating my office, free of charge. I worry a little that he just likes to be around the boys. I have had a long talk with him about keeping the decor totally butch, and he's attempting to do so—however it's an uphill battle for Lance. He's already had to remove the old English riding scenes and replace them with Neiman prints of the Olympics, to his great dismay. And I've queered...or is that a Freudian slip...the mauve and yellow carpet and mauve and red coverings for the office chairs and sofas. Even though to my great surprise I kind of liked the way he put the color chips together. Who'd a thought it?

I've had to threaten him with evisceration to make him stop calling me 'darling' so he now calls me 'stud-nutley' which may be some kind of light-in-your-loafers code, but in mixed company I guess it's better than 'darling,' or 'Braddy Boo.'

I leave Lance hanging the new prints and grumbling, in a sweet tone, about my preference for plain colors, then idle into Santa Barbara to have breakfast. Rather than take the freeway, I stick to the beach, then turn up State Street. As usual, Lower State is an eclectic bunch, from street people pushing shopping carts to the trust fund set in three hundred dollar jeans with holes in the knees and even the buttocks—the ladies with a patch of sweet tan butt cheeks or a flash of pink or blue string briefs showing through well placed rips. Some of whom are trying to look like they really are one of the 'people' by driving open topped beat up jeeps, shiny Hummers, or by peddling fat tire bikes while sporting two hundred dollar tennis shoes and three hundred dollar haircuts.

It's *huevos rancheros* at Sergio's, one of my favorite Mexican restaurants in a town with two dozen from which to choose. Two Hispanic couples sit across the room, nice looking girls with overweight boyfriends, working off hangovers with steaming bowls of menudo, topping it with chopped cilantro, chopped onions, and chasing it with sweating ice cold bottles of Bohemia. Two U. C. Santa Barbara coeds are two stools down from my seat at the bar, bell bottom jeans a little incongruous with bikini tops, announcing that they're heading on down to the beach, to flounce and bounce the volley ball, and showing the world the perfect blemish free skin of the pre-twenties—except for the butterfly tats each of them sport, only half showing above the dipping belt line of the jeans. As hard as it is to do, I ignore them, and the fact there are no discernable tan lines.

Eating a casual breakfast, I take my time, as I can't make the next call until after ten.

If there's one thing this particular animal dislikes, it's being awakened before ten, as he's up every night until three or four in the morning.

At exactly ten, I call T-Rex. He answers as always to a pre-noon call.

"What the fuck are you doing calling me at frigging sun up?"

And, of course, he has no idea who it is, and I'm sure cares less.

"Sunup was four or five hours ago. How's your bank account?" I ask.

"After last nights crap game, it's slim and fucking none. What's up?"

"So, five bills a day for who knows how many days might work into your busy schedule?"

"When and where, Bulldog?"

"Meet me at the office at noon, I'm heading to LAX to pick up Cocoa and I'm dropping you off in Malibu on the way for a twenty four hour surveillance...maybe more. Bring a lunch or two, a pound of jerky, and a hydropack of water...and your bag of tricks. This may take a while."

"Why don't I take my own wheels?"

"You know damn well a car parked on the street for two days in that kind of a neighborhood will attract too much attention. We don't want the badges snooping around."

"Okay, okay, just don't leave me hanging. Noon I can make."

T-Rex, Thomas Rex Pollack, is a little guy for this kind of work, a couple of inches short of six feet and only one eighty soaking wet, but as his nickname says, he's a mouth full of canine teeth, and a body primarily sinew...and tough as six pit bulls and with a lousy two percent body fat, but more importantly, there's no back up in him. His one eighty is mostly rock-hard muscle; stainless steel bone; Gila lizard bite; pounding knees, elbows, and knuckles; and pure old country kick-ass mean when the occasion calls for it. If he had a spoon and wanted to be in a bluegrass band he could play the washboard on his abs.

I've seen him walk though the valley of the shadow of death a dozen times, and he's always the meanest son-of-a-bitch in the valley.

So he's good to have on your side.

T-Rex, and myself, Bulldog Bennedict—both former Marine Corps Reconnaissance who served in the same platoon in Desert Storm—are the equal of a half dozen or more of Jo Jo Bling's boys, and should be enough to solve this problem before something even more untoward can happen to the Stanton twins...God willing and the creek don't rise. And, of course, we have ex-Miami Dolphin Tupo Tulasosopo, AKA Cocoa, along for our light work.

The fact is, deep in the black portion of my heart, I hope this one comes to wet work as I hate the thought of some filthy dickhead who'd resort to using ruffies on a couple of young women—no matter how wild and wicked their reputation. I hate the thought of pricks like Jo Jo walking the same earth as decent folks. As far as I'm concerned Jo Jo Bling's lower than snail slime. What I know of Jo Jo, he's more than happy to mess the nest of his own people, as I know his own nephew overdosed. His homeboys move a ton of coke a year and at least half that much of Mexican brown, and most of it to young black boys and girls. He's a rotten son-of-a-bitch who spreads filth among the many who look up to him, idolize him, in fact look upon him as the Malibu messiah. He raps of religion and bringing his people up, then poisons them so they have no chance to rise out of the muck he's shoved their faces into. His success is built on the fact he has his heel on the neck of thousands of young browns and blacks, and a few whites, in L. A.'s South Central, and God knows where else.

I truly hope to stomp Jo Jo's nuts into a grease spot on the Pacific Coast Highway right in front of his multi-million dollar estate, but I know deep in my twisted heart that won't be enough for me. Nothing brings out my wolf like a cowardly self-serving predator who preys on his own, particularly with prayer. I'd really like to put a .44 between his squinty eyes and make a hollow headed Cyclops out of him.

It was all I could do not to take on the second assignment Stanton offered, but I don't kill for pay, I never have and never will. If I kill, and I have had to three times—always in self defense.

I have no compunction about ridding the earth of scumbags who've proven time and time again that the world would be a better place with the worms working their rotting flesh. I hope and pray Jo Jo Bling comes out shooting so whatever Cocoa, T-Rex, and I have to do—hope to do—is legal and final, and Jo Jo finds the hell he's brought to so many right here on God's green earth.

No compunction is a bit strong, as it's always taken me a while to justify taking a life...it comes back to haunt one in dreams and nightmares. Then you've got to wonder, had the other guy won, and I'd become worm food, would he be having nightmares. I doubt it, and reconcile it as I have time and time again. However, when you get past being revolted by the warm permeating stink of blood and guts, it's probably time to become a Buddhist and find a place to meditate.

Ridding the world of Jo Jo would cause me lots of grief, for our confused contemporary society thanks every rotten scumbag is entitled to three hots and a cot, a TV, and a weight room, and my PI's license and Bail Enforcement badge doesn't give license to kill. That kind of twisted thinking is only one of the many reasons California is broke and it's prison system is a production line for recidivists. If this should come down the way I'd really like it to, it would likely be a year of courthouse grief—and cost every dime we make—if we have to shoot our way in and out with the girls...but it might be worth it to rid the world of Jo Jo and his pack.

Now, with that out of my system, I resign myself to doing the job I'm being paid to do. I've got to put the bit in my teeth and charge forward...bring the Stanton twins home safely, and let the law handle Jo Jo Bling if I want to make any dough out of this deal, particularly any dough I get to hold on to. Damn, damn, damn it. But I can lapse into dreamland once in a while.

The bikini top girls are at the register paying at the same time I hit there.

Robby Rodriquez owns the joint, and works the register with his *frejoli* enhanced Hawaiian-shirt-enclosed belly laying on the register shelf, and smiles under his General Zapata mustache when one of them asks me, "You headed down State towards Stern's? We could use a ride."

Two hard-bodies giving me the sweet eye, and I have to be at LAX in a few hours.

Chapter Four

D arlin', I'd love to have you two straddle my ride," I give her my most suggestive grin, "but I'm on a Harley and it just wouldn't be fittin'." There's something about the Levi's and sweatshirt that makes me fall back into the lexicon of my Texas upbringing.

"Well," she says, batting big blues warm enough to melt a glacier, "maybe next time."

"Next time, for sure…if you can handle a sensitive guy like me?"

They giggle, and the bikini tops bounce alluringly as I pocket my change and head out. However, it makes me think of the Stanton girls, and my resolve strengthens.

Now, to drop T-Rex where he can reconnoiter the Jo Jo palace then go on south to gather up Cocoa.

Before T-Rex rolls into the office, I get a call from my friend-informer, Marcus the barman.

"Hey, those two a-hole's you maced were back in the place last night, trying to find out who you are and where you are."

"So, do they know?"

"Not from my lips, but I think they got a good take on your ride from the guy at the station next door. Did you fill up…."

"I did, and I paid with a credit card, so if they've got a brain…warn them off, will you, Marcus. I don't like trouble in my own town."

"I already told them you'd left lots of old boys flat on their backs, but I don't think they were impressed. They gave me a really bad time and know I know more than I'm telling."

"They got names and addresses, and maybe, but I doubt it, jobs?"

"All I know is Frank and Toby. The Frank guy is the tall one, and Toby the smaller smart ass. Sometimes Frank calls Toby Scooter, or maybe Skeeter. I really haven't paid much attention to the dumb fucks."

"No address, no jobs?"

"All I know, my mon."

"Don't sweat it. We'll take it as it comes. If they give you any more guff let me know and I'll find them before they find me and let them know I'm not all grace and mace. Thanks for the heads up."

"My pleasure, my mon."

All I need is a couple of dickheads showing up at General McClanahan's or having to get their butts whipped on the sidewalk in front of Lucky's or Café del Sol. I don't take much work in my hometown just for that reason…it doesn't pay to mess ones own nest and scare the locals.

But I've got a bad feeling about these two as I get the impression their too stupid to let bygones be bygones. They'll take a little more persuading.

It's a little over an hour and a half to Zuma, a Mecca for the sun-bleached beach boys and girls, and another few minutes beyond to the point that's known as Dume. The point consists of a couple of rolling square miles west of the Pacific Coast Highway, an eclectic mix of scattered structures from beach shacks to mansions, and scattered humanity from beach bums to billionaires. Most the beach front and rocky coast frontage, is, of course, of the millionaire or billionaire mansion variety.

Jo Jo Bling's place is among the higher end variety, near the point on the south facing coast.

It's a tough place to recon from the land side; there are no real hills to climb to get a good visual, so it means T-Rex will have to trespass on Jo Jo's property, or on one or both of the two estates flanking. The good news is the point is covered with vegetation. Lot's of green both short and tall, enough so it's made a few landscapers in the area financially independent. The bad? Dogs. It's seldom the owner of a five acre or more estate with a residence full of quality artwork, high end electronics, and mama's furs and jewelry, selects a lhasa apso or toy poodle to guard the joint. Rottweiler's and pit bulls would likely be the choice of the dope dealer set, let's hope the neighbors are more into golden retrievers or Portuguese water dogs, breeds more likely to lick the grandchildren rather than rip their throats out, and at worst bark at an intruder hoping he'll toss a ball or frisbee.

T-Rex has slept since the moment we drove out of my office parking lot. We are in my van, with stick-on signage announcing Joe Jenkin's Plumbing and HVAC, with a smudged out address as to town, and

3564 Main Street as an address...no phone number. Doesn't every town have a Main Street? No one seems disturbed by a plumber cruising his or her neighborhood, and the van and signage has oft times served me well. However if one peered inside, and saw the chains, cuffs and eyebolts rather than valves and fittings and roto rooter equipment, one might become a little more concerned. The van's used to pick up skips while busy at the bail enforcement side of my life, and the chains and eyebolts to keep them secure on the way to lockup.

I wake T-Rex and listen to him grouse as we near our target, but in moments he's filled his coffee cup from my thermos and is attentive. After all, he's the one going to the slammer for at least a night for trespass, while the law tries to figure out who he is and what he's up to, should this go sour.

We cruise the road a half dozen times, as if we're a couple of doofus plumbers looking for an address, when in fact we're looking for the best spot to observe Jo Jo's crib. The interesting thing about homes on the beach, or on harbors, inlets, or keys, is that, even though worth millions, many of them are second homes. The car dealer in Indiana has done well and has a place to escape to where he can watch the boats sail by and forget a thousand complaining customers. We do note a lack of basic common sense in the family to the east of Jo Jo's pad, their mailbox is stuffed full and with my binocs I can see a half dozen papers in the circular drive a hundred fifty yards from the road. They aren't home, and haven't had the good sense to stop the paper and the mail.

I drop T-Rex off while at a slow roll and he disappears into a long line of thick white and pink flowered oleanders. I make a couple of more passes up and down the road, giving him time to get settled in, then shoot him a text on the iPhone.

" A okay," is the message that comes back, so I head for the highway.

Traffic, as usual, is a bitch, but I thread my way through Malibu, Santa Monica, and to LAX. Cocoa knows I'll be circling the parking lots and waiting for his very obvious bulk to present itself at the curb. Six foot six, three hundred fifty pounds, with a billiard-ball-bald head the size of a small watermelon, is hard to lose, even in the LAX herd.

He appears near a rent-a-car pick up area, a place crowded with jostling travelers, his bald pate covered with a stylish pork pie hat. Giving me a wave then an uplifted index finger the size of a corn cob tells me he needs a minute, so I watch patiently and with interest, as he's carrying two oversize bags and working his way to a Hertz bus. I know how my *compadres* travel, and know these black monster bags are not his. His is a small rolling carry-on now stuffed under his arm. He pauses and lets a little old blue haired lady pass to the front of his path, then follows and hands her huge bags to the bus driver.

She digs in a bag and tries to hand him a fiver and he extends both hands, palm out, warding her off. To my surprise she leaps forward and throws her arms around his keg sized neck and almost has to leap off the ground to give him a smack on the cheek. I can see by his expression he's embarrassed, as you can't see Cocoa's Hershey chocolate skin redden. Disconcerted, he walks in front of a limo on his way across the two-lane one way to where I'm parked against the left hand curb and the driver has to slam on his brakes. Mohammed, the chauffeur, shakes a fist at Cocoa, fires off an indistinguishable foreign tirade, and I laugh, knowing Cocoa could probably turn the limo over should he take umbrage. Instead, he tips his porkpie hat at the guy and proceeds in front of the limo to where I await, pops open the sliding door on the side of the van, throws in his rolling carry on, then jumps in the passenger side. The van perceptibly sags when he nestles into the bucket seat, which disappears under his bulk.

"Doing your white knight thing, I see."

"That some kind of a racial slur?" he asks.

I gun it away from the curb, laughing. "Merely an expression, Cocoa, my man. Why didn't you take the five?"

"Nice lady. Scared her to death when I picked up her bags. Black dude four times her size grabs her goods…. Guess I shoulda ask did she need some help. But I could see she did…them bags was big as her."

"You're a nice man, Charley Brown." I dodge a hotel van, then head for Century Boulevard.

"Another racial slur?"

"You on some 'I'm a poor black man' kick. Who the hell are you talking to, sucker?"

Chapter Five

Sorry, honkie." He laughs, then gets serious again. "Some ten dollar cigar skinny wimp a-hole on the plane tried to get my seat, saying I was wrong place, but I had my boarding pass and it was right there...8A...then the little wimp, 'bout your size, complained what was I doin' in only one seat. Said I shoulda had to buy two. He ask the steward guy to set him someplace else. Almose hurt my feelings. Why would a guy chew a cigar when he knows he can't light up?"

"You're here, so I know you didn't do your John Henry and pound his skull down between his shoulders. And don't be calling me a wimp."

"Nope, no pounding, quit doing that stuff...unless it be work, a course."

"Good thinking."

"Who's Charley Brown?"

It took me all the way back to the Pacific Coast Highway to explain to this twenty five year old mountain of a man who Peanuts, Charles Schulz, and the rest of the characters were, and about the deft social commentary of the strip.

Then he asked me who John Henry was, and I had to sing him the part of the song I remembered, which wasn't much, so he declared he'd find it on the Internet. He does make the comment, "Another bad ass black man," and I can't disagree.

Cocoa doesn't talk much, but when he gets on a subject he's worse than a backyard full of four year olds for asking questions. Like a Great Dane worrying a bone, he'll wring everything you know about any subject you bring up, until you beg for relief. And he listens until you run out of info then asks another penetrating question. Consequently, he's a lot smarter than he might appear. I surmise that his mom, who alone raised him and his six brothers, couldn't afford a Sunday paper, or he'd know Peanuts if not John Henry. Just feeding Cocoa, sans brothers, would bust the average household budget.

When we got back to Dume Point I make a swing by Jo Jo's to check on T-Rex. I shoot another text, "whats haps' with the iPhone and get a "Say wha?" right back.

"Any luck."

"Nope."

"Manana," I text, but don't get a return. So we head for Santa Barbara. T-Rex can text as quick as the average high-schooler, faster with one thumb than I am with all ten of mine, and I'll hear from him if things heat up. None the less, I'm scheduled to pick him up tomorrow an hour after sundown, when he'll start to get low on supplies and long on appetite, mostly for a couple of shots of Jack with a Bud chaser, if I know my T-Rex.

As we roll up into the parking lot of my office, I get a text tone from my phone. "Two fox blnds, matching the pics, sun n by pool, undr the ey of one-ton blk lady. Blnds healthy, happy and mucho loaded."

I went right back at him. "Blk woman, yng or old."

"Yng."

I shoot back, "Email me pics of blnds and fat lady."

And get back, "10-4."

As we walk into the building, I ask, "Hey, Cocoa, want to make a move on a chocolate flavored walrus woman? T-Rex says she's mucho delicious." Only a small lie.

"Jus' mo' woman to love," he says. Now I got to figure out how to set that up.

After a few minutes I text T-Rex again. "If blk woman lvs advise."

Just at conventional business closing time, my text tone sounded off again. "Blk woman cked out. Must be paid hlp."

So, when we pick T-Rex up tomorrow, we'll take two vehicles, and Cocoa can tail the black lady and see his handsome bulk can catch her eye. Good thing he likes 'em large. Of course, what would he do with a hundred pounder other than smother her.

Now, to find an all-you-can-eat-buffet so Cocoa doesn't wipe out this month's wages. Sounds like he might have to put on a few pounds to make weight against Jo Jo's babysitter, or whatever she is.

However, I've got one more call to make before I switch off the lights.

"Herbert Handly," he answers.

"Handy man, Bulldog here. I need some help."

"I thought you were calling me Sparks?"

"Okay, Sparks, I need some help. Thought you didn't like Sparks?"

"Didn't know it was a reference to all those ol' world war two radio men. Now I think it's cool."

"They were the closest thing to the computer geeks of their time. You're the twenty first century equivalent of the best of them, my young friend. You wanna grab some chow with Cocoa and I, and get up to speed on a couple of gigs?"

"I just got up. Not up to speed, but out of the sack. Flew in hyperspace all last night. Sushi?"

"God, no. I said Cocoa. He can eat five hundred bucks worth of sushi. Golden West Buffet, out near your place in Goleta."

"Okay, you're on. Twenty minutes."

"May take us a little longer with the traffic. Get us a table."

Sparks is a nineteen year old computer science student at University of California at Santa Barbara, and from what I've seen of his work probably should be teaching most of his courses. He's a prodigy, who's already in the masters program, and probably only hits about twenty percent of his classes, all of which are slam dunks unless they grade on attendance. Most of his time is spent in a dungeon of a second bedroom in his apartment, eyes on a half dozen monitors arrayed around the small room. You'd think his heroes would be Steve Jobs and Gates, however the walls are plastered with Lady Gaga, Christina Agullera, Rihanna, and the Black Eyed Peas.

He's at a table meant for four, as promised, a plate piled high with salad and fruit is already half-demolished. He's a vegetarian, except for the occasional bite of chicken or fish, like many of our misguided university youth.   Who am I to complain, more t-bones for me.

Without bothering with a greeting, he raises his eyes from his plate and fishes a pen out of his pocket protector, poising it over a tablet already in position beside his plate. "What's the gig?"

Cocoa heads for the food line as I fill Sparks in. "All you can get on Grenwald G. Stanton," I have to spell everything for Sparks, as mundane things like spelling are not his long suit, "and his wife and daughters, Britney and Roberta, a.k.a. Bobbie. Then on Jo Jo Bling, rapper, a.k.a. Mohammad Jamal and before that Jimmy Oliver Jefferson."

He's writing away between bites.   "You got that?"

"Got it," he mumbles, mouth full. "I know that cat…don't think much of his music. But I got it."

"Next case, Alvin…Al…Poindexter, dot com soon to be billionaire. Engaged to Ronnell Oldstrom, who's actually the wife, or so I'm told, of Barney Oldstrom. Got all that?"

"No sweat."

Cocoa returns balancing three plates, each six inches high. We're going to be here a while as I know he'll go back at least twice. By the legs, thighs, wings, and breasts piled on one plate like a blowdown of timber in the national forest, I'm sure the kitchen will have all their chicken roasters roaring away to supplement the now vacant spot on the serving table.

Sparks, a pair chicken legs sticking out of one shirt pocket, excuses himself. He's falling off the vegetarian wagon, obviously. There's nothing Sparks likes better than a computer challenge, and he's off to his cavern to start a half dozen computers humming while Lady Gaga makes his ears ring. The Asian lady behind the cashier's desk gives him a dirty look as he passes, and points to a sign "No take out" on the wall. But Alvin ignores her and is gone.

To my great surprise, looking over Cocoa's huge shoulders, I see my old bar buddies, Frank and Toby, each with a plate full of food and each sucking down a beer.

This is not the time nor place to teach them a lesson in respecting their betters, so I shine it.

They're still there when Cocoa finally leans back and discretely belches. "That'll get me to breakfast," he says, and gives me a silly grin. A few hundred years from now some paleontologist will find that pile of bones in an ancient landfill and think he found the midden of a whole tribe of coastal bird eaters. He'll be disappointed when they're proven to be chicken bones and not those of sea gulls, pelicans or pterodactyls.

Cocoa excuses himself to the restroom and I head for the cashier to pay the check. A middle aged lady with dyed red hair the color of a bright copper penny eyes me with watery green peepers over half-glasses as I hand her my American Express.

"The house lost money on your friend there. Don't bring him more than once a month, okay?" She's smiling, but I think, serious.

"He's from Florida, so you're safe."

"Thank, God."

As I'm signing the check, I can see Frank and Toby slide out of their booth. Seems they've spotted me. They stride my way, with purpose.

"If it ain't Benedict, still-a-dick. Hope you're headed out to the parking lot," Frank says with a smirk, from ten feet way.

Toby adds, "And you pull that pussy mace this time, dickhead, we're gonna shove it where the sun don't shine."

I give them a casual smile. "You guys are on my dance card, but not today."

"You got no choice," Frank says. "Outside, or right here, right now."

About that time I see Cocoa exit the hallway containing the bathrooms. He's headed my way, and is behind the two overgrown, overblown, halfwits.

"What's up?" he asks, when he comes even with them.

Chapter Six

Something for another day," I say to Cocoa, whose fists are now balled at his sides, his neck beginning to bulge like a hippo in heat.

Toby and Frank eye Cocoa up and down as their eyes widen, giving way a couple of steps to make sure they're out of Cocoa's reach. It appears he may be the size of both of them together. When Cocoa gets primed for action, he begins to breathe a little like a locomotive building up steam. It's disconcerting, and a little frightening if you're anywhere near whatever track he might rumble along. And his breath count is rising as he assesses the situation.

"Now, what was it you two wanted?" I ask, my casual grin getting toothy.

They spin on a heel and head for the door, and Toby says over his shoulder, "Later, dip shit. You'll be alone one of these days, and only moments away from the emergency room."

"One of us will be," I call out loud enough so they can hear as they push through the door.

"Something I should know about here?" copper hair asks.

"No, ma'am. It's all under control."

"You want to go out the back door?" she asks, giving me a concerned look.

"You're too sweet for words, but they won't be waiting outside. They've already had one lesson, and don't want another, particularly one from my large friend here…although he's probably way too full to be much help."

"Damn well should be," she mumbles.

"Humph," Cocoa manages, expelling some boiler pressure, and we head for the door, exiting just in time to see the two bikes roar by and peel out of the parking lot, but not so quickly that I don't get tag numbers, nor miss Frank's extended middle finger.

I ignore Cocoa's, "Who was those guys?" until I can get to the van and jot their numbers on the small pad I keep in a keeper on the sun visor.

Then I turn to him as he's settling in and making the van ride slightly tilted to the right. "Those guys are just a couple of local hardheads who are dying to have them busted, again."

As we head home to the General's estate and my gardener's shack in the back, I call Sparks and give him one more job, the tag numbers and instructions to get me all he can on the two misfits, Frank and Toby.

General McClanahan is on his back patio, picking a few cymbidiums for his dinning room table, as we wheel the van into the parking pad next to the gardener's cottage where I call home, and looks up, seemingly disturbed. I am normally in my Mercedes when home, which I've left in my office parking lot.

"Oh," he manages as we step out of the van, but he's still eyeing Cocoa with some dismay.

I walk his way and Cocoa rumbles along behind. "General Tobin McClanahan, this is my friend and associate Tupo Tulasosopo, former defensive tackle, Ole Miss, more recently of the Miami Dolphins till his knee went a couple of years ago…friends call him Cocoa."

The general's thin hand is lost in Cocoa's. "Nice to meet you, Cocoa," then he turns to me with a smile. "Cocoa does your light work, I presume?"

"Yes, sir, about like the B 52's did yours. Cocoa will be with me for a couple of days, General. Don't be disturbed if you see him around."

"He'll keep the cougars and bears away. Nice meeting you, young man." He laughs, and goes back to his orchids.

As we walk to the house, Cocoa asks, "Cougars and bears?"

"The place backs up to the national forest, and, yeah, the cougars come on down to dine on a house cat or lap dog once in a while. Bears don't bother much."

"You kiddin'," he says, and I wonder if I've finally found something Cocoa fears.

"No joke."

"There goes my walk. You got a gym close?"

"Not too far, five blocks from the office. You can hit it in the morning, after we take a run on the beach. You don't like cougars and bears?"

"I don't like nothin' hangs in the forest. Hate snakes. Don't like no sharks either. Some really big sharks in Somoa…one ate a big piece of my Uncle Kalepo. Lucky he a big man with some butt to spare."

"And I was gonna teach you to surf."

"Not happening."

I leave Cocoa in front of the TV watching The Simpsons reruns with the hide-a-bed sofa pulled out, fully expecting it to be broken flat in the morning, and retire to the second room in the one bedroom abode, and am asleep in a heartbeat.

Cocoa is still snoring away when I rise with the sun. The shower in my cottage is too small for Cocoa, so after I carefully wake him, from a distance, I suggest he use the gym or the one in my office, which is four feet square, as I often do if I'm going to run on the beach or hit it hard at the gym.

We both pull on work out clothes and take a hanger with our work duds, but the phone rings before we get out the door.

"You up?"

"Up with the birds. What's up, Sparky?"

"Got your files finished. Five hours last night. You owe me two hun fifty."

"Meet me at the office in an hour and a half."

"Roger that," he says. He's taking the Sparks thing to heart.

Almost as soon as I hit the red disconnect, the phone chimes again. The generic chime, an unknown caller.

"Quiet Ops," I answer.

"Mr. Benedict?"

"You got him."

"My name is Poindexter, and I understand you've been inquiring about my private affairs. Is that true?"

Chapter Seven

I'm a little taken aback as I figured I'd have to run Poindexter down to turn him into a client. This could be good...then again....

"I've been informed about some activities of your associates that may be of interest to you, Mr. Poindexter. I have not been snooping into your business...." I wait for a response. Getting none, I continue. "Actually, I planned to get in touch with you tomorrow."

"I have nothing to talk with you about."

"And you know that how?"

"I had a conversation with a bartender...Marcus...whom I understand you are friends with, and he's informed me of your business, if you can call it that. I call it some kind of bottom feeder activity, preying on other's feelings of inadequacy or possibly their indiscretions. I have no indiscretions, Mr. Benedict. Nor do my associates...associate...if that's what you wish to call her. I want nothing to do with that kind of thing. Don't call me."

I don't give him a chance to hang up. "Mr. Poindexter, I understand you're about to undertake an initial public offering?"

He's silent for a moment, then guffaws. Then asks, "And what would you know about such things, Mr. Benedict?"

"Mr. Poindexter, I've worked for some of the larger and more successful companies in the U.S., and abroad, so I have a smattering of knowledge about such things." Again he's silent, so I continue. "I do know that any indications of...of indiscretion, imprudence, impropriety, or even folly on your part will be looked upon with a jaundiced eye, or worse with a dismissive one, by your underwriters...and even your accounting firm. Even if that indiscretion is on the part of someone who conceals that fact from you."

Again, silence, only this time he interrupts me when I start to speak.

"I'll meet with you, Mr. Benedict, but only to dissuade you from interfering further in my affairs."

"I assure you, Mr. Poindexter, I have no intention of interfering in your affairs in any way. So, no, I won't meet with you at my initiation. I've done all I can and you seem to think I have some motive other than to be of service in my capacity as a security consultant. If you decide you want to be assured that you'll have no interference from anyone else in completing your underwriting, which I assume will add many zeros to your personal net worth, then you give me a call. Tomorrow would be good, and then we'll talk more. Good day, Mr. Poindexter." I disconnect without awaiting his reply. There are times when a smattering of rudeness is appropriate.

I seem to have niggled his interest, or more likely concern, as my phone almost immediately rings. And as it had the first time, the call is 'undisclosed caller'. I presume it's Poindexter, so I shine him on. I'm not merely being fickle. If he spends the night wondering what I know, he'll become more and more interested in meeting face to face…and probably less reticent about paying the Quiet Ops fee, which in his case will be substantial. I have to be careful with him as I don't want to seem to be blackmailing the guy. He's in love, and love often overrules, in fact overwhelms, common sense. In my business you often have to be convinced that you're doing the client a good turn as well as providing a service, and keeping him from getting fleeced by this young blonde hussy is a good turn, and may assure him a billion or so from his public offering to boot.

Jogging on the East Beach with Cocoa is like running with an elephant seal, however being in the weight room with him is a little more than merely humbling. Having wrenched a shoulder badly while in Desert Storm, I still have to favor it. Even then I bench press two eighty with a rep of ten…and then Cocoa adds another two twenty and does five reps of ten. That's twenty five thousand pounds he just threw around, even if a little at a time, in case you need help with your math. Funny, he doesn't look that well tuned, but large heavy girthed men hide lots of sinew under that layer of pizza and beer. They have to, merely to carry their own weight. I've seen him pick a two hundred twenty pound guy up over his head and throw him over a Mustang, and not scratch the sunroof.

He's amazingly strong, a little like having a Caterpillar D8 on your team.

Sparks is waiting in the parking lot when we get to the office. And he's got a smile on his face and a two inch thick file under his arm; a good omen.

As we're ascending the stairs, he's overflowing with information. "The guy named Frank is Frank

Havlicek, and he's a pretty bad som'bitch. Just got out a year early from doing a nickel in Tehachapi for assault on a police officer...beat the hell out of the guy. And his buddy, Toby, is all nickel and dime stuff...a couple of DUI's and a petty theft for which he did a couple of months county time. He's been busted a few times for dope but only using, not dealing."

I stop him as he's going to go on for an hour about the guys I'm least interested in. "Hold on, how about Jo Jo the Bling and Poindexter."

"I got a ton of stuff on Jo Jo, including his associates, and they make Frank and Toby look like choir boys. If a guy named Alonzo Bohanson is still his bodyguard, there's a warrant on him for statutory with a fifteen year old, and another for assault, and another for aiding and abetting a felon in an escape from the Pritchess Detention Center at Castaic. His pic and rap sheet is in the file."

We enter my office and gather around my circular claw foot oak table which serves as a conference table. Each of us takes a seat.

Cocoa asks. "You got a Coke. I'm dry."

"In the little fridge under the counter."

He fishes out a can and returns to the table, overflowing one of the four captain's chairs.

"Use a coaster, Tupo."

"My name's Cocoa," he says, giving me as dirty a look as I gave him when he sat his Coke can on my newly finished oak table.

"And Poindexter?" I continue.

"A cool guy. You'd probably think he's a nerd, but he's done some super computer stuff. He did a codec on videos that compressed them exponentially."

"Cool," I say, having no frigging idea what he's talking about. "And his girlfriend."

"Married, twice, with a baby, actually now about three, a girl, that her mom is raising in Oregon,…Redmond the last I have on her. Ronny baby did a month in Portland for soliciting and was arrested in Seattle and released on her own recognizance, and skipped, so there's a warrant on her in Washington…and Sacramento. She also skipped an O.R. in Sac, along with her hubby, Barnaby."

"Perfect," I say, with a smile.

"Perfect?" Sparks asks.

"Perfect. If they skipped there was probably a bond on them, and if there's a bond, I can get a contract and jerk their chain. It's probably too late for the bondsman to recover anything, but if I offer a freebee he'll jump at me jerking their chain and returning them to custody."

"Oh. Anyway, it's all in the file. But that's not the best of it."

He's smiling like the proverbial Cheshire cat.

"So, what's the best of it?"

"Jo Jo hangs with a guy named Jethro Tull; the only white guy in his entourage. And he's got a murder rap back in Detroit. And he's on the state's most wanted list. Seems he snuffed a city councilman who was trying to keep things honest in Motown. Drowned the guy in his own Jacuzzi. Forced a fifth of rum down the guy, then held his head under water. Would have gotten away with it…drunk guy drowns…had it not been for a nosey blue-hair neighbor who liked looking down on the councilman's pad from her second story window. The Detroit cops made the guy easy. How many guys weigh three hundred who have a dragon tattoo from their scapula to the crack in their butt. I did a facial recognition on a guy who was in three different Beverly Hills man-about-town pics with Jo Jo, which is how I got on to him. Looks like Jo Jo has the guy on the payroll as a bodyguard. He's a big guy...not quite as big as Cocoa here...but a really big guy."

"You did good, Sparks." I rise and go to my desk and dig in the credenza behind it and find a See's candy box I use to hide some cash, and dig out three Franklins from a few hun I keep under the chocolate creams, then return and stuff them in Sparks' shirt pocket. "There's a little extra for a good job. I'll read this stuff this afternoon and may have some more questions."

"Cool. Call me after five as I'm going to get some more zees."

"You got it, if I need to."

As Sparks heads out, my text tone goes off on the phone. "Im made. Sht city."

Chapter Eight

L et's go." I yell to Cocoa, grabbing the file Sparks put together, then heading for the closet which has a hidden door that disappears into the paneling next to the credenza behind my desk. Lots of weapons and other folderol line the walls; but I grab the duffle bag, my bug out bag, that I keep at the ready at all times; my wind breaker off a hook; and head for the door with Cocoa on my heels. He has his ditty bag in hand.

"T-Rex?" Cocoa asks as we take the stairs three at a time and head for the van.

"You got it, and it sounds like he may be in trouble."

"I got no weapon," he complains.

"Yes, you do, in my bag is enough for a squad."

He does dig an eight inch switchblade out of the bag and pockets it.

By the time I reach the bottom of the stairs the phone goes off again, this time it's *When The Saints*, it's T-Rex. I poke the answer and can hear shouting on the line, and T-Rex yells, "hey, asshole," then it sounds like the phone hits the pavement. Muffled sounds, then the phone goes dead, as if someone stomped it into splinters. I immediately redial, but get four rings before it goes to answering machine mode. It's off, or out of commission.

I run for the Mercedes, with Cocoa lumbering behind. I have it started and in gear by the time he's able to throw his gear in the back, put the passenger seat back, and squeeze in. I'm peeling out before he gets the door shut.

The first call I make is to Monique, who, luckily, is in the Palm Beach office. I explain what I want, and she goes to work.

We would have had to make this drive to pick T-Rex up from his recon in a couple of hours, but not at the speed I'm traveling, risking a stop by the California Highway Patrol, the CHP. I keep it at 85 mph, which is normally acceptable on a clean clear California freeway, even if the signs say 65, but the stretch between Santa Barbara and Ventura on Highway 101 is busy, and with the California economy in the tank, is rough as hell and badly in need of maintenance and the cops take special notice of speeders as the pot holes and dips can throw and unwary driver off course in a heartbeat. Luckily, it's a clear dry day and with a little providence the CHP boys are cruising the many beaches along the route, enjoying the tans on the surfer girls.

When we make the turn onto Highway 1, the Pacific Coast Highway, the situation is a little different, it narrows to two lanes with an occasional third passing lane after you pass Point Mugu, and the cops are more vigilant. Then when you hit the twenty mile long city of Malibu, it's all eyes out for black and whites of the L. A. County Sheriff's office, who handle police work for Malibu. Luckily, we're before the beaches begin to cool down and clear out and before the Mercedes, Porches,

BMW's, Bentleys, and Rolls Royce's begin to return to their play land in the land of milk and honey: from Beverly Hills, Santa Monica, and Hollywood. So we make good time.

Even flying low it's still almost an hour and fifteen minutes before we make the turn to Point Dume, and the Jo Jo Bling compound.

Cocoa has been reading the file to me as we progress, and I know there's a personal phone for both Jo Jo's cell and house. I request the house number and dial it in while I'm doubling the speed limit on the surface road heading for God knows what.

"Jo Jo, please," I say to the woman who answers.

"This is Chandra. What you want with Jo Jo?"

"This is Brad Benedict. Tell him to get on the line."

"Jo Jo don't just 'get on the line.' You tells me what you want and I tells him…maybe. How you get this number?"

"What I want is an excuse not to blow his ass into next week, tell him that, and make sure you tell him it's Brad Benedict."

I hold until we're only a couple of hundred yards short of the compound.

I can hear some breathing on the line, then finally, "You that asshole what hauled Jimmy John McDoon to the lockup."

"That would be me, Jo Jo. As you know, he's doing a well deserved twenty." He doesn't respond, so I continue, "You got some things of mine."

"Oh, yeah, what's that?"

"An associate of mine, six foot, blonde crew cut, gray eyes, lots of mouth."

"Damn straight he gots lots of mouth. He keep it up we send him south." Jo Jo has a habit of talking in rhymes, one of the few rappers who's able to actually rhyme his lines.

"Jo Jo, you know I'm not a fan so ditch the rhymes. Where's my man? And while we're at it, you might as well hand over the Stanton twins."

"You guy is a burglar man. He lives and he's going to the can."

"He gets hurt and I have you for dessert." That's the best I could do under the circumstances.

"Cut the cheap shit, Benedict. This asshole was taking pics. We had him for a paparazzi, till he pulled a piece, then we lit him up like Christmas lights."

"Was he on your property?" I slide up in front of his gates, the dust swirling around us.

"That you up front?"

"Yeah, it's me. Let us in and we'll talk."

"Fuck off, honky, and die. We swat you like a blue tail fly."

"Enough with the rap crap. I asked you, was he on your property?"

"Don't matter, I say he was and I got ten niggers, one of them my Sunday Baptist church goin' sister, here swear straight like I say."

"Get him out front, and the girls—"

"That what this is all about, big-meat black man shaming you white boys by deep dickin' a couple of you little ho's?"

"No, this is about you using ruffies and needles to get them to follow you into the pile of shit that's your life. Their momma and daddy want them home."

He pauses for a long moment, then I can hear an audible sigh. "I think I open them gates and you can come on up. I got a pitcher of good Cap'n rum and coke here and we can have some sip time and lip time, and you see how these two blonde slits with the pink clits love being with they big daddy Jo Jo."

He no more than finishes saying it and the gates swung open.

"Dig those two Glocks out, Cocoa," I instruct after I disconnect, as I ease forward. I have on my bail enforcement office black windbreaker so I can belt the automatic behind my back without it being seen, not that I think I'll actually get in with it, but Cocoa is still in an Omar the tent maker size tee shirt, loose cut jeans, and ankle high boots.

"Second thought, you grab the stub nose thirty eight in the ankle holster. Strap it on under your sock deep in the boot as you can get it."

The material Sparks dug up on the compound described it as French Mediterranean, however Jo Jo is probably responsible for the paint job, a garish pink which at least almost matches the color of one of the variegated roof tiles. It's obvious he's an *Architectural Digest* aficionado. By the time we roll the hundred yards up to the covered porte-cochere, we're ready to exit the Mercedes. I leave the keys in it and step out just as the massive carved front door opens and two very large goons, one white—who I make immediately—one black, step out, and they are not bashful about the weapons they carry. In fact, the black one motions us forward with an automatic Mac 10.

It takes Cocoa a moment to negotiate his way out of the Mercedes, and as large as the goons are, I notice both their eyes flare a little as they see the man who's brow is deeply furrowed as he glares at them.

"Ain't gonna be no guns at dis party," the black one says, and motions us up against the wall. He hands the Mac 10 to his partner then pats us down, but misses the ankle holster Cocoa wears, he does however find the switchblade, and pockets it. He relieves me of the Glock.

"I want that back," I snarl, but he doesn't seem impressed.

He shrugs, and stuffs it into his belt under a protruding belly.

The white boy, whom I've made as Jethro Tull, with a semi-auto in hand—looks like a 45 ACP—leads and the one with the Mac 10 follows us inside. I'm a little surprised to note that the inside is tastefully done. A couple of Renoirs, or good replicas, grace the entry, along with a John Seward Johnson bronze, a *trompe l'oeil* painted statue; a life-size grizzled old black man sleeping on a park bench with a bottle of wine balanced on his chest and a newspaper, *The New York Times* covering his eyes and the top half of his face. It might be a copy of Johnson's style, but if so, it's a damn good one. On the other hand, it's far from his normal subject matter. Still, I'm impressed.

They lead us through a great room and into a game room with a variety of stuffed heads of African antelopes lining the walls along with a massive cape buffalo. A pool table with carved legs centers the large room. Jo Jo is perched at an eight seat oak bar, clad in a purple velvet running suit over a yellow velour top, smiling as if the canary has perched on the rim of his cat litter box and he's ready to spring.

"Where's my man?" I ask, not returning the smile.

"That burglar man.   We holding him for the pigs."

"So, you've called the cops?"

"Not yet, we wanted him to sweat a while.   But we do our civic duty pretty soon."

"Bring him and the girls and I'll get them out of your hair."

"You rude, dude.   Who this Uncle Tom you draggin' along?"

Cocoa hasn't said a word, but then he seldom does.

"This is my younger brother.   He's a pest control specialist from up in Santa Barbara.   We heard you had a real problem here at your place, so I brought him along to see if he can rid your place of some of these rats and cockroaches, need be."

"This be your brother?   Then there be a nigger in your mama's wood pile."

"Let's cut the bull, Jo Jo, and get my man and the girls out here."

"What I tell you your man had a accident and done slipped and drowned hissef in the bottom of my pool?"

Chapter Nine

Cocoa's steam is rising and he takes a step forward, and the Mac 10 across the room comes up. I give Cocoa my outstretched palm. "He's not that stupid, Cocoa." And then turn back to Jo Jo, who's smiling, showing off a gold front tooth with a half-caret diamond inset, while pouring himself another rum and coke from a tall carved pitcher that might just be Waterford crystal. "You want some of this to drown you sorrows, losing a friend that'a way be a hard load to tote?"

"You asked me 'what if' so I'm obliged to tell you that we'll burn this place down around your ears, with you in it, should my man be drowned, as you say."

Jo Jo guffaws loudly and he slaps his velvet-covered thigh. "You talk strong for a man wif' a auto pistol shoved up twix his lily white ass cheeks. You about to get one of them…what you call them…colonoscopies, and you still talk shit. You got some brass balls, my man."

"Just get him out here. You may not have called the law, but I did while we were outside your gate, and told them there was an officer down. You know they watch and worry about your crib and are looking for any excuse to bust your door down. You'll hear the sirens any minute. Least a half dozen uniforms will soon be at your door."

"You fuckhead," he shouts, and comes to his feet. "I be rippin' off your head and pissin' down your throat!" Then he suddenly calms and turns to his man. "Jet Man," Jo Jo instructs, "Drag his honky ass up here."

"Them girls too?" Jethro asks.

"Stop thinkin'," Jo Jo snaps, "and do what I tell."

The one with the Mac 10 is still in the room, but has stepped back well out of reach. I'd guess he's done some security work before, maybe even trained as a cop.

I'm smiling inside. My earlier call to Monique was to get to the bail bondsman who lost a couple of hundred thousand when Jethro Tull skipped town. You can't bust a skip without a contract from the bondsman, but I'm willing to take a chance on that contract merely being on my iPhone in the form of a Page file, should the opportunity arise. He won't pay a dime for the recovery, unless he can get the court to refund some of his losses, and that's doubtful. However, he'd love to see Jethro Tull pushing weights in the Alger Maximum Correctional Facility in Munising, Michigan. And it will gain me a lot of points with him, and he'll owe me. That's worth something, better than nothing.

"I'll take that rum and coke now, Jo Jo."

"Fuck you. You call the law on me…."

"I didn't. I was bullshitting you so you'd bring my man up. No hard feelings."

To his credit, his frown fades and is replaced by another gleaming diamond studded smile. He turns to Cocoa, "You want a shot, big man?"

"On the twelve steps," he says.

"Good for you, demon rum de downfall of the black man." As he spoke he picked up a paring knife from a small cutting board on the bar and carved a piece off a lime and squeezed it in the drink he was mixing.

"I'm Samoan," Cocoa says, furrowing his brows at Jo Jo.

"Dat make you less black?" Jo Jo asks with challenge in his tone.

"Or more, maybe. More everything when you be Samoan. I show you some day, *pukio*."

"Doubt you get the chance, island nigger. What's a pu..pu...whatever you say?"

Cocoa merely smiles, his teeth white as a new ping pong ball.

T-Rex, in leg restraints—large cable ties around each ankle and strung together with another so he can only take six inch steps—and with his hands bound behind him by more cable ties, is pushed into the room hard enough that he falls heavily and umphs losing half his breath. His eyes are both swelling and one is closed, and he's got a lip that's fat enough that he won't be eating comfortably for a while.

"You okay?" I ask.

"Fucker's tased me," he mumbles. "I had 'em cold till then."

"Yeah, yeah. You on their property?"

"Nope."

"Don't matter," Jo Jo interrupts. "We say you was."

"It's like this, Jo Jo," I say, moving to the side away from the guy who's now sitting in an overstuffed chair across the room, the Mac 10 still cradled in his arm.

"Like what?"

I take a bar stool, and now have Jo Jo between me and the doorway were his man leans, large semi-auto in hand.

I can lie with the best of them when the situation calls for it. "Like I did a GPS search on T-Rex's phone, and he was at least fifty feet on the neighbor's side of the fence, and that's in my phone's memory, so you got nothing on my man."

Cocoa interrupts us. "You got poison ivy 'round here?" he asks. I notice he's been scratching his thighs.

"Hell no," Jo Jo says. "Ain't no poison ivy in California. We got poison oak here." He guffaws again. "You get into the poison oak? Don't be scratcin' your sack or your balls swell up like beachballs." That makes him slap his velvet thighs and howl.

Cocoa's scratching lower and lower on his legs, and I begin to get his play. He ambles toward a pair of French doors leading outside, mumbling, "I got to get outside. Too hot in here," which takes him past the guy in the chair with the Mac 10. The one they'd called Jet Man—for whom I hope I have a contract as he's Jethro Tull—is leaning on the jamb of the doorway leading to the great room, where he'd appeared with T-Rex. He's got a semi-auto pistol, dangerous, but not nearly so ominous as the Mac 10.

Cocoa scratches his way toward the French doors, shaking his ass like he was in Pilates, then stops and madly scratches at the calf just above the snub nose, lifting his pant leg a little as he does so. Jo Jo and his two goons laugh at Cocoa's antics, but the laughing stops suddenly when he jerks the 38, cocking it in the same motion, and jabbing it in the goon's ear who is seated with the Mac 10 in his lap. He manages to get it up, trying to train it on me, but I've worked my way behind Jo Jo.

I snatch up the paring knife, while Jo Jo's attention is on Cocoa, and shove it under Jo Jo's chin, making him lift his eyes to the ceiling and cry out like a cat who'd just had his tail caught under a rocking chair.

The white goon in the doorway pans his semi-auto back and forth from Cocoa to Jo Jo and I, looking confused.

"Tell them both to put the iron on the floor," I instruct Jo Jo, jamming the paring knife a little deeper under his chin to make the point, with the point.

"Do it," he says, his eyes wide as a stallion staring at a hot mare.

Neither of them do so, and Jo Jo commands again, "Damn it, put 'em down!

Cocoa says quietly, "This little 38 ain't much, but her flat nosed dum dums will poke a little hole into you ugly head and come out size of a rugby ball."

The Mac 10 is gently placed on the floor between the goon's splayed legs, and the guy in the doorway bends slowly and puts his semi-auto on the floor.

"You two, come over here and take a seat with Jimmy or Mohammad or Jo Jo or whatever the hell you want to call him."

The seated one eyes the Mac 10, but Cocoa shoves the 38 deeper in his ear and he winces, rises, and moves toward the bar. The one called Jet does the same, tripping over T-Rex still prone on the floor. T-Rex tries to give him a double kick with his cable tied legs, but it's futile as Jethro jumps forward.

I move away from the bar so as not to get between them and Cocoa, then stride over and pick up the Mac 10, and swung it on the three now seated at the bar as I move and kneel to cut T-Rex free. He rises, looking angry as a starving pit bull, as angry as a guy with one closed eye and one blackened and puffed one can, so I lay a heavy hand on his shoulder. "Hang on, we've still got business to do."

"I really, really want to fuck them up." He is tensed and his tattoos are rippling with the bunched muscles beneath.

"Lots of time for that later."

Before I finish the sentence, a heavyset young black woman fills the doorway to the great room. Her eyes widen and she spins on a heel, surprisingly light footed for a very big lady, and disappears even more quickly than she'd appeared.

"Chandra!" Jo Jo yells after her, but she doesn't slow.

"Bring the twins up here," I command Jo Jo.

"I got to get on the phone intercom."

"Do it."

He picks up a phone from the end of the bar and pokes in a couple of numbers and I can hear phones in other parts of the house ringing one long and two shorts.

It rings several times before someone obviously lifts a receiver and it stops.

"Chandra, bring them girls up here." He pauses a moment, then "No, this ain't gonna be no shoot out. Just bring them up then you can go bake some cookies or som'tin."

There is no conversation while we wait. Finally, the very large black lady, who I knew from Spark's work to be Jo Jo's younger sister, appears in the doorway, with a sallow appearing bleary-eyed blonde girl behind peering over her shoulder. The big woman steps aside, and gently urges the girl past.

"You Britney or Bobbie?" I ask, keeping my voice as friendly as possible under the circumstances.

"Britney, who...who are you?"

It was obvious the girl is _{WAS} strung out on something heavy as she is slurring badly.

"I'm a friend of your mom and dad's, and they want you to come with me. Where's your sister?"

"Sister...Bobby you mean?"

"Bobby, I mean. Where is she?"

"Sleeping."

"Sleeping or passed out?"

"I wanna go back down." I presume ~~with~~ _from_ that the house has a basement, and that's where the girls have been staying.

"Please, let's get your sister and I'll get you on a plane back to see your parents. They've been worried sick about you girls."

"I've been meaning to call...or write...or text...or something." She eyes Jo Jo, seemingly having trouble focusing. "Where's my cell, Jo Jo. You promised...."

"She don't want to go wif you," Jo Jo says adamantly.

I growl at him. "She's so screwed up she doesn't know what she wants."

"She a free white woman of legal age, and she don't want to go. Do you Brit, my baby girl?" He's eyeing her threateningly.

Chapter Ten

Her dazed eyes widen a little, then she smiles stupidly. "No, I want to stay with my Jo Jo man." She turns to him, in a dope stupor. "Let's party, Jo Jo?"

"Okay, darlin'. We'll party, soon as these honky motherfuckers and they Uncle Tom get down de road. You ain't welcome here no mo," he says, and smiles widely, flashing the diamond studded gold tooth.

"You need to come with us," I say more adamantly to the girl.

"No way. It…it's gonna be party time with my daddy man, Jo Jo."

"Your real daddy wants you home."

"Tell that stingy mo'fucker to leave us be," Jo Jo says.

With that, I turn to Jo Jo, fearing he's won this round, but there's still something I have to do. "I've got to see the sister and know she's okay."

"Shit got to be it got to be," he says. "Chandra, take this loser down stairs and give Bobbie a poke so he know she be ready to party again soon."

I hand the Mac 10 to T-Rex, and instruct him strongly. "I don't want to have to explain to the cops why we've got a bunch of dead assholes scattered around," then I turn to Jo Jo, "Don't irritate him, he's got a short fuse and if he blows it'll be all over the room."

Jo Jo merely shrugs, and I nod to Chandra. "Let's go give Bobbie a prod and make sure she's still at the party."

She leads me through the great room, into a hall, to the end of it and down a flight of stairs. I'm madly making mental notes of the layout of the place. We pass a couple of closed doors which I push open, then she pushes into a third. It's a decent room with a private bath, and three four foot wide windows no more than a foot high at ceiling level, probably just above ground level outside. Bobbie is sleeping on a queen size bed, the covers askew, her nicely tanned body exposed to whomever. It's damn near flawless, except for a two inch pink flamingo tattoo on her otherwise perfect left butt cheek, and except for the fresh tracks on her arms. I roll her over and she moans lowly, and half-opens her eyes. I can't help but notice that this girl, who was so perfectly groomed in the many pics I've studied, needs a shave in a most personal place. A five-day bush is returning, proving, however, that the twins are natural blondes.

"Bobbie, I'm here to take you home."

"Home," she mutters. "Okay."

I pull her to her feet and Chandra reaches inside the bathroom door and comes out with a terry cloth robe, which we get on the girl and get the belt tied. She stumbles along, me guiding her, until we reach the door to the game room.

Jo Jo is on his feet and commands Britney, "Tell her she ain't going."

Britney crosses the room and lifts her sister's chin. "Hey, Bob'o, you and I are staying with Jo Jo. This guy works for the ogre, and we are not going back there."

Bobbie lifts blurry eyes to me. "We not…we are not…going back there. Brit says…. So le…let me go back to sleep."

I let her ease to the floor. As I told her father, I can't take them against their will.

"This isn't over, Jo Jo," I say in my most ominous tone, but he's not impressed and gives it right back to me.

"Damn straight it ain't over. I may jus' call the man and tell him you done broke into my crib and banderished a firearm and assaulted my friends."

"It's brandished, you dumb butt-fuck." I'm letting my disgust get the best of me, which I seldom do, so I turn my attention to the problem at hand. "Chandra and Jethro here are going to walk us out to the car."

"Fuck you," the big man known as Jethro says, but before he can get it all the way out, Jo Jo is agreeing.

"Do it, Jet Man. Let's get these assholes down de road so's we can go back to livin' large." He gives me a winner's condescending laugh.

Cocoa and Chandra lead the way, I follow with Jethro by my side, and T-Rex brings up the rear, with the Mac 10 sweeping our six.

I can't help but smile as Cocoa is talking sweet nothings, or so it seems, to the girl, and she's actually seeming to blush. Chubby girls—I'm being kind here—are particularly cute when they play coy.

When we get to the car, I command, "Cocoa, ride in the back with Tull—"

"Bull shit, I ain't going…"

I give him my most winning smile. "Oh, yeah, you're going, big man. We'll let you out at the highway, just up the road. We need some insurance."

"Bull shit," Jethro says, then adds, "How'd you know my last name?"

"No bull about it," I say, and ad, "Jo Jo told me. Why, you embarrassed about it?" And shove him, hard, toward the rear passenger side door. He balks, so I drop and give him a hard karate kick to the back of his knee, and he folds and leans up against the door, both knees on the blacktop driveway. "The next shot is to the ribs, big man, and I can break a four by four with that kick, at least three ribs will go unless you get in and set quiet."

"Asshole," he mumbles, but struggles to his feet, opens the door, and slides in.

"See you, mama," Cocoa says, giving a wave to the girl, who looks coy and batts her big browns at him. He circles around the back of the Mercedes and wiggles his way into the driver's side rear seat, next to Jethro. T-Rex waits until I get behind the wheel and get it fired up, watching the other goon who's now in the doorway, hands on hips, no weapons in sight. They won't start anything with Jo Jo's sister in the line of fire. I gun it, spinning the wheels, and in seconds we're down the road heading for the Pacific Coast Highway. I pull into a motel driveway, just before we reach the highway, and tell Jethro to climb out and kneel down, again on both knees.

"What the fuck," he mumbles.

"Just do it," I command. "You're a dangerous man, I don't want you delaying us." I play on the asshole's ego.

Both T-Rex and Cocoa follow. I dig into the compartment between the seats and come up with a set of cuffs and hand them to T-Rex through the passenger side window. "Hook him up."

"Bullshit," Jethro complains more loudly, but puts his wrists behind him, thinking he's going to be set free, even though he's being cuffed.

It takes both T-Rex and Cocoa to get the big man back to his feet.

"Now, put him back in the car," I say, and Jethro looks surprised, then tries to bolt. T-Rex sinks a right deep into Jethro's gut and the big man folds, then again goes to his knees, only to catch the right knee of T-Rex coming up, which spreads Jethro's nose over his face.

"Damn it, Rex, now he's gonna bleed over over my car."

There's a McDonald's sack among the floatsum and jetsum along the road, and T-Rex gathers it up, recovers a paper napkin, and with a smile on his face rolls a couple of tubes and not-so-gently, shoves them into Jethro's nostrils, then he and Cocoa get him back on his feet and again shove him in the back seat, hands cuffed behind his large girth.

That done, I dig out my cell phone and check to see I've got a Page file from Monique, and I do. I don't have time to open it, and can only hope it's an agreement from Jethro's bondsman so my actions here are legal. But I'm not going to prove it up until I get back to my office where another copy should be in my fax.

What a day, no dollars earned, lots of trouble stirred up, and the day's not over. At least we know where the girls are, and that they're alive.

I'm not a mile down the road before my phone rings again, unknown caller.

"Quiet Ops," I answer.

It's Marcus, the bartender. "Hey, those two assholes broke up the bar and that's not the worst of it, they broke my arm."

"Christ, Marcus, I'm sorry."

"I had to tell them."

"Tell them what?" I ask, alarmed. I'm hoping he didn't tell them where my office is located.

"Where you live."

Chapter Eleven

W hat!" I'm shocked, as I had no idea Marcus knows where I live. I don't advertise it around the Santa Barbara bar scene.

"That little blonde with the butterfly tattoo on her boob, Kitty something. You took her home a couple of months ago. She was braggin' to the whole bar about being at the general's mansion."

I normally take women to my office, which has a bathroom, shower, and pullout—all the required facilities—but I guess the little blonde needed impressing, and just driving up the colonel's driveway a quarter mile is enough to impress a diva, much less a little dream of a real estate lady.

"Jesus J. Christ, Marcus, couldn't you have lied." I gun the Mercedes as it looks like it's going to be as quick a ride home as it was coming. And me with a skip in the car and one I have no idea is or is not a legal bust. I could be the one ending up with three hots and a cot. If the file on my phone is not a contract, a citizen's arrest would be my only grounds, and those grounds are as shaky as one of California's regularly scheduled earthquakes.

"I did lie, Bradley buddy, and I'm good at it, until they threatened to break my other arm and damn

near did.   I'm at the emergency at Cottage
Hospital…they may be headed your way, my mon."

"You got insurance?" I ask, fearing I may be
morally obligated for a several thousand dollar doctor
bill, as the whole thing sort of comes back on me.

"Damn right I do.   Good insurance, but I'm
gonna be off work a while."

"Okay, we'll work something out.   I got to call
the General.   I'll be in touch."

I ring off and immediately find General Tobin S.
McClanahan's number.

He answers, and I'm hoping it's from Birnam
Wood, his country club where he spends a good part of
each day.   "General, you playing golf?"   I'm hoping
against hope.

"Nope, messing with my orchids."

"This is important, listen closely.   I have a
couple of guys who are looking for big trouble and they
may be heading for the cottage."

"How big, this trouble?"

"Pretty big.   You don't want to be there when
they arrive.   Call the sheriff and ask them to send a
car—"

"I've got a nice 12 gauge that has never been
fired.   I've been looking for an excuse to try it out on
something.   Varmints will do just fine."

"Please don't do that, general.   I'll take you bird
hunting first chance I get.   These guys are bad news and
I don't want to bring you trouble."

"Brad, when I rented you the place I knew what
your business consisted off, and it amuses me.   I don't
get much excitement anymore—"

"Please, general, for my sake. Call the sheriff and request a car. I'm still an hour away down the coast or I'd handle this. Please."

"Oh, okay. Damn, you ruin all my fun."

"You promise?"

"Brad, when the general says he'll do something—"

"Thank you, sir."

"Ten four, get off the line so I can do what I say I'm going to do."

"Yes, sir," I say, and hit the disconnect.

"Where the hell you taking me?" Jethro asks. His tone a little apprehensive, like he thinks we may make a stop to deep six him in the Pacific.

"You're on your way back to Detroit, my man. Seems you missed an appointment with the judge."

"Oh, shit. You one of them bounty hunters?"

"Renowned, here and abroad," I say, some amusement in my voice, but it fades quickly as I have to get to the cottage and make sure the general has kept his word, although I think it would take an act of war to make him break it.

"Fuck, fuck, fuck...." Jethro is mumbling. I hear a thump and glance into the rear view mirror to see that Cocoa has given him a very stiff elbow, and Jethro's eyes are bulging a little.

"You watch your language, Mr. Tull. I am a Congregational Christian from the beautiful Islands of Samoa, and I don't like that kind of talk," Cocoa says, quietly but with authority.

Come to think of it, I swear very little, only in the most stressful of times, and I don't think I've ever heard Cocoa swear…now T-Rex is another thing altogether.

I'm going straight to my cottage as I have to protect both it and the general. However, I hate to do anything other than deliver Jethro directly to the Santa Barbara Sheriff's Department and get him processed. Having a skip or perp in the car when you're on other business, and getting him hurt or worse could come back to cost a lot of money. California juries don't seem to take into consideration that the guy may be a child rapist, ~~and~~ you're responsible for the injury of someone in your protection no matter his crime; and a guy unable to defend himself because he's hooked up with your cuffs is unable due to your action.

Part of the game, under the pressing circumstances.

Chapter Twelve

Again I get an unknown caller ring. "Quiet Ops."
"Let's meet." It's Poindexter, the lovelorn hopeful Internet billionaire.

"Glad you called, but I'm in the middle of something that's imperative. I'll call back when it's over."

"You know, Benedict, I think you're not just a bene dick but a real dick. I don't know why I even called."

"And that's your call, Mr. Poindexter. But if I was working for you, you'd want me to pay attention to my assignment...and that's what I'm doing right now. Do you want me to call back or not?"

"Yeah, yeah, but you don't have my number."

"Mr. Poindexter, information, among many other things, is my business. I not only have your cell number, I have the unlisted numbers of your home, your home in Tahoe, and your home in San Carlos, Mexico. Do you want me to call back?" I'm glad I glanced at the work Sparks delivered.

"Yeah," he says, and disconnects.

I'm immediately both worried and relieved to get a glance of a sheriff's cruiser with the lights flashing as I wind up the driveway and approach the general's house.

Then laugh as I see Frank Havlicek and Toby O'Brien, wrists hooked up, looking very disgusted, on their knees in the driveway. A surprisingly fine looking blonde sheriff's deputy, uniform barely able to hide her feminine curves, stands behind them, legs splayed and arms crossed, in Doberman Pincer mode, while a male officer talks to the ~~colonel~~ *General.*

I had Cocoa read the file on Havlicek and O'Brien to me on the drive down, and my attitude toward the boys has changed somewhat.

I park far enough back from them so they can't see into the Mercedes, and instruct T-Rex and Cocoa to watch over Tull while I talk with the entourage in the driveway.

As I approach, the general makes an introduction.

"This is Brad Benedict, who's my tenant. Brad, this is Sergeant Fredrickson and that's Officer Petrovich."

I shake hands with the Sergeant, then move a few steps, circling Frank and Toby, and extend a hand to Officer Petrovich, who's got emerald green eyes that must be contacts. If not, I'm in love...hell, even if they're fake, I'm in love. "Hi, I'm Brad."

"Petrovich," she says, and I'm a little disappointed I don't get a first name.

"You got a first name, officer...just for my records?"

"Oh, sure. It's Annie, Annie Petrovich."

I nod and return to the ~~colonel.~~ *General.*
"Fuckhead," Frank says as I pass.
"Watch your mouth," Annie says with a tone that would curdle a guy's gonads.

"You're looking good, Frank," I say as I pass, then ignore him.

"So, did they make any real trouble?" I ask Fredrickson.

"The general here watched them kick in the door."

I glance over and see my door standing open, and the jamb torn away. "Bad boys. Sorry I wasn't here."

"I'm not," the general says, a sly smile on his face. "You should know I was keeping my word and leaving, but they arrived before I could escape." His smile is a little mischeivious.

I return the smile, only mines a bit tighter. "You didn't move too quickly, I suppose?"

"I'm getting older, Brad. Not as quick as I once was."

The Sergeant speaks up. "The general here had them on their knees, coming to Jesus when we arrived…with that twelve gauge over there."

I glance over to see a beautiful double with engraved gold on the receiver, leaning up against the orchid hothouse doorjamb.

I give the General an evil eye and shake my head.

He puffs up. I guess he's not used to getting an evil eye. "They kicked the damn door in, Brad. They're lucky I didn't blow their balls off."

"So, you gonna charge them with something?" I ask Fredrickson.

"That's up to the general."

The General eyes me. "What do you want to do, Brad?"

"Let me have a chat with them. We're they armed?"

"There was a 38 police special under the seat of their car. They each had a fist load. The tall one had brass knuckles, the short one a roll of quarters. Looks like they were planning to kick the hell out of someone, you I guess since it's your place...but like I say, the pistol was in the car under the seat."

"The fact is I kicked the hell out of both of them a few days ago. Not good enough, I guess." I nod and walk over and eye each of them in turn. "Fellas, you are way out of your league here. You can go to jail for malicious mischief or maybe even B & E, or I can assure the officer and the general that you are through trying to avenge your ass kicking—"

Frank snarls, "Ass kicking hell, you maced us."

"Whatever. It was you on the ground then, and it's you on the ground now. So, how do you want to play it? I'd suggest you do a couple of things."

"What's that?" Toby asks.

"First, I'd apologize to the general, and these officers." I glance up and see Officer Annie looking a little irritated. She's not approving. I continue, "Then I'd pay for the damage to the door. Then I'd haul ass to Cottage Hospital and apologize to Marcus and make arrangement to pay his bill, and pick up his tab for the six weeks he'll be mending."

"Marcus..." Frank mutters. "You know about Marcus."

I ignore him. "And then I'd look me right in the eye and assure me that I'll never see your dumb asses again. So, what's it going to be?"

Toby turns to the taller man, speaking low enough that the officers can't hear. "Frank, I told you this was a piss poor idea. You only been off parole for two months. They'll shove it up your butt and mine cause I'm hanging with you. Get to eatin' crow."

"Yeah," Frank says. "Okay, okay. Can I get up?"

"Officer?" I turn and ask Annie, who's across the driveway.

She walks over and grabs one of his arms and I grab the other. Frank turns to her first. "I'm sorry, I shouldn't have caused trouble."

Annie is not smiling. "If I had my way you'd be getting hosed down and de-liced in the lock up."

Frank walks on over to the general and Sergeant Fredrickson. "Hey, I apologize for causing trouble. You really a general?" he asks.

"Yes, and it's hey, sir, to you."

"Yes, sir. What branch, sir?"

"Air Force."

"I was an airman, mostly at Beale up north, but did a tour in Desert Storm."

"I rotated through Beale, but was at the Pentagon during both Iraq engagements," the general says, and eyes Frank a little more carefully, then adds, "Glad I didn't have to ventilate your hide, airman."

"Me too." Frank turns to Fredrickson. "And to you also, Sarge. Sorry about the trouble."

"Next time, you'll be scrubbing toilets in the county lockup in a heartbeat, for at least a few months of heartbeats, understand?"

"Yes, sir."

Officer Annie had helped Toby to his feet and he followed suit. She unhooks them, and they stand rubbing their wrists.

I step in front of them before they head for their old truck. "Your gonna check with my office and see what you owe for the door, and pay the general, via me, the same day. Right?"

"Right," they both repeat.

"And now you're headed for Cottage to check in on Marcus, right?"

Again, in unison, "Right."

And they are gone, driving away in an old Ford pickup.

"I hope you did the right thing," Fredrickson says, shaking his head.

"I have some background on those guys. Frank Havlicek has a bronze star from action in Iraq, and an honorable discharge. He's drawing disability. He did six months in the hospital for CSR."

"What's CSR?" Officer Annie asks.

"Combat Stress Reaction…used to be called battle fatigue. That buys him lots of points from me. Now if he'll just stay out of my way. Some Pakistani in L.A. gave him some crap and he flipped out and put the guy in the hospital with some busted facial bones. He did a nickel in Tehachapi for assault, so I'll watch him." I don't bother to mention the Pakistani was a police officer, and that Havlicek threw the cop's gun though the windshield of another approaching patrol car.

"I'm going back to my orchids," the general says.

"And we're going back on patrol," Fredrickson says.

"You did the right thing, Brad," the general says as he's walking away.

Fredrickson waves over his shoulder as he heads for his cruiser.

Officer Annie starts away to join Fredrickson, and I can't help but note that her ass is as superior as her eyes.

"Hey, Officer Annie," I call, stopping her.

Chapter Thirteen

Y es," she says, pausing and turning to mesmerize me again with those emeralds.

"You like Mexican food?"

"Doesn't everybody," she says.

"I'll be at Café del Sol after work. I'm buying."

"I go there a lot. Haven't seen you there. Not that I'd notice." It's a smart ass remark, but not so when accompanied by a coy smile.

"You will tonight," I hope my tone is not too hopeful. One doesn't want to seem over eager.

"If I see you, I see you. And by the way, even on my deputy's salary I can buy my own tacos and beans." She, too, waves over her shoulder as she walks to the car, where Fredrickson is patiently waiting.

I guess I should have suggested The Stonehouse Restaurant at San Ysidro Ranch, where John and Jackie Kennedy celebrated their honeymoon; maybe she's a five star diner as well as being a five star looker. And maybe I can't afford her. Only in Santa Barbara or Montecito would a sheriff's deputy be a five star diner. She's probably a trust fund baby playing at being a cop. Then again, she's got a hint of a southern accent. It may be that she's country solid.

We stop by the office so I can check my fax. Thank God, my agreement from Jefferson Bail Bonds in Detroit is in the basket. The remuneration part says ten dollars and other good and valuable consideration, so it's a valid contract. I laugh, a little sardonically, as the day hasn't been a total bust.

I look for Officer Annie while I'm delivering up Jethro Tull to the sheriff's department, and filling out a ream of forms…but no such luck.

It's late suppertime by the time I finish, so we head for the Café del Sol, two doors from my office. I don't give T-Rex and Cocoa any choice, as it's my favorite place, and it might just be Officer Annie's should she have any interest in you-know-who. Why any intelligent man would choose to chase a woman who carries a sixteen shot nine millimeter, a sap, and mace, is far beyond common sense, but sometimes the little head rules.

They go on in while I spend an hour on the phone with Mr. and Mrs. G. G. Stanton, and Mr. Stanton is not happy. In fact, he's screaming about half the time while I'm trying to make him understand the problem. He goes through every thing from threatening to sue for the return of the advance to hiring a bunch of gangbangers from Miami to come and "do the job right" to quote him. I keep talking sense to Mrs. Stanton and finally get him calmed down, at least to a low roar. I promise to call again after we make another run at them, which I hope to do tomorrow.

As it's Friday night, the place is rockin' and rollin' and full of folks looking for good food and fun.

T-Rex, puffed up and black and blue, gets more than his share of stares, and he one-eyes them right back as he has one eye still tightly swollen shut. We manage to find three stools at the bar, and when T-Rex asks a guy to move over so the stools can be together, the guy wisely is polite enough to do so. Rex's patience is a little on the thin side. He doesn't like looking like the victim of a train wreck, and is eager to return the favor to just about anybody.

Aleandro, the bartender, gives him a smile and asks, "You a friend of Brad's, I see. You guys try and arrest the Ram's defensive squad, or what?"

"Nope," I say, "just a normal day's sparring match at the gym. Rex here drops his left and it leaves him open."

"Fat frickin' chance," T-Rex growls, and Aleandro slips away to pour his order, a shot of Cuervo Gold with a Dos Equis back, and Cocoa's tall Coke with a squeeze. I settle for a Jack Daniels and water, figuring on having a beer with my supper. Two's normally my limit, even when within walking distance to the office.

There's a group outside on the patio, and as a cool ocean breeze is beginning to come in over the Andree Clark Bird Refuge, they are filtering inside, filling the place even more. And what do you know, Officer Annie is with a half dozen folks, a couple of others I recognize as Santa Barbara County Sheriff detectives. John Espinoza is an old friend and Harold Laukenbach is something just more than an acquaintance. John was in the Corps and involved in Desert Storm at the same time as T-Rex and I.

Officer Annie looked great in her uniform, but nothing compared to the tight white slacks and blue knit fitted top she now sports. Curves, in all the right places.

I catch her eye and she wanders over as the others head to the back and gather around a couple of tables they pull together.

"Mr. Benedict the bounty hunter," she says even before I have a chance to say hi, "have I been hearing some stories about you. You didn't mention that the guy in the car was a skip from Detroit...and a really bad boy, or so the scuttlebutt was."

"All stories about me originating from County Detectives are bald face lies, I'm sure. Whatever it was, I didn't do it. However, the guy in the car was and is a bad boy. Hope you all keep a tight rein on him." I rise and offer her my seat. "By the way, officer, you look dynamite in civics."

"Thanks. But no, thanks. I promised to have something to eat with the gang. And our jail is pretty damn tight. I imagine we can hold on to him until he gets transferred out."

Cocoa and T-Rex are staring at Office Annie, probably awaiting a proper introduction, but I'm way to busy trying to get more than just passing attention from the lady.

"Great," I say, with my most charming smile. "Hey, we're gonna have something ourselves. Maybe we can grab an after dinner drink, and I'll straighten out all the lies Laukenbach and Espinoza are telling you."

"Maybe," she says, and gives me a wave over her shoulder as she heads for the table.

We're just pushing our plates back—and I mean plates as Cocoa has polished off two entrées—when she and her crew have finished and are walking out.

"Drink?" I ask as she passes.

"Next time, bounty hunter. No bounty on this bod. You may be working the wrong case. Besides, all cops are a bad bet."

I laugh, but am crying inside. I guess my most charming smile was not nearly charming enough, so I add, "Maybe, but I'm a privateer."

"As in pirate. I heard that. Face it, private cops are worse."

"So, you're a cop. Are you a bad bet?"

She ignores the question. "Next time." She waves over her shoulder and is gone.

Espinoza is the last of their party to pass. So I stop him. "Hey, big John, tell me about Officer Annie?"

"Nice lady, good cop, came here from Bakersfield or Fresno or somewhere over in the valley. Other than that...oh, yeah, she doesn't mess her own nest—"

"Meaning?"

"She's been hit on by all the single guys and half the married guys in the department, and so far as I know, no takers."

"So, she's single?"

"A one horse *caretta*. Never seen her with a guy."

"She's not—"

"Never seen her with a woman either." He guffaws. "What, you writing a book?"

"Nope, just queuing up."

He laughs. "Brad, me lad, it's likely to be a long wait, 'cause it's a long line."

"And looks like it might be worth waiting for. Tell her what a fine guy I am, old buddy."

"Fat friggin' chance. I already told her you've got six kinds of clap and genital warts to boot. I'm in line myself. However, good luck, *amigo,*" he says, pokes me in the shoulder, and follows the rest of them out.

Fresno or Bakersfield? The San Joaquin Valley is half expatriate Texans and Okies, shades of *The Grapes of Wrath*...just right for a Texas boy like myself.

Damn it, I've forgotten to call Poindexter. It's not like me to forget something that may well be worth five or even six figures. So, I walk out front under the stars—no moon up yet—and search into my phone's received calls, and, of course, it's an unknown caller with no number. I stick my head back into the bar and move up between T-Rex and Cocoa.

"Hey, I've got to walk over to the office for a minute to get a phone number out of the file."

T-Rex looks over his shoulder. "We ain't going nowhere I know of."

As I cross the parking lot, a low sedan who's backed into a parking space hits me with its lights, then spins its wheels shooting forward. Not only does it *not* swerve to avoid me, but centers me with the hood ornament. I dive like a tight end into the end zone for a nearby flowerbed, and the sedan blows by, missing me by inches.

I roll to my feet, spitting leaves and debris from the beds, and try and palm my pistol at the same time I'm trying to read a plate number...but of course as I was only heading a building away to Café del Sol, my sidearm is left behind in the office, and the sedan has fishtailed onto the road and behind the line of cars in front of the café...and is gone. No plate number...hell, no I.D. on the car at all, except a two door, and dark. So much for eye witnesses.

As I'm brushing off, I see flames through the second story windows of my office, licking upward already above the windowsills. As I'm running for the stairs, I remember the extinguisher in the trunk of my Mercedes, and hit the auto-trunk-opener and have it in a heartbeat, and run for the stairway, at the same time dialing 911. As I crash through the door I realize that there are four points of origin for the fire. Arson.

I'm inside and have three of them beaten down, but the extinguisher is depleted, by the time the first truck arrives, and the fourth site, on top my desk, has grown to the ceiling and the heat and fumes are pushing me out the front door when the guys in the yellow fire-resistant suits are clamoring up the stairway and shove me aside and charge in, already dragging an inch and three quarters fire hose.

I'm now worried as hell as there are several thousand rounds of ammo and an odd variety of stun and flash grenades in my hideout room, opening via a concealed door behind my desk. Some of my stash is not exactly legal.

Son of a bitch, I think, as I move over beside a captain I know from Little Joe's, a bar and café, up on State Street.

"Sam, you guys were quick. If this thing gets away from you, there's live ammo, etcetera, in an adjoining room."

"We'll have it knocked down before it goes through any walls...but thanks for the heads up. We were returning from another call, and only four blocks away. Lucky for you."

"Don't know if you can call this crap luck, but thanks. I'm glad you were close. I smelled a propellant when I opened the door."

"Yeah, that was a bad move by the way. I don't know how long that fire had been going, but if it was starved for oxygen, the backdraft could have both lit you up and blown you clean off that second story landing. You're ugly enough already, and would be a real sight with your nose and ears torched off."

"Yeah, thanks. I knew I was taking a chance and stood back against the wall when I opened her up. I could see lots of flames, so figured the backdraft hadn't built up much. It flared, but didn't blow. By the way, looked to me like four different ignition spots in the office."

"So, you know a little about fires…you're not just a pretty face. Max already radioed me. Arson guy is on his way. You're not needing some insurance dough are you?" He's smiling, but I get the feeling he's only half in jest.

"Don't have enough insurance to pay for the pencils and copy paper, much less the stuff of real value, plus it's at least ten grand deductible. Some asshole tried to run me down as I was walking back to the office. I imagine that's our boy."

"Any idea who?"

"Let's see, I've made over two thousand arrests, and provided the proof for two or three dozen guys to get serious time. Hell, there are dozens of guys, and a few gals, with hard-ons for me. You're guess is damn near as good as mine."

I glance over his shoulder and see Officer Annie slipping under the crime scene tape that's already up.

Sam, the fire chief, slips away to a pumper before she sidles up.

"I heard the call on my scanner. That mess up there your office?"

"It is, or was. And yes, it's a mess. What the fire didn't screw up the fire extinguisher and the water did. I'm in for a grungy clean up."

"What   started   it?"

"Or who…arson, if my guess is right."

"You   shouldn't   make   so   many   friends, Benedict."

"Somehow I don't think it was a friend."

"I'd give you hand with the clean up, but I'm on tomorrow. Still, I'll buy you a drink next door when you're done, after work."

"It's a date."

"No, it's a drink. But I'll see you there." She waves over her shoulder and heads back to her ten year old BMW.

It's three A.M. before Alex MacAndrews, the county fire department arson expert is through with his workup, and me…at least for a while. I'm banned from the place, now considered a crime scene, until at least tomorrow afternoon, as they are bringing in a canine team to locate the propellant. The arson guy worked me over, as it seems my being in the proximity of the fire, and the owner of the contents, put me right on top the suspect list. And no one at the bar saw the sedan try and make me part of the landscaping. I leveled with the arson guy, but I feel I'm still not out of the woods with him. Some private dick must have once got the goods on him before a very expensive divorce. Who knows? Probably he's just doing his job.

I've let Cocoa and T-Rex take my Mercedes back to the cottage, so I drive the van home. T-Rex is in my bed, the presumptuous son of a bitch, even though I've asked him to stay close and not head all the way back to his garage apartment in Goleta. And I'm beat up, so I backtrack to the Montecito Inn, rent a room, and crash.

And I still haven't called Poindexter.

Chapter Fourteen

It's eleven before I've had my coffee and dial Poindexter.

"So, you finally got around to me," he says upon answering the phone. Obviously he knows the caller. Sometimes not having your number on the unidentified caller list saves the preliminaries.

"Had a few special problems last night."

"So I heard," he says knowingly, making me wonder. I had the late morning news on the tube and saw nothing yet about the fire. Guess it wasn't impressive enough, or I'm not, to make prime time. "Dissatisfied client?" he asks.

"Can't ever remember having one," I say, giving him a smug tone, along with the lie. "So, you have your own sources. Maybe you don't need my help."

"Let's meet for lunch, say Brophy Brothers?"

"If you don't mind me in my jogging duds. I need a run and that's about right from here, besides it's tough to park there."

"Sure. Jogging clothes are fine. You run over. I'll have my driver drop me off."

It's his turn to be smug.

I jog over, working up a good sweat, and pause at a vending machine on the dock to get a bottle of water, and let the sweat evaporate before I climb the stairs to Brophy Brother's second floor restaurant and bar.

He's at the bar with a dozen others, most of whom are eating there as well as drinking as the place is packed as usual. He's watching for me and nods when I top the stairs clad in a Nike jogging suit and an LVPD bill cap—a gift from a Vegas detective after I turned a perp over to them. A perp caught in the overflow of my arrest of his buddy, and one whom I had no contract on, so he was no value to me, except the satisfaction of seeing him hooked up in the back of a patrol car. So it was a gimme to them. Poindexter waves at the hostess and she leads us out to a tight rail-side table overlooking the marina.

Wasting no time, he glares at me with ice blue eyes, "Benedict, I think you're blackmailing me. You're threatening to expose something to my board or my underwriters, and I damn well don't like it. Isn't there some kind of professional organization I can get you thrown out of?"

I don't know if he's trying to be funny or is serious, but I'm tiring of him. I have not even warmed the chair before I upend and finish the water bottle I've brought in, then rise again. "Look, Poindexter. If I walk out of here you'll never hear from me again, nor will your board nor your bloody underwriter. Marcus said you needed help. If you don't, it's no sweat off my gonads one way or the other. Now, it's totally up to you."

He eyes me like a bull at a bastard calf, so I shrug and I give him my back and start out, reach the stairs, and am half way down before he catches up with me. "Hey, Benedict, hold up."

I stop and turn. Even with him almost two stairs above me, I am about eye to eye with him, putting him at about five foot six. I smile inwardly as the blonde must be a half-head taller than him, for sure that much in the five inch heels I hear she wears everywhere.

"So, what's it to be?" I ask.

"What are you going to charge me for this so-called service."

"Tell you what I'm going to do. You buy lunch and I'll give you a half-page report, no more obligation. If you want to go on for the full boat it'll be a grand a day not to exceed ten thousand. You'll get several pages and pictures, and all the answers you need to either go ahead with this lady, or run for it."

He looks at me in a different light.

"I figured you were looking for ten times that."

"I get paid for the amount of work I do and the time spent, unless there's a hell of a lot of risk involved, then there may be other considerations. I'm beginning to think you're way more trouble than this job is worth." He's looking a little sheepish, so I soften my tone. "Is it lunch, or do I continue my run?"

"Let's eat," he says, and spins on his heel and starts back up the stairs.

I pick his brain until my cioppino and ice tea, and his fish and chips and dirty martini, are done, then my phone clangs with an unidentified caller.

"Benedict," I answer.

"You got a minute," and I recognize the voice.

"Officer MacAndrews?"

"Actually it's Chief MacAndrews."

"What's up? Is the crime tape down so I can go to work seeing what I can salvage?"

"It's down and we may have a lead."

"Quick work."

"Luck," he says, and I'm beginning to like him, even though he gave me a hell of a bad time.

"How so?"

"A black sedan damn near ran an old lady in a Bentley off the road, or I should say her driver off the road, coming out onto San Ysidro Road, about the time you said you had to dive into the bushes. She was spittin' mad and got a partial plate and phoned it in. We're working on it."

"How about filling me in, so I can work on it too?"

"It's police and fire department business."

"Hey, Chief, it's my business…or I should say was my business before this a-hole doused it in gasoline and made it half a business, or whatever it was he used—"

"Gasoline. He was no pro. He even left a pick in the lock. Hard to figure someone was breaking in…."

"So, how about that number?"

"We'll handle it. Go do your clean up. Watch for the building inspector as he'll want to condemn the place as unfit for habitation unless you convince him otherwise. He's due over there early afternoon. I'd be there if I was you."

"Thanks for the heads up. You sure about that partial plate."

"Dead sure."

I hit the red button on the phone, pick up my notes, and excuse myself, thanking Poindexter for the lunch and telling him I'd be back in touch, pause on the walkway below to call T-Rex and Cocoa, and get a surprise when Monique St. Marmont, my Palm Beach partner answers my cottage phone.

"Stretch, what are you doing here?"

"I talked to the boys last night and they filled me in on the twins, and the little overheating problem at the office. You okay?"

"I'm good, still tasting gasoline and smoke, but no harm done. Kick those two in the butt and have them join me at the office. You probably need some shut eye after the midnight flyer."

"I'm good to go," she says. She's always amazed me as to how little sleep she requires to get by.

"Hey, this is gonna be dirty work—"

"I'll supervise," she says, and I know that means she'll be up to her elbows right along with the rest of us.

I give a buddy a call at a tool rental place, and he offers to deliver a truck and trailer to the office for the clean up. On the jog there, I get a wild idea, and stop to give the sheriff's department a call, and leave word for Officer Annie. I'm going to find out if she's more than merely a pretty face, nice boobs, and fabulous ass.

She returns the call just as I come even with the bird refuge.

"Hey, I need a favor?" I ask with unabashed gall, puffing a little as I do so.

"Do I owe you a favor?" she asks, and I can hear the humor in her voice.

"Nope, not yet, but you will some day."

"So, what?"

"Some nice observant lady in a Bentley almost got run off the road last night, probably by the same guy who damn near made a hood ornament out of me. She got a plate number and phoned it in to either your shop or SBPD. I need that partial plate number."

"And no one else will give it to you, because you're a civilian and it's police biz?"

"You got it. But I've got sources and methods you honest cops can't use."

"And you've got tight lips?"

"Loose lips sink ships, and I don't want any of us to go down into the cold briny blue. Particularly you, as you look too good in the uniform and I'd hate to have to give you a job, as that would make you off limits."

She laughs, then adds, "I'll call you, and yes, you'll owe me big time."

"Super big time, I'll even let you off on the drink you promised. I'm buying."

As I'm waiting for the truck and my crew to arrive, I plop down on a bench over looking the lagoon at the bird refuge, just across from my burned up office, and spend a little deep thinking time. Who's on top of the arson suspect list? The two goof balls who I kicked the crap out of in the saloon actually owe me for not having them hauled to the hoosegow, so they don't head the list, at least not yet. Jo Jo Bling is probably pissed about losing his bodyguard, and the drubbing we gave him and his boys in his own living room. And hell, even old Poindexter was royally pissed at me, and could be covering his ass by meeting with me. He did know about the fire even before it hit the news. Then there's about two or three dozen other perps and their friends and relatives who think they have a beef with me. It's a bit of a quandary, but the partial plate may just get us on the right track.

I give up on the mental gymnastics, and fulfill another obligation by calling my beat up buddy Marcus the bartender, and commiserate with him. He's home, watching baseball, and happy as a clam as he's on pain pills and Budweiser. He was surprised to get a call from Frank the arm breaker and more surprised by Frank's offer to pay his medical bills, but I'm pleased the guy was a man of his word. I have renewed faith in Air Force pukes. I tell Marcus to call me when he feels like doing a little one handed office work, and he promises to do so.

The truck arrives about the same time as my crew, and we spend the next two hours cleaning up and sorting scorched and burned stuff that will have to be gone through, when the building inspector arrives. I give Monique a wink, and she unbuttons the top three of the blue work shirt she's borrowed from T-Rex, and charms the guy until he'd drooling all over himself. He makes sure there's no structural damage then agrees to come check the place out in a couple of days, after we've have time to get it cleaned up.

It pays to have competent, and sexy, associates.

I watch as T-Rex is cleaning the credenza behind my desk, finds a box of See's candies, looks inside the scorched box to see a melted mess, then throws them in a garbage sack. I'm glad I'm paying attention and yell at him to bring them over. He looks at me like I'm nuts, but fishes the box out and walks across the room and hands it to me.

"You need a chocolate fix that bad?" he asks.

I dig in the box and flip the now solid mass of chocolate over and peel twelve unscathed hundred dollar bills off the back side, and give him a grin. "Ben Franklin likes chocolates too. ...Mad money."

"Your buying dinner," he says, over his shoulder, as if I wasn't buying anyway.

"Well flip for it," I say, but he knows better.

He shrugs and goes back to work.

It's almost six before we finally break and head over to Café del Sol for a well-earned drink, and only moments later, in walks Officer Annie, looking fine sans uniform.

I make the introductions, then ask, "Do I owe you dinner and a cocktail or six?"

"Or sixteen," she says, with a giggle, and gives me a buss on the cheek while surreptitiously handing me slip of paper, with three letters and a number. She smells as good as she looks, lime and jasmine I'm thinking, and I'm pleased to note that she gives Monique the once over and I'm wondering if that's a little jealousy I see in her, emerald, with an occasionally flash of turquoise, eyes. A good sign. While she and Monique chat it up, I get my mind straight and immediately dial up Sparks and employ him to glean what he can from cyberspace. Three letters and one number of three—and eye witnesses are notoriously bad at remembering plate numbers—and a dark sedan, is not much to go on, but he's a whiz kid, so I have high hopes.

We have a couple of drinks, I give my Montecito Inn room key to Monique, and she and the boys head out while I'm trying to convince Officer Annie to slip over to the Biltmore, over looking the beautiful Santa Barbara Channel, for a nightcap. My evil intention is to check in there on the mere chance of getting lucky, something and someplace I wouldn't normally choose as I'm sure it's a five hun gamble in the five star Biltmore...or maybe more. But like I surmised earlier, she's a five star lady.

She agrees, but warns me, "I'm a five date girl, Benedict, and very, very seldom does anyone get past the fourth date. And like I said, this isn't date one."

"Come on, Annie, I bought drinks and dinner. That ought to count for date one."

"Nope. A date is when you pick me up at my door, daisies in hand."

I can't help but laugh. "You are an old fashioned girl. I'm a rose man myself...will that work?"

"You bet, a dozen might even get you lucky in four dates."

"Wow, I'll bring five dozen if a day is knocked off for each doz. Let's go have a cocktail and see if the piano bar is humming."

It's worth a giggle out of her, then she asks, "They have a piano bar? I love piano bars, particularly if they know lots of Sinatra."

"I knew, it, we're meant for each other. So, you've never been to the Biltmore. Then this is definitely a date."

"We'll see. I'm following you in my car."

"You are a suspicious sort. Am I the first date you've had with a guy riding in the front with no handcuffs on?"

She laughs. "Nope. I put handcuffs on my dates after I get to know them better."

"That may be more than I want to know."

"Being suspicious goes with the job...mine, and yours, I imagine. Let's go."

I've got to spend a little time cleaning up in the Café del Sol men's room, but manage to get duded up at least up to Biltmore gardener level. I've still got my Mercedes, so at least I look like I can afford to buy a round or two, and luckily out of it's trunk I pull a clean windbreaker with a Sandpiper Golf Club logo on over my clothes, loaned to me by General MacClanahan. Maybe they'll think I'm a poorly dressed golfer, and as the same guy owns the Sandpiper as owns the Biltmore, they'll likely overlook my ash-soiled attire.

She's a woman of her word, as even after two more drinks at sixteen bucks a pop, and three dances to old Sinatra tunes, she allows me only a good night kiss as I push the valet aside to open her car door. But the kiss is a deep-wet-winner; this lady knows how to whet an appetite. At least I didn't check into the high dollar joint and am not down another five hun. She speeds out of sight in the old but spotless BMW and I head for Motel Six.

My phone jangles with Sparks identifying ring, the theme from 2001 A Space Odyssey, before I reach the motel.

"What's up?" I answer. "You got something on the plate already."

"Nope. Did you ever tie up with that Poindexter guy?"

"Sort of. Not the deal I want yet, but it's moving forward."

"Doubt it."

"What?"

"Dead."

"What?"

"He's a dead dude. Toes up."

Chapter Fifteen

What happened?"

"Somebody stuck him and shoved him off his balcony and he's a dead puppy. Head bashed in on the rocks, at least that's what I get off the SBPD computer."

"Where?"

"His beachfront house over on Shoreline, a couple of lots north of Santa Cruz...you've got the address in that first report I did on him."

"Thanks." I hang up and head for Poindexter's place, and hope I know whomever the detective is that's pulled the gig, and know it'll be easy to locate from the rotating red lights in the street. And I was going to head back down the coast to make another run at springing the twins, which is the only paying gig I've got going, particularly now that this little bread and butter job is obviously in the tank. This may set me back a few hours, and has sure as hell set me back a few bucks.

There's no love lost between Poindexter and I, but the guy sure didn't deserve to get a gut full of shiv, a mouth full of ice plant, and a bashed in head. I am pulling up in front of his place, where the meat wagon and a half dozen patrol cars are parked, when my T-Rex ring lights my cell.

"What's up?" I answer.

"A couple of Santa Barbara dicks just left here, looking for you, and not smiling."

"What's the beef?"

"Seems this guy Poindexter you were hustling for work bought the farm."

"Yeah, I just pulled up in front of his ten million dollar pad. Sparks gave me a heads up."

"Don't expect a warm welcome. Seems you're on top the suspect list."

"What the fuck?"

"My sentiments exactly. You want us over there?"

"No, God no. I'll handle this."

"Good luck."

As I double park and exit my Mercedes, Harold Laukenbach, the SBPD walking scarecrow dick that was having supper with Annie and her group, strides toward my vehicle. With his Adam's apple protruding like a walnut, and the veins swollen on his forehead, he steps in my path. "You're wanted for questioning, and we're about to put an all points out on you."

I can't help but smile, which seems to make his Adam's apple and veins protrude even farther.

"As you can see I'm not hard to find."

"Spin it around, smart ass, and put your hands on top the vehicle."

"Fuck you, Laukenbach."

He drops his hand to his side, flipping his coat back. I step into him and clamp a hand on his wrist, keeping him from pulling his weapon, and eye to eye, snarl, "Have you lost that pile of mush you call a mind?"

"Get your hands off me, Benedict, or I'll take you in right now for assault and obstructing justice."

Over his shoulder I see John Espinoza's beer barrel body striding up.

"John, tell this dipshit to stop trying to flash the brass on me. I'll be happy to hand my weapon over to you, then kick this asshole into next week."

He again tries to disengage his semi-automatic from his holster, and I hold him in place.

"Brad," Espinoza says in a calm tone, "let him go. John, keep your weapon holstered or *I'll* kick your ass."

"But—"

"No buts about it,…Brad, two finger that Beretta out and hand it over. Let's all go get a cup of coffee and you can try and explain why this guy warned his staff about you."

"Warned his staff?" I ask, a little astounded.

"Yeah. Now the weapon?"

I do as John suggests, letting Laukenbach's wrist go and stepping back, starting to two finger my Beretta out of my shoulder holster. He palms his weapon and starts to level it on me, but this time it's Espinoza who grabs his wrist, far more gently than I would have.

"Don't prove you're a complete asshole, Harold. Let's head down to iHop and you can stuff down another three thousand calories while I gain five pounds just watching." He takes my weapon with his other hand and shoves it in his belt, letting Laukenbach's wrist go. Harold looks indecisive for a moment, but finally re-holsters his semi-auto and glowers at Espinoza.

"Whose partner are you?" Laukenbach asks.

"Yours, Harold. That's why I'm trying to keep you from making a damn fool of yourself, or worse getting your ass kicked all over the street with half the force watching. Now, let's go get that coffee. If it makes you happy, Harold, Brad will ride shotgun and you can sit in the back so you can keep an eye on him, okay?"

Laukenbach merely furrows his brow and heads for their unmarked, and as John has suggested, climbs into the back seat on the passenger side. He is a complete asshole and if he wasn't Espinoza's cross to bear I would wipe up the pavement with him, as I'm sure I could antagonize the prick into taking the first swing while off duty. Oh, well, life is full of little obstacles.

I get in, but can't help but ask, "How about I get a look at the crime scene first?"

"Don't push it," John says, starting the car.

"Yeah," Laukenbach's voice rings from the back, "you probably already saw it up real close."

I keep my mouth shut and hook up my seatbelt.

John makes small talk the four miles to reach the nearest iHop, which seems to irritate Laukenbach even more, but as soon as our coffee lands on the table, asks, "So, why does this stiff's general manager think you're our bad guy?"

"I let it be known via a mutual acquaintance—"

"Who?" Laukenbach demands, opening a shirt-pocket size spiral notebook and posing his pen over the small paper.

"Marcus…let me think…Marcus Somoza, or Fomosa. It think the latter. He works out at the Roadhouse…or did before he had a recent accident—"

"You push him over a rail too?" Luckenbach snaps.

"He broke his arm. I have his home number in my phone."

"Dig it out," Luckenback grumbles, as if he's hoping I'm lying, then repeats me, "You 'let it be known.'"

"That I wanted to talk to Poindexter, whom I heard was getting set up for a fall...and protecting folks is my business."

"Protecting them over the rail onto the rocks." Laukenbach still has a very smartass tone. He obviously wants to pick the low hanging fruit on the suspect list, and thinks I'm it.

"When did Poindexter take this swan dive?" I ask.

"Sometime this p.m. We'll know more when the crime scene types have a little more time."

"I was working my ass off cleaning up after an office fire. Three of my people were with me so it's an alibi easy to verify."

Luckenback laughs. "Three of your people who'll lie for you in a New York minute."

"Probably," I reply, then add, "however they don't have to lie this time."

The waitress arrives and sets some Godawful concoction of hot cakes and canned fruit and caramel sauce, all topped with whipped cream, in front of Laukenbach, and I'm pleased that he'll have his mouth full for a while.

"God," Espinoza mutters, "that has to be five grand of cals."

"And would gag a maggot," I add, but Laukenbach is not phased.

Laukenbach gives him a superior grin, his mouth too full to speak, as John sips his black coffee, then John turns to me. "So, Brad, why are your prints all over the crime scene?"

Chapter Sixteen

B ullshit," I say, figuring they're trying to lead me to say I'd been there.

"No bullshit," John says with sincerity. "They got your prints. A clean set, which they sent in via a digital picture and got an immediate hit from your PI license. You were there."

"I was not there, John. As God is my witness I've never been in any of Poindexter's houses."

"So," Laukenbach mumbles with his mouth full, "your prints were there but you weren't. You got to explain that one to me, Sherlock."

I shrug. "I had lunch with him. Maybe he was playing detective and brought something from the restaurant. Who the hell knows…but I've never been in that house."

They merely stare at me as if I'm a lying son of a bitch.

"So, where were these supposed prints of mine?"

John starts to answer, but is interrupted by Laukenbach, "that's telling him too much. Don't give away the dozens of places we found them. All you'll do is help him make excuses."

"Shut the fuck up, Harold," John snaps, then turns to me. "We only found them one place."

"Yeah, on something he could have hauled in. You didn't find them on the furniture, door knob, window sill, or kitchen counter...right?"

"Right. We found them on a water bottle *on* the kitchen counter."

I think for a second while they study me. Then smile. "A water bottle I took to lunch with me. I jogged over and stopped down below to let the sweat dissipate and to wet my throat. I left that bottle, Crystal...right. He hauled that bottle back, playing detective, obviously wanting my prints for some reason. He wanted to find out if I had some skeletons in the closet as he knew I had a lot on his girlfriend, who had him by the short hairs with her talents and looks, and he was hung out a mile if he hooked up with her. She's a bad act...."

"So," John asks, "hung out how?"

"He was getting ready for a public offering, an IPO, and they run a fine tooth comb through your background and associates. We'd discovered he wanted to marry her, panting like a dog in heat, and she was already married. Part of the service I was offering...."

"Right," Laukenbach snarls, "and the service included pushing him over his railing. Why don't you come clean, Benedict."

My fuse is getting a little short. "You truly are a dumb s.o.b., Harold. One print on one plastic bottle hardly makes a case. How the hell did you ever qualify for detective, when dickhead should be your highest ranking?"

He starts to try and stand, but John pushes him back down in the seat, then slides out of the booth. "Let's get back to the scene and find out who killed this computer geek. I've had enough coffee and enough bullshit from both of you."

"I'm ready," I say, slipping out of the booth.

Laukenbach jams two more bites in then adds, with a disgustingly full mouth, "Make the fucker walk back." He slips out of the booth.

"Ride in the back," John says to me. "I don't want you two fist-fighting while I'm trying to drive." Then he puts his hand on Laukenbach's shoulder and in a friendly way, guides him to the door and out into the parking lot in front of me. "Harold, you can make anybody walk you want to...when you're driving. Climb up front with me and you won't have to look at Benedict." He turns to me, "And you keep your pie hole shut."

"Yes, sir," I say, but can't help but laugh, which I can see riles Laukenbach. Then I get serious again. "So, his girlfriend was nowhere in the neighborhood?"

"What girlfriend?" John asks.

"Come on, the one I mentioned...Ronnell, goes by Ronny. A flat fox of a little blonde, but I think she may be half rattlesnake. I had a small assignment from Poindexter to check her out. That's what the lunch was about."

"No girlfriend in sight. However there is a small part of his very large master closet with women's clothes...only a couple of feet worth, suggesting a more than occasional visitor, but not a live in."

"Size three or less, I'll bet?"

"Didn't check...yet. You got a phone and address for this Ronny?"

"I do, but it's back at the office in my files...what are left of them."

"And what else is in Poindexter's file?"

"Not much, yet, but more to come from one of my guys."

"And you'll hand it over?" Laukenbach snaps. "It's evidence."

"It's my file, Harold," I say in a less than friendly tone, then add before he gets pissy, "but, yes, I'll give what I have to John."

"Let's go there now," Laukenbach says as we pull up in front of the crime scene.

"We got better things to do," John says. "Brad will bring the file to the shop in the morning...right Brad?"

"You got coffee and donuts...which I know you do...and I'll be there."

"I think—" Laukenbach begins, but John interrupts him.

"He'll be there in the morning."

We unload from the car and I give it another try. "How about letting me check out the crime—"

"Forget it, Benedict," Laukenbach growls, and John agrees.

"See you in the morning," John says.

"Gentlemen," I say, feigning a salute. *"Por la manana."*

"Hasta la vista," John says, mimicking Schwarzenegger, with a wave, and with Laukenbach glowering at his partner both of them head for the house where the crime scene team is still hard at work.

I lean on my Mercedes and give Cocoa a call. "Hey, you guys get ready to leave for Malibu again in the morning, and take Monique along. I've got a command performance at the Santa Barbara P.D."

"Is this your one call from the hoosegow?" Cocoa asks,

"Nope, I'm headed home...or is T-Rex in my sack again?"

"Nope, he's downtown somewhere, riding your bike."

"Oh, crap. I just got it painted from the last time he laid her down." T-Rex is good at lots of things, but riding my Harley doesn't seem to be one of them. And I love my Harley.

"He promised to stay sober."

"Right, and the sun will rise in the west tomorrow. Wish you would have dissuaded him."

"Last time I tried to dissuade him he broke my pinky finger before I choked him out."

"Right. Do your best to get what you'll need together, and throw it in the Blazer. I want some time with you and Monique...and T-Rex if he gets back...when I get in." I disconnect. At least I might beat him to my sack. He'll come back full of booze and sleeping on the floor will be no trouble for him. I remind myself to invest in one of those blow up mattresses, and swing by WalMart and grab one as it's just off the highway.

To my surprise, my Harley is parked in front of the cottage when I wheel up the driveway, and the three of them are drinking coffee in my tiny kitchen. I brief them on what I want to come down in Malibu in the morning, and let Monique drive the Mercedes back to the Montecito Inn.

We make it in the sack by midnight.

I wish I was able to lead the pack to Malibu, but I'm also interested in what went down with Poindexter, and I promised John Espinoza.... And John's not a guy to whom I'd want to break my word.

Now, to get back to the paying client, and get those girls out from under Jo Jo Bling's needle.

Chapter Seventeen

ROUSE

I ~~kick~~ the boys out of the sack at 6:00 am and call Monique, which gains me a less than complimentary remark, something about the status of my birth, but serves to get her up and going. We agree to meet at the Montecito Café in her hotel, as it's quiet at breakfast and we can talk with some privacy.

Laying out the plan for their trip to Malibu, I wait for comments or suggestions, and get none, so we head for the office where they'll pack some equipment and change the magnetic signs on the van from Joe Jenkin's Plumbing and HVAC to Coastal Internet & Electronics before hitting the Pacific Coast Highway. Thus they'd have an excuse to be climbing poles and following phone and power lines, or even going up a tree to do some trimming, obstensibly away from phone or power lines. Aw, the wonders of modern electronics. While they are getting ready I get a wild idea and make a phone call to Frank Havlicek. My boys have both been made by Jo Jo and his crew, so I need a fresh face.

"Yeah," he answers his cell.

"This is Benedict. I heard you met up with Marcos?"

"I did. We're square…at least will be when we raise a few bucks to pay his bills."

"You were an airman?"

"Yeah."

"So, were you a grunt or did you have some skills?"

He laughed. "You don't get far in the Air Force without some skills. I was an electronics guy on the UH-72A Lakota Light Utility helicopter for awhile, then was transferred to the F-16, and was damn good at it…until they lobbed some mortars into LAS-Anaconda. …And fucked me up pretty good."

"Are you working?"

"Between jobs."

"Can you use two fifty a day, for a part time gig that might be reoccurring?"

He is silent for a long moment. "What kind of gig?"

"Surveillance. Installing some equipment."

"I'm trying my damnedest to stay clean…since you gave us a break I've been trying to rethink my life. This gig…nothing illegal?"

"You might get a trespassing charge if we screw up."

"I can probably handle a misdemeanor. When and where."

"My office is two doors down from Café del Sol. You know the Mexican restaurant on the freeway side of the bird refuge. I need you as soon as you can get here. You'll be working with three others."

"On my way."

I hope I'm not making a mistake, but I read people pretty good, and don't think so.

The crew gets on the road in the re-signed van by 9:30 and Monique follows in the Mercedes, which leaves me the ~~Bronco~~ *Blazer* or the Harley to ride to SBPD to meet up with Detectives Espinoza and Laukenbach. It's a beautiful coastal morning, the islands clear across the channel, the temp mild, so I head out on the Harley.

The P.D. is on E. Figueroa, a couple of blocks east of State Street, the main drag. Parking is a problem damn near everywhere in the city of almost ninety thousand, so I take my chances with the fifteen minute spaces on the street. Odd's are the meter maids are harassing the tourists downtown rather than hanging out in front of the typically Spanish style building that houses the P.D. The 19th Century old California architecture is slightly prostituted by the array of antennas and communication folderol behind the red tile topped mansard of the two-story structure.

I check in at the front desk and the overweight pince-nez-spectacled sergeant gives Espinoza a call. He's front and center in a heartbeat.

"You promised a donut," I say, in lieu of a greeting.

"Bullshit. You mentioned a donut. I didn't promise a rat turd."

"So," I ask as I follow him up the stairway, "does that mean you don't have a donut, won't share a donut, or that Laukenbach has eaten all the donuts…and probably the rat leavings?"

"His nose is still out of joint, so go easy on him today."

"Fuck him, to coin an expression of yours."

"Yeah, right." He waves Laukenbach over to a conference room that he ushers me into. A coffee machine, at least, graces a built in counter, with small sink, at the end of the room, which houses a table that will seat ten.

"Good morning, Detective," I say, in my most polite tone as Laukenbach joins us. John Espinoza is pouring us all coffee.

"You want a donut," Harold says, so I guess polite pays off.

"Had breakfast, thanks," I say, and take a seat across from them.

"So," John begins, after he sits a cup of black coffee in front of me that resembles thirty-weight engine oil which already has forty thousand miles of use, "your prints didn't show up anywhere else. The cleaning lady had been at Poindexter's house half a day yesterday, so everything was pretty well wiped down. Whoever visited him was most likely gloved as we didn't get ka ka in the way of prints, other than Ronnell's, so it figures she was there...but we did pick up a couple of footprints in the flower bed next to the low wall where we figure he took flight. Three different sets of prints, male sizes...big sizes, maybe elevens or twelve's, one of them we figure was Poindexter."

"Well, that's something. How about the girlfriend?"

"You bring us a file?"

"I did, what I have on Ronnell and her husband, Barnaby. As I asked, how about her?"

"She's missing...so far. No one answers at the address we got for Barnaby."

"Did you get inside?"

John turns to Harold, who's being surprisingly cordial. "Harold, how about grabbing the file off my desk."

He looks momentarily irritated, but leaves the room.

"We have no grounds for a search warrant, without a real haggle. I was thinking maybe you'd drop by their place and see what you can see…through the window of course."

He knows damn good and well that I won't settle for merely doing a peeping Tom act. But he won't outright condone what he knows I'll do.

"I'll handle it. You got anything on Barnaby."

"He's got a warrant…in fact both of them do…out of Sacramento, so I have an APB out on his old Cadillac, but we couldn't see in the garage. Hell, it may be there. Nothing yet on either of them. I can probably get a warrant in a few days, after we've made a gallant effort every other way…but the Oldstrums could be in Honduras sunning on the beach or diving for scallops by then."

Harold returns with the file, and John makes like he's looking for something there, then eyes me again. "Okay, that's about it. Thanks for coming in. We'll go through this stuff and see if you've got anything we don't."

I rise. "Okay, if I turn up anything, I'll shout out."

"Do that," Harold says, his tone only slightly antagonistic. He must have slept well last night, or his hemorrhoids aren't bothering him, or something.

I make it back to the Harley before I'm attacked by the meter maid, although I've barely exceeded my time, and head back to the office. The Harley attracts too much attention and I want to change to the ~~Bronco~~ before I visit the Oldstrum abode. And I need to pick up some tools, and give the file Sparks provided me a quick study. I want to make sure I recognize Barney baby.

The Oldstrum place is one of those circa 1950 three bed one bath places in Goleta, to the north of Santa Barbara, best known for University of California at Santa Barbara. There are a few older neighborhoods, still pricy by most the country's standards, but not fancy by any means. I've checked the ownership of the house, and find it belongs to a guy I've met a couple of times at Café del Sol, or maybe Brophy Brothers, or Joe's, or hell, somewhere, Julio Estovez who's rumored to own over a hundred houses around the city and nearby county. So Oldstrum is a tenant, which doesn't surprise me.

Theirs is on a cul-de-sac, nicely painted with what looks to be a new paint job. I pull right into the driveway and up close enough to the garage door, the old swing out type, that it can't be opened. The house is in good shape, but the yard is overgrown, the mail box full, and there are more than one throw-away flyers littering the front porch. There's a card stuffed into the crack between front door and trim, but it's merely a landscaping service wanting work.

I give the front door a few raps, and am not surprised when no one answers, nor do I hear so much as a squeak from inside. While I'm waiting I put my phone on vibrate and kill the ringer.

I give the neighbors the once over, and don't see a nervous nelly eyeballing me through a window. So I ease around the side of the garage, use the heavy screwdriver I've brought from the office to pop the small hasp off the gate rather than mess with the padlock, and make my way through into the rear yard.

I'm pleasantly surprised by not being surprised by a pit bull at full charge, but there is a dog house, and evidence of a large canine peppering the walkways and grass. My phone vibrates in my pocket, but I ignore it.

The back yard is in as poor shape as the front, but one thing is really out of place. There's a burnt steak on the b.b.q. and a half-full glass of what might have been a whisky and water on the little shelf next to the grill. I bend over and give it a whiff without touching the glass, and think I've guessed right. Cheap bourbon. Looks as if someone was interrupted before they could get their steak cooked, or their drink downed.

It's got the hair up on the back of my neck.

Chapter Eighteen

It's time for gloves, so I pull on a pair of cheap rubber ones that the ladies use when dealing with household chemicals and cleaning stuff, find the back door locked, can't see anything through it—a Hollywood door with upper half as window—or the other back windows, well curtained, so I dig my picks out of my back pocket. Thank God Oldstrum, or the landlord, is too cheap to have invested in good locks, so this one takes less than a minute.

No air conditioning, and even though it's only Santa Barbara normal eighty degrees, it seems warm inside, and that odor.... It's not death, but it's slaughterhouse disturbing.

And it only takes me three steps into the kitchen to discover what it is. My phone vibrates again and I all most jump out of my skin, even though it doesn't ring. I ignore it.

The kitchen is a mess, pots and pans and broken dishes cover the floor.

My intuition was right on, right down to the breed. There's a dead pit bull on the floor among the flotsam and jetsam, his belly split, his entrails spilled on the linoleum floor. On closer inspection, I can see that the back of his head is blown away. His mouth is gaping open, and I realize he'd been shot through that opening as there's a bloody crease on his tongue. I can picture him lunging at his killer, his mouth *posed* to tear out an interloper's throat, but he was stopped short by a nine millimeter or maybe larger. Why they opened his gut is anybody's guess...and my guess is pure meanness.

I raise my head from the dog inspection to see a small dining room off the kitchen, and face down on the chrome and Formica table, his arms splayed out, a pool of dried blood beneath the head, appears to be the man of the house. A half dozen beer bottles sit around on the table and one rests on a windowsill nearby. I note under the table that his ankles are bound together with what looks to be a man's black pant's belt.

Seems the guests took umbrage with their host. And their host I recognize: Barnaby Oldstrum.

On closer inspection, I see there are ligature marks on his wrists—or maybe cuff cuts as they most likely would have left him tied, but wanted to take their cuffs with them. And there are several cuts on the half of his face I can see, and black marks. Burns? He really did make his guests angry.

It's cheap beer...maybe that's what got them so pissed, but I doubt it.

Again the phone vibrates, but I need to get a look here and get the hell outside before I'm caught and busted for b & e, so I ignore it. I'm glad I had the forethought to use rubber gloves, as I've had enough fingerprint problems.

Then I notice an even more nasty indication that his guests were incensed with him. There's an electric flat iron on the floor, and its cord has been cut away with only six inches left attached to the appliance. Behind our unlucky host the missing cord is plugged into the wall, and by the way the business end is split with plenty of copper showing on both halves, and from the burns on the back of his neck, and burn holes in his shirt, I'd say his hair should be finger-in-the-socket on end. But it's not, in fact he has very little hair, and what he does have is cut very short.

His tongue is slightly distended, and I can see he even has electrical burn marks on lips and tongue.

A pair of jumpers from a Ford battery would have worked much better, as they could have hooked the clamps to his nuts and probably not killed him, but a one ten from the wall...obviously serious overkill.

This old boy died hard; paid heavy for his many sins.

They were either very upset with him, or wanted him to tell them something and he needed encouragement. Or both.

Now I'm wondering if they didn't eviscerate the hound in order to make a point with the dead guy. See what's going to happen to you, buddy!

Doing a quick recon of the house, I half expect to find Ronnel, the wife, in the same condition as Barney, but the house is clean...after a fashion. I should say sans Ronny, as the house is actually pretty filthy, and has been tumbled by pros. Even the attic access cover located in the hall is on the floor, indicating there was a total search of the premises. I do find pieces of Ronnell; thank God, expendable pieces, as a handful of blonde hair is in the bathroom, and the bathroom door has been kicked open. It doesn't bode well for Ronnell.

I do take a quick peek into the garage, and note the old Cadillac is resting quietly.

I decide it's way past time to take my exit. But before I do, I jimmy the curtains on the dining room windows so there's a slight opening—so an outside observer could have seen in. Returning to the ~~Harley, I perch thereon and~~ *Bronco* make a couple of phone calls, chasing down the landlord's number, then the landlord.

"Mr. Estovez, you have a problem, I think…"

"Aren't you the bounty hunter guy?"

"That, and other endeavors. We've met before, if you recall. I have reason to believe you have a problem at one of your properties."

I don't expound, other that to suggest he doesn't want to clean up after a cadaver which has occupied one of his places, seeping into the carpet, for a week or so before the neighbors get a whiff of the problem. Maggots are very difficult to get out of a carpet.

He agrees to be here in thirty minutes or less, saying something about this not being his first rodeo.

Finally, I can see who's wearing the numbers off their phone trying to call me so I search the missed calls. Monique. I return her call.

She sounds satisfied with herself, and is purring like a cat having its belly scratched. "Hey, I made a new friend of Mr. and Mrs. Goldstein, Jo Jo's neighbors to the west. Your new employee, Frank, is busily putting cameras up in their sycamores getting a good view of the neighbor's back yard. We've got the hyperbolic mike trained on Jo Jo's bedroom slider, and T-Rex and Cocoa are on the trail of a big black Denali and will get one of the GPS Tracksticks under a fender the first chance they get. It's being driven by the sister, so maybe Cocoa will have a chance to cozy up to her."

"What's the story with the Goldsteins?"

"No problem. Good citizens. I flashed the brass on them and they didn't bother to ask what department or anything. They were more than happy to have anyone after Jo Jo and his boys. Seems they play their music a little too loud, have barking dogs, and occasionally have sex in the backyard with 'loose women.' Can you imagine?"

"I can. Nice there are some helpful folks left in the world...and some loose women."

"I'll ignore that. Mr. Goldstein did suggest I come up with twenty bucks for the electricity we'll be using. He said he'll check it against the same month last year to make sure that's enough." She laughs, then continues, "Seems you don't get an ocean front property in Malibu unless you count your pennies. I'll be back in a couple of hours. My work is done here."

"Have you seen the twins?"

"Happily sunning themselves by the pool, stoned as an unfaithful Iraqi wife caught in the act, and topless to the dismay of Mrs. Goldstein. However I sense that is to the great pleasure of Mr. Goldstein...which is, I imagine, one of the reasons Mrs. Goldstein is so totally peeved...so to speak. After I told her my maiden name was Schwartz, and my former married name was also Goldstein, she warmed right up. Of course that was after she made sure I hadn't been married to either of her, and I quote, worthless brothers-in-law. Then I was treated like the returning prodigal daughter."

"You actually don't mean 'prodigal.'"

"A figure of speech...and why don't I?"

"It means wastefully extravagant. Mr. Goldstein wouldn't approve."

"Well, aren't you the little edition of Webster's."

"Big edition, thank you. However, great work, Stretch. Sounds good so far. If it's just you and me by super time, the sushi is on me, and I want to fill you in on this local gig...not that it's a paying gig, but it's interesting, and I want to ride it out."

Within five minutes after Estovez arrives, I give John Espinoza a call, and he and the troops head our way.

He and Luckenbach are the first to arrive, and walk over to where I'm still perched on the bike. Harold is in his normal cheerful mood.

"Benedict, you are like a vulture circling these murder scenes," he says.

"You think?"

"I think, ...only vultures don't do their own killing, and I think you do."

"Merely following up a lead, Harold me lad."

"Bullshit. You don't have a case to follow up. You may be merely interfering with justice, and giving me an excuse to bust you." He turns to John, who's looking a little disgusted. "What do you think, J.E.? Let's haul him in and sweat him a while."

John lowers his voice as two more patrol cars have already pulled up. "He's doing what I asked him to do, Harold. Now zip your lip for awhile."

"What?" Harold snaps.

"Lip...zip, please. I'll fill you in later."

Harold looks even more disgusted, but shuts up.

"You didn't leave tracks, did you?" John asks.

"Light as a feather, I am. Besides, I entered the residence in question at the invitation of the owner. I merely peeked in the window prior, of course—as it would have been illegal to break and enter—saw the scene, and called you gentlemen as any good citizen would. After calling the landlord, following him inside, I repeat, at his invitation, and confirming the gentleman you sought had become a corpus delicti...which he obviously had, as none of us were meant to get our kicks from one-ten-volt licks. Maybe twelve to twenty-four hours dead would be my guess."

"So, now you're C.S.I.?" Harold says sarcastically.

"Sure, isn't everybody now that we get about ten hours a week of it on the tube." Then I turn back to John. "By the way, you can cancel your APB as the Cadillac is in the garage...of course I couldn't see it, but I could smell it."

Harold lets out an exasperated 'humph,' but doesn't bother challenging his partner's suggestion to keep a zipped lip.

"Can you come in tomorrow and make another statement?" John asks. "We'll be here the rest of the day."

"Come on, John. I've got to make a living, and flapping my jaw at your joint doesn't pay any bills. Let me go to work and maybe I'll turn something up for you guys while I'm trying to pay my bills. By the way, the electric box in the garage is standing open. When you check the scene you'll see they must have popped the circuit breaker a dozen times or more."

"Sounds nasty. When you get a free moment, write it down, sign it, and drop it off...no later than noon tomorrow," John says, giving me as much leeway as he can. "Now, get out of here." ~~Blazer~~

I hit the starter on the ~~Sportster~~, and see John mouth a "thank you." ~~I settle my helmet on and~~ give him a nod, then am out of there.

Now, I wonder, where's Ronny? All her men are dead, so I hope she's at the local jeweler trying to hock the five caret rock, but I fear something far worse. Of course Ronny may have a third man on the scene. I'm sure she attracts them like flies to a pasture patty. If she's in the hands of the guys who did Barney, I don't envy her.

As I'm roaring down the freeway, I realize I have not gotten my email from Stanton confirming my deal with him. As I suspected this guy is going to be trouble with a capital tee.

Of course, I've got his hundred and he's yet to have his daughters.

If I call him now he's likely to be well into the cocktail hour in Florida. And I don't need sass, I need my agreement. So I think I'll call him early in the morning, while he's still groggy from those five pm martinis or gin rickeys or whatever the half billion dollar set drink.

Chapter Nineteen

Monique and I are halfway through a couple of tall bottles of ~~Hot~~ ^warm^ Saki, a pair of soft shell crabs, and a pair of rainbow rolls at Sakana Sushi, a half mile from the office, when my phone hits a few notes of *When The Saints*, and I know it's T-Rex.

"Hey, where are you? We're back at the office, such as it is," T-Rex says.

"Just finishing our supper. We'll meet you at Café del Sol in a half hour."

"We're hungry. We'll join you—"

"No, no way, we're leaving in five. Go next door and order. I'll be there in time to pick up the tab."

I kill the call and Monique eyes me. "They wanted to join us. We'll be here awhile, unless you're going to gulp your Saki." She smiles. "If I didn't know better I'd say you wanted me all to yourself."

"No question about it," I say with a mischievous smile. "However, even more I feared picking up a sushi tab for T-Rex and Cocoa."

"Real nice."

Now it's my turn for the mischievous smile. "You trying to get me to break my rule?"

She gives me a coquettish one in return. "What rule's that?"

"You know damn well what rule. The don't-mess-your-own-nest rule."

She laughs. And she's got a great laugh. Then says through a grin, "I'm funnin' you, Bulldog. I don't need any more of your kind of grief."

"Grief…. Now I'm offended."

"Okay, your hit and run tactics."

"Scalded by a woman scorned," I say.

"Now I'm offended," she says, but she's smiling. "As memory serves, I scorned you, but I know how that creative memory of yours works."

"Okay, okay, you scorned me by going to work with Quiet Ops. And I'm still heartbroken." I'm only half lying. There's only one way a man can win this kind of exchange, and that's to totally kowtow and agree, and I quickly do.

We finish up and in minutes are parked in front of the Café del Sol.

The cleanup and construction crew working on the office agreed to work a double shift, so I head over to check their progress, agreeing to meet her inside where the boys await. Lance LeRoy is there, hands on hips, eyeing me like I've just murdered his sainted mother.

"All my work—" he starts.

"Lance, look at it this way, I'll have a wad of insurance money, and won't you have some fun. But first we've got to get the basics and get back in biz."

"Well," he says, never taking his hands off his hips, "since you put it that way…how much money?"

"Not nearly as much as you're used to here in Montecito, so don't get all in a tizzy. Let's just get things back where we can work."

"But work in a sublime atmosphere." He flashes me his best Cheshire cat smile.

"Yeah, a cheap sublime atmosphere."

"Brad, Brad, Brad, sweet boy, cheap is not a word in my vocabulary. Thrifty, I can live with."

"Thrifty then, Lance. And don't 'sweet boy' me. Got to go."

"Bye, bye, Brad. We're going to have such fun."

It's my turn to give him a look, and it's not a sweet one.

On quick inspection I'm happy to say in another full day we'll be back at work on our own territory, smelling fresh paint, still putting up with Lance, I'm sure, but back at work.

As I get back and am turning up the sidewalk to the restaurant, I recognize the older BMW pulling into a parking space.

And she's still looking fine, blonde hair pulled back tight accented with a black ribbon, this time in an above-the-knee short black skirt and a red satin top that shimmers in all the right places. I get a glance at plenty of svelte leg as she swings them out of the low BMW. I'm amazed that she can navigate the pavement, which is a little rutted, in five inch spike heels.

"Officer Annie," I call out as she nears.

She flashes those brilliant blues on me. "Well, shiver me timbers, if it isn't Montecito's number one pirate."

I've got a timber that she makes shiver, but skip mentioning it. "You fresh out of seeing another sequel to Pirates of the Caribbean, or what?"

"Nope. I just heard another Brad Bennedict pirate story. Something about earning a couple of hundred thou by stealing a yacht from a Mexican *Federale* General. You're a regular Blue Beard."

"I think it's Black Beard, blue beard is a fairy tale, and trust me, I'm no fairy…and it wasn't stealing. Returning it to its rightful owner, from whom General Castinoza filched it for the mere indiscretion of having a couple of ounces of Mary Jane onboard. Rich folks indiscretions are my biz, the monied, the troubled…as most of them seem to be."

"Sounds like an exciting time was had by all."

"Not nearly as exciting as when I safely delivered it to John Solinger Esquire and the prick tried to stiff me for the second hundred he owed. Said I got the job done so quickly that a hundred was enough."

"The attorney?"

"One and the same. He knew I wouldn't try and sue him, so I finalized him instead with some info he didn't know I had, and he paid in a New York minute. Cha-ching."

"Care to give me the rest of the story?"

"Nope. Confidentiality agreement. And Big John would just love me to violate it so he could come after me."

"What an exciting life you lead."

"It was just another day in the life of Quiet Ops, out-running since we couldn't be out-gunning a Mexican gun boat. Not a particularly quiet day…but another day. Am I buying your supper…say as date three?"

"Nope. I'm meeting the crew. But since you offered, and since I do need some excitement in my life, I'll count your sincere offer as date three, four, and five…if you'll be around in a couple of hours."

I'm seldom at a loss for words, but this one made me catch my breath, and she laughs. "Cat got your tongue?"

I don't say, 'no, but you're going to get it.' Instead I manage, "No, no.   And yes, yes, I'll be around."

"Cool. I've got the day off tomorrow, so I'll expect your full attention tonight, big boy."

"And you'll get nothing less, lass."

She heads on into the bar, leaving me licking my lips. When I follow, she's already headed to the rear where she's joining a dozen of Santa Barbara County's best, including my buddies, Detectives Espinoza and Laukenbach.

Cocoa, T-Rex, and Monique are at an up front table near the windows, and there's just enough of the lingering sunset to color the sky. What a place to live.

I sit and eye the boys. "Well?" I ask.

"A good day," Cocoa says. "And maybe day after tomorrow will be better as we got some *vasti* boys there."

I've picked up enough Samoan slang to know *vasti* means dumb or stupid. "Why's that..a good day, I mean?"

T-Rex offers, "Jo Jo is appearing at the Hollywood bowl for some fund raiser with a couple of other rapper groups, and he'll either have the ladies with him, or leave them home. Either way, we'll have a chance to get next to them."

"I'll get Sparks on the Hollywood Bowl. When do we know where the girls will be?"

This time it's Cocoa's turn. "My new best lady friend, Chandra…ain't that a pretty name…personally poked her cell phone number here in my little cell phone, and I promised to give her a little poke in return. But she ain't taked me up on it yet. I have been invited to partake of a telephone conversation tomorrow, and should I be so lucky, she will join me at Neptune's Net for a few pounds of the fruit of the sea. Food there ain't as good as back in the Islands, but it ain't half bad either."

"Good, as I have to talk to their dear old daddy tomorrow. And Grenwald will be straining at the traces if things are normal." Then I turn to Monique. "How did Havlicek do?"

"He's great. Did his work efficiently, no bellyaching, no problems. By the way, I paid him in cash and you owe me a cool two fifty."

"Soon as we get back in the office. Can I hire him again? We'll need more warm bodies if we end up making some kind of a play at someplace as big as the Hollywood Bowl."

She shrugs. "I don't know his skills, or his guts, but so far I'd say hire away."

As soon as we finish, I suggest to the boys they give Monique a ride back to the hotel, as I need the Mercedes. She gives me a funny look, glances over her shoulder and eyes Officer Annie and the group at the back of the room, then gives me a knowing look.

"Come on, boys. I'll buy one round at Lucky's before I get my beauty sleep."

And they're gone.

I park myself at the bar, and wait.

It's another hour before the table full of sheriff's office employees breaks up and heads for the door. Laukenbach is in the lead, and by the look of him, in his cups. He stops at my rear, and I turn enough to keep my eyes on him. He's standing, hands on hips, a smug sneer on his hatchet face.

"If it's not the circling buzzard."

I ignore him, as Espinoza is about even with us. "How goes the battle, John?" I ask.

"Okay," he says. "We found Ronnell Oldstrum's car. Some blood in the vehicle. It's being typed now and will go out for DNA."

"What do you make of it?" I ask.

"Fuck if I know."

"Anything else from the crime scenes?"

"Nope, whoever pulled these two off...they're pros."

Laukenbach can't leave it alone. "I make of it that you got in her pants which got you crosswise with her old man, and got real pissed and did him in a way that made him hurt, then she cold-shouldered you cause you were such a sadistic son of a bitch so you did her too. Where's the girl's body?"

I seldom lose my temper, but I could feel the heat creeping up the back of my neck. I shrug at John, shaking my head in disgust, again trying to ignore Harold. "Can't you keep a leash on your yap dog, John."

Harold is more than just a little drunk, and takes a round-house swing at me. I easily slip the blow, push him away, and get to my feet. But he's going to insist on taking a visit to la la land, and tries another. This one I duck, and he spins almost all the way around. I manage to cast a quick glance at John, but he's smiling and has backed away a couple of steps, with his arms folded. He, obviously, wants the vicarious enjoyment of watching Laukenbach getting his ass kicked.

"You mutherfucker," Harold manages, and this time works up the good sense for a straight shot at my nose. I slip it, catch his right wrist, and spin the arm against the shoulder joint, at the same time sweeping his legs, and he's upended. He goes down hard, unfortunately catching the sharp edge of a table with his head. He still hits the floor hard, and his eyes roll back in his head.

"Fuck," I manage under my breath. I meant to put him down, but not down and out awaiting a trip to the MRI.

The blood is pooling under his head. Obviously he got a pretty good cut from the edge of the table.

John is at his side, on one knee, and turns Harold's head to view the damage, then quickly has a green cloth napkin pressed on the cut. Harold opens his eyes and tries to rise, but John has a meaty hand in the middle of his chest. I'm watching him carefully, as he is carrying in a shoulder holster, but to his credit, he seems to have no interest in pulling his weapon. John bends closer, and I hear him say quietly. "You fucked up, Harold. You need about fifteen stitches. Let's get out of here before this becomes something that goes in your jacket."

"I want to kick his ass," he mumbles, unconvincingly.

"You better wait a week or so," John says with a sly smile.

Harold is still a little bleary eyed, but not so much he doesn't get it. He took a drunken swing at a civilian who was sitting peacefully at the bar, in front of three dozen witnesses, and worse, got his butt kicked in front of a dozen or so of his peers.

I'm good to go, I figure.

John turns to Annie, who's now caught up with the action. "I'm driving John over to Cottage Hospital in his wheels. Will you follow in mine?"

"Yes, sir," she answers quickly, and now I'm not good.

She shrugs at me. I'm seriously thinking about kicking Laukenbach in the balls, but he'd not know what for, nor would John, and then I'd surely have to go to the lock up to cool off.

"Where will you—" I start to ask Annie where she'll be later, but she gives me both hands, palm out, stopping me short.

John hauls Harold to his feet, passing the job of compressing the head wound on to the victim, and they start out. All the rest the sheriff's crew give me an 'I'll get your ass for that' cold eye as they pass, and only Annie pauses.

"We're back to date three, Black Bart," she says under her breath.

I sigh, and manage, "I thought it was Blackbeard..." and again am a little speechless.

I watch that great ass disappear out the door, and now wish I could kick my own. Instead I turn back to the bartender. "Jack, three fingers, neat."

Remembering Espinoza saying he was right in line to make play for Officer Annie, I wonder if I've been out-flanked?

Another long cold night in paradise.

Chapter Twenty

Even though my team left long before I manage to find my way to the cottage, they are yet to arrive, so I beat T-Rex to my bed. The last thing I do before sweet dreams is give Sparks a call, knowing he's normally doing his night owl stint on the computers. I put him on the Hollywood Bowl gig, knowing he'll most likely have the latest plans pulled from the files of the Los Angeles Building Department by morning, the schedule of the rent-a-cops who are now working there, and probably their medical histories and what kindergarten class they attended. By morning we'll know all we want, and need, to know about the Bowl.

I also ask him to follow up on Barney Oldstrum, and to try and find the unlucky bondsman who bailed Alonzo Bohanson, Jo Jo Bling's second bodyguard. I want a contract on the boy as it will give me lots more leverage if I have to charge the ramparts again.

I need to know who might have been angry enough with Barnaby to do him, and am wondering if the dot com wunderkind, Poindexter, didn't merely get caught in the overflow of something or someone who had Barnaby in their gun sights. I've got that bone stuck in my craw and am not going to spit it up until I can swallow and digest it.

Or it will niggle at me the rest of my days.

I'm up at six, make a quick cup of coffee, and give Grenwald G. Stanton a call, nine a.m. his time. He answers on the second ring.

"Stanton."

Without the courtesy of a hello and presuming he'll recognize my voice, I caution, "We're on my regular cell, so chose your words."

"You have my daughters?"

"No, but we have a concrete plan." Only a slight prevarication. We have a very rough plan in the early planning stages.

"Then I have nothing to say to you."

"Where's my agreement?"

"I emailed it, and the printed version is in the mail." His 'I'm offended' tone is not convincing.

"Mr. Stanton, that's right up there with the check's in the mail and I won't come in your mouth."

"My, God, Bennedict, you can be a rude son of a bitch."

"Only when someone stiffs me. And you've had days to get the email here, much less the written agreement."

"Word is you had a fire in your office. You don't suppose it got lost somewhere in that melee?"

"Mr. Stanton, let's not banter or b.s. Get the agreement here and I'll get your girls back to you."

"You do that, and if you don't, I'll see you in court and be getting my hundred thousand back. And if that doesn't work, there are other ways…."

I ignore the threat, but feel the heat on the back of my neck as I continue. "When can I expect my email? If you sent it once, merely pull that email back out of your sent file and forward it to me. I'll see the date it was originally sent, and know you're a man of your word, then you can expect another phone call from me and an apology. How's that for a plan?"

"I'll email you today sometime."

"Fine."

"Fine," he replies.

His 'fine' obviously means 'fuck you,' but before I can reply, he hangs up.

Cocoa is coming alive on the now broken down pull-out, and T-Rex is up from a pallet he's made himself on the floor. It's Friday morning and I often have breakfast with the general on Friday morning at Birnam Wood Country Club, so I'm not surprised that by the time the boys have made their morning visit to the necessary room, there's a rap on my door.

As suspected, it's General McClanahan. "Breakfast at the club?" he asks.

"General, Cocoa is still here and another associate, Rex Pollack, an old Marine Corps buddy from Desert Storm. How about we take you to the iHop instead?"

He laughs. "Probably hard to get a poached egg on a bed of thin sliced lox and a parmesan roasted tomato on the side at iHop. Custard filled hot cakes smothered in jam or chocolate sauce are not on my diet."

"Odds are," I offer.

"Catch you next Friday?"

"Let's plan on it." And he's gone. The General never tarries, and wisely avoids my entourage invading his very exclusive country club.

"Did I hear iHop?" Cocoa yells from the kitchen area, where he's priming himself with a few pieces of toast. As iHop is about the cheapest place to fill Cocoa's enormous tank, I concede.

I poke in Monique's cell and we agree that we'll pick her up for breakfast.

When we pull out of the driveway onto East Valley Road, I notice another vehicle wheel onto the road a couple of hundred yards back. I get a tingle up my backbone, and have long ago learned to pay attention when I get a tingle. When I turn left onto Hot Springs I watch, and the four-door black Cadillac makes the same turn. For the hell of it, I pull up and park in front of Manning Park.

"What's up?" T Rex asks.

"Don't know," I reply.

The Cadillac passes. The windows are so tinted I don't get a look at the occupants, but can make out there are four males. They turn the next left onto Santa Rosa Lane, and disappear.

I give them time to get well down the road then continue. Sure as hell, they are parked, now facing back our way, a half block down the road, and by the time I get a block past Santa Rosa they're sitting at the stop sign and soon make the turn following us.

"We've got a tail," I say.

"Stop," Cocoa suggests, "an we kick some *muli lapo'a*."

I presume that means ass, but ignore it. "Let's not play our hand yet. Let's let them think we haven't made them."

"No fun," Cocoa says, but I drive on and have soon pulled into the driveway at the Montecito Inn, and have instructed the parking attendant that I'm merely picking up a guest. Monique is seldom, if ever, late. And in moments she appears, a cup of coffee in hand, and joins Cocoa in the back seat of the Mercedes.

As we pull away, I see that the Cad is parked across Coast Village Road, the main drag near the freeway; the Montecito Inn being sandwiched between. And, of course, they pull back onto the road after we're a block past. I'm beginning to wonder how sloppy these guys are. I fill Monique in as we cruise at the 25 mph speed limit. These guys are not the FBI nor skilled operatives, obviously no more than sloppy amateurs. We're about a mile from the office, so I head there.

"You got to get on the freeway to get to iHop," Cocoa cautions, his stomach ruling as usual.

"I want you two guys to climb in the van, then let's see what these boys do. We'll also find out if they have a back up team. We'll take separate routes to iHop and see who gets the privilege of being tailed."

"Okay," Cocoa says, satisfied he's headed for breakfast.

We do as planned, and Cocoa and T-Rex drive away in the van, and are not followed, so far as I can tell. The Cad sticks with Monique and I.

We backtrack and pick the freeway up as the boys have headed down E. Cabrillo along the beach. The Cad follows us.

The closest iHop is just north of downtown on the main drag, State Street, and we are lucky to find a parking place in their small lot. We've beaten the boys there, so we park, go inside, and get a table for four. Somehow we've lost sight of the Cad, but I'm not surprised to see it idle along after we get seated. They find a parking place on W. Valerio, the side street. Two of them exit the rear of the car and are soon inside, and find seats at the counter. They're Hispanic, one's pudgy and middle aged, one younger with a pock marked face to rival the moon, and both are wearing jackets even though it's already in the high seventies.

I presume the bulges in their jackets are not bean burritos.

Chapter Twenty-One

We've barely gotten our coffee when Cocoa and T-Rex enter. Cocoa takes one look at the booth and grabs a chair from another table, as he'll never fit.

We take a leisurely breakfast, while Cocoa takes two, and, as we're out of earshot of the boys at the counter, go ahead and talk over the forthcoming opportunity to snatch the girls away from Jo Jo Bling. Cocoa is to meet Chandra Jefferson, Jo Jo's sister, on down the coast for lunch, and should learn more about Jo Jo's plans then, if he can wrangle any info out of the lady. It's my hope Jo Jo plans to leave the blonde twins at his compound at Point Dume, as squiring them away from there, even if he leaves a couple of bodyguards on watch, will be much safer than trying to worm them out of a place filled with a twenty thousand mad-as-the-mad-hatter rap fans. And we have to convince them to go with us, only putting as little pressure on them as possible. We can't have it appear we took them against their will.

When we've finished our discussion, I go onto the problem of the two ~~thin-faced~~ Hispanic ~~boys~~ at the counter, and the two in the Cad across the street.

"This time I want T-Rex to take Monique in the van, and Cocoa will go with me in the Mercedes. Let's see if it's Monique who's being tailed or me. They might have followed me this morning only to find out where Monique was hanging her hat." I turn to her, "You haven't pissed anyone off lately, have you, Stretch?"

"Nobody in California," she says, with a shrug.

"Let's go. See you two back at the office. See if you can get the tag number on the Cad as we leave."

We ignore the boys at the counter and follow the plan. The Cad follows me back to Mission Street and back to the freeway. So I'm the person of interest for the four Hispanic boys. Interesting as I can't remember pissing any *chamacos* off lately. Although one of the guys at the counter was pretty old to be called a punk.

My phone rings with a text before we get back to our turnoff at E. Cabrillo, and T-Rex informs me of the tag number. It gives me an excuse to give Officer Annie a call, which I do, and after a short lecture on who's an officer of the law and who's not, she agrees to run the tag for me. As we're pulling into the office parking lot, she rings back, and as I suspected the car is from Hertz. Not much help there, except we might assume they're from out of town, probably out of the state. I avoid asking Annie how her trip to the hospital with Harold and John went, as I'm not sure I want to know.

The car's a rental, the occupants Hispanic, and Sparks has ripped into the car companies computers and discovered it's rental location as LAX. I wonder, could they be Cubans from Florida?

Again, interesting.

Sparks calls and brings me up to speed on the bondsman who bailed Alonzo Bohanson. Unfortunately, it's a guy named Joel Steinman, and Steinman and I have crossed paths before, and not in a good way. However, that doesn't mean he won't give me a contract on his skip, so I tell Sparks to get me in touch with him, then I get the bad news…Steinman is out of the country and can't be reached as he's on Safari in Africa.

Everyone enjoys having four ugly boys with bulges under their arms trailing them. It won't be too long before I begin to get nervous and my good looking boys and I are forced to turn them upside down to see what shakes out. I wouldn't be surprised if one of those things is a cell phone with some calls back and forth to and from one Grenwald G. Stanton, aka G.G.

Conrad Wilson, my contractor, is still in the process of cleaning up the office, but we horn in and start putting things in order. I only have to listen to Conrad for a half hour while he bitches about having Lance LeRoy giving him hell about every nail.

Thank God Lance is somewhere else making some other poor soul's abode or office sublime.

In an hour, we're settled into the three desks, with T-Rex catching up on his sleep on the office sofa. I dig some cash out of the safe and repay Monique for her advance to Havlicek, which reminds me to call him and get him scheduled to help us tomorrow. He agrees and asks, "Skeeter got laid off. Can you use another hand?"

"Skeeter?"

"You know, Toby O'Brian, the guy that was with me when we got busted at your place."

That takes me back for a minute. "You can vouch for this guy?"

"Yeah, he's okay. He's not much with his fists, but he's willing."

"Okay. Tell him no weapons. And you also…no weapons."

"Got it. See you in the morning."

Then I call my buddy Marcus, with the broken arm, thanks to Frank Havlicek. "How's the wing?" I ask.

"Good, not paining me much any more. Still healing."

"You want some work? I may need another pair of eyes on a job tomorrow. It may last well into the wee hours."

"How much."

"Two fifty for the day. All I need you to do is watch and use a radio."

"This legal?"

"So far that's the plan."

"Where and when?"

He too, will meet us at the office in the morning.

My last call is to Sparks, who agrees to bring over all he's gathered on the Hollywood Bowl. I'm still hoping that the Bowl is not our target, but if it turns out to be, then we have to be ready.

He arrives and we start working out our alternatives. If the girls are in the audience, or backstage, or if there's a party somewhere after the event it will be an alternative place—info we hope Cocoa will glean from his lunch date. The later we make our move on them the better, as the more the girls partake of whatever dope they're being provided with, odds are the easier they'll be to convince. Had they been away from Jo Jo the first attempt we made, they would already be in under mama's wings in Florida. This time I mean to make it happen, even if G. G., Papa Stanton, stiffs me, which I'm now sure he'll try to do.

And I can't afford to have that happen, as I cut a check for twenty grand to the contractor, and can only hope against hope that my insurance company is going to reimburse me. I plan to get Jo Jo to come with the dough, even if the insurance company comes through, as reimbursing them will put some points on my scoreboard and maybe score me some work from the insurance company later on. This new plan for reimbursement of the fire damage is due to some new info Sparks has brought along with the Hollywood Bowl package—it seems the partial license plate of the car escaping the fire belongs to a black Trans Am belonging to one of Jo Jo's occasional employees. We didn't see this guy when we were at the house, gathering up T-Rex, but we now have made him thanks to Sparks and his facial recognition software. Santiago Morales, known as Spider to his friends, who's also been with Jo Jo at some social events.

Again, interesting info. And good ol' Spider has wants and warrants in Phoenix, and coincidentally, was arrested for suspected arson, but the case wasn't made. Otherwise, nothing too serious—assault and evading arrest—but good trading material for the twenty large now owed to yours truly. That, when taken into consideration that he's already a two-time loser for dope, makes for excellent negotiating material. I'm smiling.

We spend the rest of the day getting the office back in order, while Cocoa takes the Mercedes and heads down the coast to lunch with Chandra, Jo Jo's sister. He's not back by the end of the day so we hit the Café del Sol for some chow, and my secret hope that Officer Annie might be on the scene. The chows good, my luck's not. Finally, at nine after we've had a couple of beers and supper, I text Cocoa.

What's up?

And he comes right back.

Gettin lucky. Sleep good. C U morn.

Well, it sounds like he's tucked in for the night.

T-Rex has been staying close to us, but has decided to head back to his garage apartment in Goleta to feed his goldfish and sack out; Monique, driving the van, is still expensively ensconced in the Montecito Inn; consequently I've got the Harley and the cottage to myself for a change. Tomorrow could be a really big show so I decide to spend some quiet time. Besides, I need to give the Poindexter killing and the Ronnell Oldstrum missing person cases some thought, and probably get Sparks back to work on them. I know when something niggles and niggles at me that I'm missing something, and Poindexter tickles my curiosity every time something else isn't pressing for think time. Then there're the four scumballs in the Caddy who are dogging my tail. If they are a back up team hired by Grenwald G. Stanton to make sure I'm getting things done, that's one thing; if they are a second team hired by him to do what I was hired to do, that's another altogether, and it could cost me a hundred fifty grand...not that I think he'll pay up easily none the less. But if another team brings home the bacon, he'll sure as hell not pay up, and I won't have much of a case with which to press the issue. I'm sure there's no email or fax awaiting me attesting to our agreement.

Either way, the greaser team will get in the way, and I don't want to worry about them while I'm worrying about snaking the Stanton twins away from Jo Jo.

The last thing I do before I call it a night is call Sparks and get him to do a real in-depth cyberspace investigation of the recently expired Barney Oldstrum and his wife, Ronnell. At first I might have thought that old Barney boy might have shoved Poindexter over the rail, but since he was subject to an even worse fate, now I can't imagine him being the perp. The perp or most likely perps did them both. 'Why' and where is Ronnell are the questions of the day?

Just before I'm about to doze off, my phone rings with an unknown caller.

It's my detective buddy John Espinoza.

"Did I wake you?"

"Just about. What's up?"

"Murder stuff. You clear headed?"

Chapter Twenty-Two

Espinoza launches right into it. "The blood in Ronnell's car was her husband's. I'm wondering if whomever waxed Poindexter did so while Ronnell was there, but her old man was outside in her car. They dragged Ronnell out, put the arm on her old man, then drove her car back to Barney's place, tried to one ten volt some information out of him, and did or didn't, but took Ronnell with them after hubby took the road to hell. She was an ultra sexy lady, so maybe they wanted to use her a while before they did her. Of course I shouldn't say 'was', as she may still be among the living, or hell, may have been teamed up with the bad guys. Who knows? Or maybe she knew where whatever they were after was stashed and they needed a guide. Who knows?"

"Hell, that's the question of the day, and as good a story as any. Who knows? I've got a friend doing a little work on the Oldstrum's background. I'll keep you posted."

"I'm headed for the del Sol. You wanna bend an elbow? Seems my regular drinking pard is out of commission." John chuckles, then continues. "He's embarrassed as hell, by the way."

"Embarrassed because he was an asshole or because he got his ass whipped?"

"A little of both, I imagine. I doubt if he's looking for a rematch."

"Tell him all's forgiven…presuming forgiving's a two way street. I'm down for the count. I'll owe you a couple if that's okay?"

"You got it. Sweet dreams."

Now, some sleep.

Cocoa is sacked out on the pull-out—I'm happy to say he remembered the codes and made it in past the two alarm pads, one at the gate and one just before you reach the general's house—when I wander in to make coffee just as the sun is turning the sky orange over the sandstone and chaparral-covered mountains. He's snoring a little like a runaway freight train, rattling the windows, so I let him sleep. Handling the two-ton-tilly must have worn the boy out. The lights are on in the general's kitchen, so I pull on a tee shirt and some shorts and head over. Sure enough, he's already up reading the paper and sipping a cup of something. I rap on the window and he waves me in.

"Coffee?" he invites, and I'm happy to partake.

I know a little about his business investments and think I remember something about his having an interest in a prominent security company headed by an old Air Force Air Base Ground Defense colonel buddy of his, so I ask, "I remembered you have something to do with a Los Angeles security company?"

"Event Security & Safety. I've been a stockholder for years. Colonel Harold Allensworth runs the place. Over three hundred employees, last I heard."

"So, as I recall they do security for lots of different functions around L.A.?"

"You bet. Pro football and basketball...and hocky at one time. They had the Emmy's and the Oscars for a while. Lot's of high-end events at 'so-called stars' parties. Don't know if they still do as I'm really not close to the day to day management and haven't seen the colonel for a while...but I know they stay busy as they pay dividends every year."

"I've got a gig coming up at the Hollywood Bowl. I've got good intel on the place but don't want to get crosswise with security if I can help it, and things might get slightly rough."

"I'll give them a call and see if the Bowl is a client of theirs, if that helps?"

"You bet. I'll owe you big time...again."

We spend the next hour talking golf, orchids, and lonely Montecito widows; all subjects upon which he's well versed. Then I head back and throw a towel at Cocoa from across the room. You don't want Cocoa to wake from a bad dream and be in his flight path, but he wakes slow and easy like a groggy hippo, if Hippos can don a sheepish grin.

I get him rolling then call T-Rex and listen to him curse me and all my ancestors for being awakened before noon, get him moving, then call Monique and make arrangements to pick her up in forty five minutes. This time it's Sambo's for breakfast, just across E. Cabrillo from the harbor.

Not overly thrilled, I clean a bunch of stinking crab shells and trash out of the floorboards of the Mercedes while I'm waiting for Cocoa. He wanders out and looks a little sheepish. "I was gonna get to that."

"Right. The car smells like a Tijuana whore house full of hog farmers on a hot day. It's kinda lost that new car smell."

"Sorry."

"Ka ka happens, but it's not supposed to happen on the formerly clean carpets of my Mercedes. I hope your trip was worth it?"

"You bet. It's the Hollywood Bowl and an after-concert party at the old Roosevelt around the corner on Hollywood Boulevard. The girls are supposed to go along, one blonde on each of Jo Jo's tattooed arms."

"Good work. We'll go over the details at breakfast."

The Caddy picks us up after we swing out of the driveway, only this time there are only two guys. It galls me that they think I'm so stupid I can't make a tail, so I decide to rattle their chain. I call T-Rex and fill him in, then line it out for Cocoa. By the time we get to the Montecito Inn and pick up Monique, we have a plan.

We park in the Harbor parking lot across from Sambo's, and Monique and I head straight for the restaurant, jay-walking across E. Cabrillo. The Cad has sped on past the entrance to the lot, but by the time we're inside, has returned and pulled into the lot as well. I guess they didn't notice that Cocoa wasn't with us. He's joined T-Rex a half-dozen rows back from where we've parked in the row closest to the main drag.

The two Hispanic gentlemen merely sit in the Cad and eyeball Monique and I, as we take a booth near the window where we can watch the action. As instructed, the boys let them get good and bored, with us well into our breakfast, before one of them slips up on each side of the Cad. They pop the doors open and drag the two boys out, one on each side. I can see that both have been disarmed and their weapons are under the cars on each side, as I make my way back across E. Cabrillo, leaving Monique to enjoy her breakfast. So far, we aren't drawing a crowd, as both Cocoa and T-Rex have their charges in a fairly inconspicuous wrist lock, both the Hispanic boys are up on their toes, looking very uncomfortable by the time I get there.

I jump them. "Do you two think we're blind, or what?"

It's the razor thin, pockmarked-face one, who Cocoa has, who speaks up. "What the fuck, man? We're just sittin' here and you *culo* face fuckers roust us."

"You've been doggin' us like a couple of hyenas…you and your two buddies. What for?"

"Don't know what the fuck—"

"Break his wrist, Cocoa," I say, and Cocoa knows I mean to hurt the guy, but not put him in the hospital. He puts the pressure on. The guy screams like he has a hot poker running up his *culo*, and I laugh but mostly for effect. I'm concerned as a couple of old ladies have stopped on the walk under the palm trees and are eyeballing us.

I give the fat Hispanic a dirty look, "you're next, *gordo*." Then I turn back to pock-face. "Now, I ask again, why are you dogging us, *flaco*?"

"Fuck you," the guy says, to his credit, as I know Cocoa has just put a world of hurt on him. As ugly as he is I guess you have to be tough to look at yourself in the mirror every morning.

"Take their wallets, and their firepower," I instruct T-Rex and Cocoa, and they do. Cocoa rips the back pocket of pock-face away and palms his wallet, then shoves him away and goes down on all fours to fish the weapon out from under the car. The guy foolishly tries to put a brogan in Cocoa's face, but he catches the ankle and upends the guy, cracking his head a good one on the pavement. He's on his butt on the parking lot, his eyes rolling like a Vegas slot. T-Rex puts one deep into the flabby abs of the other guy, doubling him over, only then does T-Rex go down to fish that weapon out from under the car. Both are automatics, and the boys pop the clips and eject the shells out of the chambers, then follow me as I move away. They drop the automatics in a parking lot wastebasket, pocket the clips, then follow me across E. Cabrillo.

One of the old ladies is on her cell phone, so I'm sure we'll have a black and white as company in short order. As we go inside, I call John Espinoza and bring him up to speed. The two Chicano boys have fished their weapons out of the garbage—not that they'll do them a lot of good without clips, unless they're carrying a spare—and climbed into the Cad and hauled ass by the time the black and white arrives.

We're casually eating breakfast when two young patrolmen come inside and head straight for our table.

"You Benedict?" one of them asks.

Chapter Twenty-Three

I give him my most boyish smile. "Yes, sir. Sorry for the trouble, officer. Couple of guys over in the parking lot gave my friends here some trouble. We took care of it."

One of the young cops eyes Cocoa for a moment, then turns back to me. "They weren't real smart guys, were they?"

"Not real," I say, with a pleasant smile.

"The two ladies who called it in said something about some weapons...some firearms being involved?"

"As I'm sure Detective Espinoza told you, we're all licensed to carry, and we were merely advising the two gentlemen who were making trouble that we were armed so they would cease and desist, and not be surprised if perchance the weapons got exposed. No firearms were brandished."

"Not what the ladies said."

"You know how excitable old ladies can be," I say, flashing another reassuring smile.

"This wouldn't end here, had Detective Espinoza not radioed us."

"You guys about at break time? I'm buying breakfast, or at least coffee."

"Another time," he says, then smiles, "I think you owe us one." He nods and they both tip their hats and head out.

"Now, about those wallets," I say, and both boys pull them out and start shuffling through them, and making notes.

"What do you know," T-Rex says, "all the way from Miami."

"I'm not in the least surprised." By the time my breakfast arrives, my phone goes off with another unknown caller.

"Hey, *cabrone, mi tienes harto*."

"Speak Floridian if you know how."

"What?"

"Speak English, and hurry it up. My breakfast is getting cold."

"*Mejor que no me chingues*, motherfucker."

"English, or I'm hanging up and pulling the plug."

"My guys want their wallets back."

"Oh, yeah. They can't get on the plane back to Miami unless they have some I.D., can they? Maybe they can walk home."

"Fuck you."

"How'd you get my cell number? We got mutual friends in Florida?"

"I doubt you got friends anywhere. You don't give a fuck how I got your number…but I got your number, motherfucker. I'm gonna get more than that…."

"What's your interest in me?"

"Fuck you."

"Gimme a hint, or your wallets go in the garbage disposal."

"Fuck you."

"*Vete a la mierda!*" I say. I know a little street Spanglish.

I hang up.

"What was that all about?" Monique asks.

"I have a sneaking suspicion it was our friends with the Caddy. Something about them wanting to fornicate me, or at least that's what they kept saying."

"You do know how to win friends and influence people," she says with a coy smile.

My phone rings again, unknown caller. "You rang," I say.

"Okay, okay. You guys keep the dough in the wallets, but we need the other stuff back."

"Nope, we'll leave the dough. Not enough to worry about. You guys give the dough to your favorite charity, promise?" I don't get an answer, not that I expect one, so I continue. "The wallets will be in the same garbage can where the guns were dropped. But that will be after we finish breakfast and head out, and won't happen if I see any ugly Miami mugs in the area. Don't dog my trail, or the next time your firearms will be shoved up chocolate alley, understand, *mericon*."

"I'll be seeing you," he replies with an ominous tone.

"In all the old familiar places, that this heart of mine embraces," I say, with my best Frank Sinatra imitation, and hang up.

"Can I keep the money?" Cocoa asks.

"Cocoa, that's dirty dough. You don't want dirty dough. They promised to give it to their favorite charity."

"Right," he says. Somehow I don't think he's convinced.

Monique takes a moment to write down every piece of information from the wallets: names, addresses, credit card numbers, driver's license numbers, and one of them has a small phone book with two dozen names and numbers; she notes every piece of info. Both of them have a Sam's Club card with their pics thereon, and we retain those.

Sergio Foca and Rodolfo Mendez are gonna be pissed when they go to Sam's Club.

We spend the rest of breakfast, and two more hours at the office with Frank Havlicek, Toby 'Skeeter' O'Brian, and Marcus Ontiveras, my bartender buddy and new part time employee, going over our plan to snatch the girls out from under the nose of Jo Jo Bling and his bodyguards. I give the general a call, and he gives me a phone number. It's good to know generals. I've hit the jackpot as it is Event Security who's handing the Hollywood Bowl, and we have a cell phone number, and contact, and an in. I also give Sparks a call, wanting to know what I can about the two Hispanics, now that I have names, but get a recording as it's his sack time, unless he has a class. I leave instructions.

We load up, all dressed respectably in slacks and sports coats, except for Cocoa, who's in a jogging suit, the most dressed up he normally gets, and Monique who's in a dark suit that would pass for business were it not for the bling of rhinestones on the collar, and the fact it shows plenty of cleavage. Her automatic is in a trick compartment of her purse. The dress of the day for the crowd will be cut off tee shirts, sweats, and hoodies, but sport coats do a much better job of hiding side arms, belt holsters, and shoulder holsters. By two in the afternoon, we're off to Hollywood: Cocoa, T-Rex, Frank, and Skeeter in the van; Monique, Marcus, and myself in the Mercedes.

Chapter Twenty-Four

We're barely on the road before my phone announces an unknown caller.

"Bennedict," I answer.

"Mr. Bennedict, it's Patricia Stanton."

"Yes, ma'am. What can I do for you?"

"Just so you know, my husband instructed me never to call you...but I've heard from the girls...well, actually, from Roberta."

"Have they escaped?"

"No, no, nothing like that. Roberta wanted me to FedEx a gown as she was going somewhere special...but I told her I would do no such thing and that she should come home. She hung up on me."

"I'm sorry, Mrs. Stanton, but the girls are under the influence and not themselves."

She was silent for a moment, then her voice seemed to harden. "Why didn't Gren want me to talk with you?"

"No, idea."

"Are you going to get the girls back for me, Mr. Bennedict?"

"We have an operation under way as we speak."

Her voice softened. "Oh, I so hope you're successful."

"Mrs. Stanton, we've had some interference from another…another group of men. Mr. Stanton has not hired someone else?"

"Not to the best of my knowledge."

"I hope not, as they may get in our way."

"I'll speak with Gren if you'd like, but he doesn't all ways tell me the truth, I'm sorry to say."

"Don't bother. Call me tomorrow if you'd like, if you don't hear from me later this evening, and I'll fill you in."

"Thank you."

After I break the connection I'm wondering why I'm feeling like it's good to have a friend in the enemy camp. I'm working for the Stantons, and shouldn't be feeling as if either of them are the enemy.

Just as we pass the San Diego Freeway, my phone rings again, only this time I know the caller. Detective John Espinoza, who, as usual, starts talking without bothering with the niceties.

"We turned up a print," he says.

"Regarding what, and where?" I ask, not sure which murder he's talking about.

"Poindexter. There was a knife dropped into a storm drain outside his house. Some kid chasing a ball saw it, told mama, and she was wise enough to give us a call. Had a touch of blood on it…Poindexter's blood type. It's out for DNA now."

"You get a make on the print?"

"In about a New York minute. Guy who's done some serious time. Gilbert a.k.a. Chaco Rodriquez, runs with Mission Hombres, affiliated with 14th Street. They're heavy into meth and Mexican brown at the moment. We've busted a dozen of them, but there're more than that still on the street. Why would Poindexter be mixing with those scumbags?"

"I got a hunch it was the woman and her old man who were mixing with the Hombres. Any word on her?"

"Nothing."

"You got a want out on Rodriquez?"

"I do, and we know where they crib up, so I expect we'll have him shortly."

"Thanks for the heads up."

"You gonna hit the Café del Sol tonight? Harold has come to his senses and wants to buy you a drink."

"Tell him thanks. Out of town on a job…got to make a living."

"Soon then."

We swerve off the Ventura Freeway onto the Hollywood. I check my phone for the time and see it's only 2:00 pm. The show starts at eight so we'll have plenty of time to recon the Hollywood Bowl, and hopefully tie up with Reggie Alexander, who General McClanahan put me onto, and who heads up the team from Event Security who's running their op tonight. The general told me to look for a six foot four ripped cat with screaming red hair and an Aussie accent. Shouldn't be hard to find.

We grab the Highland off ramp and in a couple of hundred yards Hollywood Bowl Road.

Marcus and Monique are with me in the Mercedes, and Cocoa, T-Rex, Skeeter and Frank follow in the van, and close enough I can see the whites of their eyes. At the entrance to the bowl complex you're greeted with an impressive fountain, with statues reminiscent of ancient Egypt. We stop just inside turnoff and a guard at the closed gate approaches.

I give the guard my most officious tone. "Mr. Alexander, Event Security is expecting us. The van's with me."

He opens the gate and waves us through without comment.

I dial T-Rex on the cell and instruct them to find a spot to park out of sight of the incoming traffic, on the slight chance some of Jo Jo's boys might wander in and make one of us. I also instruct them to turn on their hand-held radios.

As we approach the bowl complex—the stage shaped like a half a bowl on it's side—the offices, dressing rooms, stage, control rooms clustered around and under the bowl, half the back of which consists of a loading dock; I decide to fade to the far side of the employee-only parking and give Reggie Alexander a call. He picks up before the first ring is complete.

"Alexander."

"Mr. Alexander, I'm Brad Bennedict...General McClanahan called about our activities—"

"Actually he called my boss, mate. Had it been me was asked, I'd a tol' you to bugger off. I don't know what your act is here but it can't...it cannot...compromise the safety and security of the event."

His voice is little more than a growl. "Let's have a little face to face time...if you have time."

"Where are you?"

"Parking lot. Employee parking."

"I'll come out."

In moments he catches my wave and is striding across the lot.

I exit the car and extend my hand and he takes it with a grip that would shame most iron workers. I flash my bail enforcement shield with the other hand, but he gives it no more than a passing glance.

"Let me guess," I say, "Commando regiment?"

His hard look almost catches a smile, but not quite. "Actually Special Air Service Regiment. That was a few years ago. Took a little lead in oh nine in Afghanistan courtesy of the ragheads, and had to out myself. Attached to a Special Operations Task Group."

"Marine Force Recon myself. You have the bearing."

His look hardens again. "So, now that we've kissed and made up, what are you gonna do to fuck up my night?"

"Shouldn't be a problem. We need to pick up a couple of stray ladies and escort them out of here. We'll do our very best to be discreet. Should all happen backstage and out of sight." I'm exaggerating as I have no idea how this will come down, but I want to give him some confidence.

"Sounds like a billabong cluster fuck in the making, and I'm the one likely to end up wet...but the boss said to stay out of your way if possible. You be dinky-di and make sure it's possible, mate."

"Do my damndest." Obviously he garnered little confidence.

"I got eighteen thousand fuckwits expected here, mostly yobbos, blackfellas, who couldn't find their ass with either hand, I imagine, and I'll be like a jackaroo herding wallabies in a windstorm…so I don't need you makin' me a hornet in a bottle."

"Wouldn't think of it," I say, only about half knowing what he's talking about, but I imagine a hornet in a bottle would be pretty angry. "But do me a favor, mate?" I ask.

"What's that?"

"How many people you got doing security?"

"I got twenty five full time employees wearing black tee-shirts with security printed front and back in white. They'll be carrying radios, and five of them carry mace. Another hundred part timers in green shirts with white lettering front and back…most of them are worthless as tits on a bull. Hollywood P.D. has at least two dozen on site. There are seven of you, right?"

I nod as he hands me seven generic backstage guest badges with clips. "Thanks. I presume you'll be giving your people some final heads up?"

"Right'o."

"Then tell them the handsome guys in the sport coats with the guest badges are the good guys, one lady with me on staff, and one hippo size Samoan gentleman in a jogging suit, and a guy with a cast on his arm, just in case things run over into the stands."

"Don't let that happen, mate. You look like a bloke can handle 'is se'f, but, trust me, I'll shove your head up your donga and you'll be cactus."

Chapter Twenty-Five

The Aussie is looking at me like he'd like to rip my head off and piss down my neck, and it's all I can do not to smile as he has made his point clear without me understanding about half what he's saying.

I stifle the smile and try to placate the big ol' boy. "Do my damndest—"

"That's not good enough. Don't let it happen. And don't put Rafferty's rules in play here, or make a Wally out of me, or put anyone in the crowd or my people in peril."

"You got it." I'm still getting about half of what he's saying...hell, less than half. But I get the drift.

"Good on ya," he says, but unconvincingly. He nods, and spins on his heel and strides back to the office complex behind and under the bowl.

I climb back in the Mercedes, smiling, and turn to Monique and Marcus. "Either of you get that?"

Marcus laughs. "That guy sounds Australian, or maybe Martian."

"Talks funny, but he's a hunk," Monique says, her smile a little on the hungry side.

"You need a cup of coffee and a piece of pie," I say, a little disgustedly, then get on the radio to the boys.

"Let's make a pass around here on foot, then go for coffee and a confab."

"Ten four," comes back from T-Rex, and in moments they pull up behind the Mercedes and we all unload, I pass out Google Earth photo maps and diagrams of the place to each of them, courtesy of Sparks, and begin a recon on foot. We're almost an hour checking the place out, each of us with backstage guest badges dangling from collars and pockets thanks to our dubious new friend, Reggie.

The orchestra pit has been set up for special-guest seating, and I presume the girls—if they're not sequestered backstage—will be among the front six rows of special seating in temporary but comfortable looking folding seats. Whereas the rest of the 20,000 will be in, from front to back: The Pool Circle, Garden Boxes, Terrace Boxes, and the least super, SuperSeats. The Hollywood Bowl features three different types of seating areas. Box seats are partitioned off for groups of 4-6 patrons and feature collapsible canvas-covered seats. SuperSeats are plastic molded seats with cup holders and are the type typically found in arena settings. The rest of hill is covered in rows of wooden benches. There is no lawn seating at the Hollywood Bowl. Two giant screens grace each side of the stage, bringing everyone closer to the action, and a huge third screen is directly overhead stage-center. The theater makes seat cushions available to guests. There are special ramp seats on the sides for wheelchairs, up close, very near the stage. The bowl complex is surrounded with California oaks, buckeye, and some non-natural landscaping.

It's a beautiful, functional venue with superb acoustics, and not a bad seat in the house.   We're satisfied.

The troops follow me to the Roosevelt Hotel, more correctly the Hotel Roosevelt, named for my favorite president...Teddy...where I know we can get valet parking and grab something in the coffee shop.

In a few minutes we've pulled together two tables and have coffee and pie on the way...except for Cocoa, who has two hamburgers, a milkshake, and a double order of fries coming.

Leaving the vehicles at the Roosevelt we wander nearby Hollywood Boulevard and end up on Hollywood and Vine, the towns most famous intersection, now a labyrinth of tourist-trap shops, but both Monique and Cocoa seem to be enjoying themselves checking out the stars on the walk of fame, so we wander the streets, taking in a Ripley's Believe It Or Not and a half-dozen other robber baron attractions, until it's time for a bite to eat before we go to work. We find a spot near the Kodak Theater that won't break the bank and each grab a sandwich and shake, then head back to our vehicles and on to the bowl.

As agreed, we leave Marcus—with his arm in a cast—just inside the gate with a radio, watching for Jo Jo and his entourage, hopefully with the Stanton girls in tow, and for anything else, anybody else, we might need to know about. I place Frank Havlicek and Toby 'Skeeter' O'Brian in the private parking lot, also with hand-helds at the ready, and with strict instructions that they are to be eyes and ears only, as they carry no P.I. or bail recovery agent license. T-Rex and I are together, the roaming take-down duo, as we're the fastest and least likely to begin a cluster-fuck that queers the whole operation and ends up with me calling my favorite bondsman to get us all sprung.

Cocoa and Monique are posted each on opposite sides of the stage in the handicapped seating, presuming the boxes don't fill up with wheelchairs and they get run out...if so they are to get as close as possible to the orchestra pit. Cocoa could be easily recognized by Jo Jo's crew, so he's cautioned to stay well out of sight, which is no easy task for Tupo 'Cocoa' Tulasosopo. Monique, on the other hand, can move right into the pit should she not be challenged by some of the performer's bodyguards or the house security or even HPD, the Hollywood police. She, too, is noticeable, but in a very good way, and who would guess this gorgeous woman had a secret compartment in her stylish handbag concealing a 9 mm Glock and a bail enforcement agent's brass badge?

Now it's the hardest part of any operation...waiting.

Our wait isn't long. The show starts at 8:00 pm and at 6:30 the concert goers parking lot is beginning to fill, the employee/performer lot is half full, and the first limo is let into the area.

Marcus, even though he can't see into the tinted windows of the limo, a white Lincoln, radios to advise its arrival. There are three groups donating their talents to this benefit for the family of a murdered member of Diamond Fang, a medium ranked group, whose remaining members are among the three groups organized for this concert. Tarver's Crib is a slightly more popular group, and Jo Jo Bling & The Homeys fill out the night's entertainment. Jo Jo has four musicians backing him up, how many are in the other groups I have no idea, but I imagine there'll be at least a dozen in each entourage, if things are normal.

To my way of thinking, the more the merrier, as the more confusing things become, and the more who can get in the way, the better.

The Lincoln is followed by a Suburban, both carrying a half dozen, three of whom are obviously bodyguards, who unload and disappear into a rear door, the only door painted bright blue among a half dozen doors leading into the rear of the Bowl. This is not Jo Jo's bunch, although I had to do a double take on one blonde in spangles and 5" heels…but she's not one of the twins.

The second radio call I get is as to a long black limo, this one a Cadillac, containing eight, some of whom are carrying instrument cases, but no blondes are among them. They, too, have a back up car carrying four who look like they were just released from a maximum security prison.

Hummer, hard to miss as it sports a Jacuzzi on the back, sans bathers at the moment. I'm not surprised to see Jo Jo, his sister Chandra, his bodyguard Alonzo Bohanson, two others whom I don't recognize, and the twins, exit the ostentatious ride. He must be feeling confident as there is no backup car, and only one bodyguard. I'd hoped old Spider, his occasional employee, would be in attendance, but no such luck.

Being by far the most famous, Jo Jo and his boys are the last act, so it will be some time before they go onstage. It's my hope his bodyguards will be worrying about him and ignoring the twins when he takes the stage. The twins and Chandra take seats in the orchestra section, accompanied by Alonzo Bohanson. When the first act takes the stage. Monique, Cocoa and I trade texts advising each other that we're on station.

T-Rex and I stay out of sight in the parking lot near the blue stage door, where a single black-shirted guard, ~~one~~ carrying a mace cylinder on his belt, checks the credentials of those trying to enter. We stay far outside as Jo Jo and his group will recognize us, and that would most likely queer the whole operation.

T-Rex is into the crap they call rap, so he's enjoying the wait, and the music, far more than I. As it's a benefit show I don't expect it to be as long as a normal show with three groups might be, and I'm right when Diamond Fang leaves the stage after only thirty minutes. Monique is advising me by text of what's happening on stage, and I am surprised by a film retrospective showing lots of outtakes of the guy whose family is getting the dough from tonight's show. That consumes another thirty minutes.

The second group, Tarver's Crib, takes the stage and T-Rex complains about being dry, so I text Monique and Cocoa and tell them we're off station for a couple of minutes, and we wander across the parking lot to the Mercedes and fetch a couple of bottles of water.

The sun's down and it's getting dark, and the parking lot lights leave a lot to be desired. But it's a comfortable seventy degrees, and that's a good thing. As the Kevlar vests we're wearing get a little warm at times.

We're only out of sight of the blue door for a few minutes. When we return, I'm a little surprised to see the security guy who's been guarding the blue door is not at his station.

"Something is not right," I say to T-Rex, and text Monique that we're back, but to be wary as the guard is missing.

Chapter Twenty-Six

I'm tuned up, tight as one of the lead guitarist's strings. When I was a kid I worked some concert security, and this guys post at the stage door is one of the most important. It should be covered but it's not, and that's just not right.

"He's probably taking a leek," T-Rex says, casually, but his eyes are scanning the parking lot alertly, then he adds, "Let's hang for a minute and let things play out."

I check my watch. "Okay, I'll give him five. I can't imagine a guy would leave this particular post without having someone cover for him."

"Cheap help, but maybe he's just inside the door, checking credentials," T-Rex says, and we wait. It's a very mild evening, so it wasn't the weather drove him inside.

When the five minutes is up, I wave T-Rex forward and we close the distance to the blue door, just as my vibrating phone gives me a text alert.

Girls headed back stage.

We slip inside the blue door and stand for a moment to let our eyes adjust. We're in a hallway with open doors to rooms on either side, and no sign of the security guy who'd been outside. The dim six foot wide hall is fifty feet long and we move forward, warily. I hear some commotion coming from one of the dark rooms off the hall, and palm my .40 caliber Glock—I've left my Beretta at the office, wanting some harder hitting firepower. Anticipating some darkness in a backstage area when preparing for this gig, I'd slipped a combat flashlight on the Glock's rail, and flip it's switch and scan the room with its bright LED. It's full of props, then I see a pair of feet. Someone is flat on their back behind a prop. I move to him, and only then see his ankles are bound with cable ties, and then that the door security guy is both gagged and bound, and seems only half conscious. We leave him and return to the hall, both now openly carrying, panning muzzles in front of us.

What the hell is coming down?

We're almost to the end of the hall that opens to a large lighted room that seems to be under the stage, a hydraulic lift rests in the middle of the room below a trap door, so someone can ascend to the stage— stairways on each end of the room ascending at least one story—when gunfire rattles as loud as if we were in an oil drum with the shooter, and both of us hit the floor, but as soon as we do, we realize it's coming from above.

By the time the echo stops reverberating through the room, we're regaining our feet, and a dozen people are descending the stairs, obviously in a panic.

In the middle of the dozen on the stairway on our side, I recognize the girls, each with a guy front and back, and they're not treating the girls tenderly, others are madly trying to get away from them, up and down the stairs. At about the same time as I recognize the

Miami foursome, they spot us. We can't risk firing into the mess of bodies piling up and down the stairs, but they have no such restraints, and raise weapons as T-Rex and I dive for the protection of the hallway. An automatic weapon peppers the opening to the hall right behind us, and lead ricochets all around us as we scramble for the outside door, screams ringing out from the girls and from the others surrounding them.

We crash through the door, and are outside, both running for a nearby vehicle and rounding it to give us some cover. We're flanking the blue door, each about forty feet away, and fifty feet from each other, when the door is slowly pushed aside.

The twins, wide eyed, each with a weapon held to their heads, come through the door side by side, followed by the four Hispanic thugs. Seems they've managed to get well re-armed. The one I've nicknamed Gordo has a sidearm at the head of one of the twins, the pock-faced one has the other covered. Both girls look catatonic, eyes flaring, mouths in a soundless scream, knees seemingly weak and wobbling. Right on their tails are the other two Hispanics, each with an automatic pistol.

Gordo hauls up short on the step outside the blue door and scans the parking lot until he makes each of our positions. My cell alerts me to a text, but I'm a little busy at the moment.

"Hey, assholes," Gordo shouts, "you beat feet and nobody gets aced."

"Release the girls and you can head back to Florida," I shout with a tough tone but I'm pretty sure I'm had by these guys. We're outnumbered, out gunned, and they have hostages for cover.

"You ain't giving no orders," he says, then says something to the guys at his rear, the auto pistols swing up, and both T-Rex and I hit the deck behind the vehicles as automatic fire cuts the air above us, and clatters into the cars, splattering glass shards like a Texas hailstorm.

I don't have to worry about T-Rex as I know that he, like myself, is finding better cover among the many cars in the parking lot.

Scrambling, staying low, I position myself three car rows away, and watch through the windows of a Toyota hybrid while the girls are forced toward a four door Cadillac.

My quandary about firing is resolved when one of the twins is shoved into the front seat, and one in the back, and before the Hispanics can follow Frank Havlicek, who's not supposed to be armed, slips out of between a couple of parked cars and my jaw drops as he fires six quick, well placed, shots from a revolver, and Gordo and one of the boys with the automatic pistols goes down. The other two open up, but Frank has disappeared back between vehicles.

I'm badly positioned and I'm afraid to cut loose on the remaining pair as the girls in the Cad are in my line of fire beyond, but T-Rex is in a better position and opens up with his Glock. The thugs still standing break back for the stage door, spraying gunfire indiscriminately behind them. One of them, Doofus I think, is dragging a leg as they disappear back inside.

Frank has disappeared like a will-o-wisp, and I have no idea if he's hit or not?

The two on the ground are not moving, but more than one gunfighter's been x'd out by a perp playing possum. Both T-Rex and I remain in place, while the girls in the Cad scream. People are now pouring into the parking lot from both sides of the bowl, so we've got to move, and do, and are kicking away the weapons and checking the conditions of Gordo and the other guy. Gordo has bought the farm, no pulse, but the other guy, Pock-Face, who I think I remember as Sergio something from the wallets we filched earlier, is still rattling breath.

"Badge up and bury the weapon," I yell to T-Rex, and both of us holster our weapons and stuff our badge holders in our coat chest pockets so the shield is clearly visible.

Among those now pouring into the parking lot are a pair of Hollywood's uniformed finest, as well as Cocoa and Monique. She arrives before the officers, and I give her a head motion toward the girls. In moments, she's removing them from the Cad on the far side, away from the approaching officers, and they are disappearing into the crowd with Cocoa covering their tail.

The Aussie gentleman with Event Security, Reggie, is close behind, and he's spitting mad and I'm sure we'd be going to fist city if it was not for the two Hollywood cops close on his heels. The first words out of Reggie Alexander's mouth are some obscene reference to my mother. I tell him about his boy, who's most likely still tied up in the prop room, and he hustles away, still cursing.

The cops arrive in strength, presuming at first that T-Rex and I are plainclothes and some of their own, and it's not until a half dozen black and whites with lights glaring, and a pair of ambulances enter the lot do they realize we're bail enforcement and not city cops. In moments EMT's are checking Gordo, then ignoring him and working on Pock- Face who's still among us, seemingly if barely as his chest is blooming red. One pair of EMT's disappear inside the bowl and for the first time I learn that Jo Jo and Alonzo, backstage inside the bowl, are among those carrying a load of lead. No one seems to know if there're dead or still hanging on. The two uniform cops are getting real nervous with our status about the time a Hollywood uniformed captain, who introduces himself as Captain Jorgensen, is on the scene, and takes over.

He's cool and reserved, gray and distinguished, and asks us politely to surrender our weapons, which we do, with equal aplomb.

I know we've got many hours in some interrogation room in front of us even though it's obvious, at least to us, that we were acting in self-defense and are both legal and licensed to carry. Frank Havlicek is another matter altogether, and I've got to make up my mind quickly how I'm going to play his participation. Having an armed felon in my employ will not go well with the authorities. In fact, it could cost me my PI license.

The good news, Cocoa and Monique have disappeared with the girls, and I hope will be winging their way halfway to Florida by the time we have to disclose why we where prowling the Hollywood Bowl.

It's gonna be a long night.

Chapter Twenty-Seven

I was surprised that after we were relieved of our weapons, T-Rex and I were placed in the backseat of the same squad car to take a ride to the Wilcox Station of the Hollywood Police Department. It gave me an opportunity to advise T-Rex to leave Frank out of the story, merely that each of us thought the other had dropped the bad guys. We can always claim that in the fray and the darkness we had no idea anyone else was shooting. It won't take long for forensics to determine that the gunfire that dropped Gordo and Pock-Face didn't come from our weapons.

I've decided to do what I can to let Frank Havlicek take a walk, as he just may have saved our chops—not that I think he'll stay free as the boys in blue are pretty damn good at what they do. I do know he served a nickel and is a felon, and as such has no right to own a weapon, and even if he can prove self-defense, he'll probably do more time. I also remember that Officer Annie or her partner reported a .38 under the seat of the truck when we had our run-in at General McClanahan's place. Frank must have claimed it belonged to Skeeter, who had no felony in his background.

It comes to light that we were there after the girls, but I claim the last time I saw them was in the Cad, and that's the truth. I make sure I don't know anymore as I don't answer the many phone calls I get, in fact I've turned my phone off.

T-Rex and I go along with forensics, who bags our hands to check for recent powder splatter from firing weapons—which both of us have admitted to doing—and watch as they fire our weapons into the water trap to determine the ballistics and which firearms caused what damage. We'll both be getting rid of the Glocks as neither of us want the ballistics or our weapons on record. One never knows.... Both T-Rex and I are firing .40 caliber semi-automatics, and I'm presuming the shots taken by Gordo and Pock Face are from the revolver I saw in Frank's hand, probably the same .38 that was under his truck's seat earlier. After fielding questions for a few hours, it's reported that the slugs taken by forensics from Gordo are .38 caliber, as are those removed in surgery from Pock-Face.

At nine AM in the morning, after twelve hours, T-Rex and I are asked/advised not to leave the state, and released after being questioned at length as to whom the other shooter was. All we gave them was a shrug, which is not well received. I check from time to time and find my phone has taken a dozen attempted calls since we've been in what was technically custody, but I won't return them until we're clear of Hollywood's best. What I don't know can't get anyone else in trouble.

They give us nothing other than the caliber of the shots that killed Gordo, not the condition of Pock-Face, or anything about Jo Jo and Alonzo. They keep what they know close to the vest.

We do eventually learn that .40 caliber slugs are not found in Jo Jo or Alonzo.

As soon as I get out of the black and white that's given us a lift back to the Bowl and the Mercedes, I give Monique a call.

"You can talk?" she asks.

"On our way to breakfast. Tell me you got the girls back to Florida?"

"It was a snap. The girls said they were six feet away when Alonzo did his job and got between the boys from Miami and the girls, and took a couple of slugs. Jo Jo, to his credit, came after them with a mike stand, and took a couple more. All this was in the wings, off stage, and the music was so loud the crowd probably thought the auto pistol was part of the show...the crowd had no idea what was going down until they announced that Jo Jo couldn't go on. The girls were so scared they would have followed a grizzly bear if it had offered to get them to safety...and they we're high as cumulus clouds and slept all the way to Florida except for the short layover in Dallas. Anyway, they're in the arms of mommy and daddy and seem happy to be."

"And our hundred and fifty grand?"

"Mrs. Stanton assured us we'd have a check tomorrow...it's only been an hour since we delivered the twins. The old man kept his trap shut, too busy lecturing the girls to join in the conversation with me, so I guess we'll see."

"Okay, we're headed back to the barn to get some shuteye. Did Cocoa go with you?"

"He did, we're five grand into plane tickets with good ol' American Airlines, so I hope Stanton pays up."

"Talk to you tonight."

We learn from the morning news that Jo Jo is in intensive care at county hospital, and that Alonzo Bohanson has bought the farm. The guy I called Gordo is actually Henri Albrech, origin unknown, however his name most likely would not have been released if his next of kin hadn't been contacted. I'm surprised at the name as I figured him for Cuban as well.

Frank Havlicek, Skeeter, and Marcus have driven the van back to Montecito and are splayed around inside asleep, near the general's gate when we pull up.

I'm both pleased and pissed. I open the gate while T-Rex pounds on the door and wakes them, and I wave them to follow. I'm waiting when Frank steps out of the car, and can't help myself.

My straight right takes him on a cheekbone and it spits blood as he lands flat on his back.

"Don't get up, Frank," I advise, waiting for my wolf to calm down.

He sits up, angry, but no so much as he ignores my advice, and remains on his butt, steaming. Skeeter stays on the passenger side of the van, eying both T-Rex and I carefully.

"Those guys would have wasted you," Frank says.

"Maybe, but you were instructed not to be armed, and you made a liar out of us. Get up and come inside and I'll dress that eye."

As we go into my bungalow, I see the general looking out of his greenhouse, and he's smiling. The old man still enjoys a little action.

I put a butterfly bandage on Frank's cheek and get the bleeding stopped, get a couple of towels and ice his eye and my swelling knuckles, then take a deep breath and we all take a seat with a cup of coffee that T-Rex has made.

"Okay, this is how it's going to come down," I say as the boys listen intently. "We've covered your ass so far. Neither T-Rex or I saw who shot the bad guys. However, when it comes down to the nut cuttin' we'll have to give up who was in our employ at the B owl which we avoided mentioning and they failed to ask. You now have to do whatever you have to do. You're no longer in my employ. I'll pay you guys what I owe you and you're on your way."

I get up and head to my small bedroom and dig some hundreds out of my side table, and return, giving two of them an extra fifty. I count out the dough to Skeeter and Marcus, then ask them to step outside.

I hand Frank fifteen hundred, and he looks surprised. "Tell anybody what I paid you and both T-Rex and I will call you a liar. If this thing goes away, come back and see me in a couple of years and I may have some work for you, but you won't be armed and I'll get my decorator, Lance LeRoy to give you a cavity search to make sure. Get it?"

"Yeah, I get it." He rises and hits the door, then turns back. "Thanks, Brad."

"No, thank you, now get out of my life."

He gives me a lame Air Force salute, then the door closes.

I turn to T-Rex. "Give them a ride, will you? I want the van out of their grasp ASAP."

"Yep."

My phone wakes me and I realize it's early in the afternoon. It's Monique.

"The fucker says he's not paying," she says, without bothering with hello.

"I'm not surprised."   I'm surprised at her language, as she seldom swears, but not surprised that G.G. is going to try and stiff us. "T-Rex and I will be back there as soon as we can get a reasonable flight. I'm going back to bed."

"See you soon."

My phone, indicating an unknown caller, awakens me late in the afternoon. I never sleep during the day, and have trouble even remembering where the hell I am. I find it and manage to get the call answered, just as T-Rex appears in my bedroom door, and stands, eying me. He's a saint, as he has a cup of coffee in hand and passes it to me.

"Bennedict," I answer.

"They've taken Gren."

"Pardon me…Mrs. Stanton."

"Yes, they've taken Gren. Kidnapped him."

Chapter Twenty-Eight

I'm on the phone with Grenwald G. Stanton's wife, the guy who's recently informed my partner that he has no intention of paying the one hundred fifty thousand bucks he owes us. Now I suddenly see light at the end of the tunnel, and the possibility of getting what's owed us. I'd rather be paid merely for good work accomplished, but that doesn't seem to be G. G. Stanton's modus operandi.

I ask, but have a good suspicion. "I'm sorry, who's taken Gren...Mr. Stanton?"

"Some very large, very ugly, very profane Hispanic men. Cubans, I think."

"When did this happen?"

"Less than fifteen minutes ago. I called you as soon as I decided not to call the police. Can you come?"

"I'm sure the police can handle it, Mrs. Stanton." I'm not sure, but it's the proper thing to say, under the circumstance.

She seems to share my doubts, and her voice weakly reflects that. "I'm not so sure. I'll have your check for recovering the girls as soon as you get here. If you'll come."

That made deciding easy. "Yes, ma'am. Of course I'll come. Next flight. I'll see you in a few hours. Did they say anything to you?"

"They said twenty million dollars or I get his head on a plate and his balls, pardon the expression, in a *picadillo*...or maybe a frittata if it's morning time...and not to call the police. I have forty eight hours to come with the money. They'll call with instructions...."

"That was it?"

"That, and something about Gren getting somebody's little brother killed."

"Yeah, somebody I told him absolutely not to hire. Monique mentioned you have an elaborate security system. Did you get any video of these guys?"

"I'm sure we did."

"I'm having a young man, Herbert Handley, who we call Sparks, give you a call. He'll tell you what he wants done with the video. Do it quickly, please."

"I will."

"That's it?"

"Short and sweet...and frightening and violent. I've never seen Gren frightened...he yelled at me, begging me to get the money, as they dragged him out. It's not common knowledge, but Gren is worth over a billion...still twenty million will be hard to put together in a short time. You don't have to catch a flight. I'll call Gren's company and they'll send the G5 for you and whomever. The plane, as it's configured, will seat sixteen."

"There will only be two of us. Let me know when and where."

"Only two?" I can hear that she's reconsidering calling the police.

"We have lots of friends and associates there in Florida, who know the customs and the territory."

Then she continues, "Santa Barbara airport, and if the plane is here and not overseas somewhere, it'll be there in seven hours or so, sooner if it's fueled up. If it's not available, I'll charter for you."

"Yes, ma'am. Private will be much better as we can carry items that might arise the ire of Homeland Security. Call Monique and ask her to get over to be with you."

"I'll do that, thank you. The girls are not much help."

I punch off and give T-Rex a winning smile. "Guess what, my man?"

"Fill me in?"

As I'm dialing Sparks, I fill him in, "We're getting paid in full for the last gig, and unless I miss my bet, we've got another very, very fat engagement."

It's mid afternoon by the time we board Janus Electronics bright yellow, blue striped, G5. Even with room for sixteen, we find a pair of facing seats with a table in between. And in seconds, have a tumbler in front of us with a well aged, peat flavored, Oban scotch wetting our throats.

A G5 would make a fella want to become a captain of industry, or king of finance, or at least the heir to some great fortune…it damn sure impressed this poor son of a Texas roughneck who never had occupied more than a three bedroom one bath abode about the same square footage as the business jet in which we now rode. T-Rex has never been one to smile a lot, but he keeps a Cheshire cat grin as Ingrid—a fetching blonde, in a mini-mini yellow skirt and blue blouse, flight attendant—serves us a medium rare filet, scalloped potatoes, and green salad along with the second three fingers of 25 year old scotch.

It's dark, overcast, hot and sweaty when we land at West Palm Beach International and de-plane at a gray and white two-story reception building. I am obliged to the pilot, co-pilot, and gorgeous Ingrid, in that they have not inquired as to what's in the four hard sided cases we had stowed in the luggage compartment, or why Janus Electronics is transporting a couple of rough old boys in casual clothes all the way from Santa Barbara to West Palm Beach…then again I guess they're paid to be discreet.

I am a little surprised that neither Cocoa nor Monique are there to meet us, but don't complain when a stretch limo drives up the jet and the pilots and driver handle our cases and small personal duffels.

This private flying is not all bad.

As nice as the back of the Mercedes limo is, I set up front with Hector, the driver, as it's time I get serious, and although I've been to West Palm Beach dozens of times, there's still plenty I don't know about South East Florida. We take Highway 80 east to South Australian, to Okeechobee, through downtown, to the Flagler Memorial Bridge, across to the barrier island, then north again to through the Island almost as far as we can go before drowning in the Palm Beach Inlet.

The houses get larger, more sheltered from the road, and obviously more and more expensive the nearer we get to the inlet end of the island.

Finally we pull into a long driveway to a tile roofed mansion facing Peanut Island. I'm not sure where we're staying, but then see Monique's Mercedes SUV parked off to the side. At least there's a friendly nearby.

Before we can shake off the five hour flight and thirty minute drive from the airport, Mrs. Stanton and Monique are outside to welcome us. She instructs the limo driver to wait, and climbs back in a pulls his cap down over his eyes.

I glance at my watch;   It was mid-afternoon when we lifted off from Santa Barbara and with the five hour flight, drive, and change of time, it's now eleven thirty.

"Can you use a drink?" Mrs. Stanton asks. Even with swollen eyes, she's a beauty. Sandy hair, long legs, a dancer's body, I have trouble deciding her age until we're inside. Early forties, I'd guess, and married to a sixty seven year old.

We go inside the two story home, which I judge to be well over ten thousand square feet, which doesn't include a guest house I spot out the back, the boat house which is four times the size of my cottage in Montecito, and the yacht, which is the better part of a hundred feet, if not a smidgen more.

I beg off on the drink and talk Merna, the maid, into a cup of coffee. I'm proud of T-Rex, normally a Jack Daniels beer back guy, as he has the same.

Even before the coffee arrives Mrs. Stanton takes a seat across a breakfast table from T-Rex, Monique, and I, and gets down to business.

"I've already given Miss St. Marmont a check for one hundred fifty thousand dollars. Now, what do you need to bring my husband home safely?"

"First, have they called with instructions?"

"No."

I set back in my rattan chair, and wait for Merna to place the coffee cups, then for her to get out of earshot. "We work in a number of ways, Mrs. Stanton, as you know, we'll give you a direct quote as we did with the girls. We work in bail recovery, and get twenty percent of the bail amount—"

"If your saying you want four million dollars, as that's twenty percent of the ransom—"

"I'm not saying that. Since you're a good client...you were pleased with the return of your daughters?"

"Of course, and you were well paid."

"No argument. We had no idea, of course, that we'd end up in a gunfight."

"I thought that's the sort of thing you do."

"It is, ma'am, but we would have charged more had we known."

"That gunfight, and the fact that man was killed...obviously the little brother of one of the men who took Gren...is the reason they got angry and kidnapped him. Or so I surmise."

I give her a tight smile, before I respond. "That's true, and had your husband not gone against my explicit instructions, those men would not have been there and there would have been no gunfight. We had only a small inkling of who they were, and they began firing at us, putting your daughters in great danger."

She looks a little crestfallen, defeated, then her voice quivers as she speaks. "I'll give you a half million, two hundred thousand in advance, the balance when Gren is delivered safely home."

It's a hundred thousand more than I'd considered asking for, and would have settled for the same amount we charged to get the girls, but I don't smile as that would be a little obvious.

"I can live with that, Mrs. Stanton, since you're a good client. Have you heard from Sparks?"

"Who?"

"Herbert Handley, our computer expert."

"I referred him to Miss St. Marmont."

"It's handled," Monique says.

"Then lets get to a hotel so we can get a few hours of rest."

"No, no, please, stay in the guest house. There are three bedrooms and your man, Cocoa I think you said, is already asleep out there. The den has excellent internet and a fax, as well as a satellite phone. I'll have my driver unload the rest of your gear and then he's relieved unless you think you'll need him tonight.?"

I give T-Rex the high sign and he goes out to help, as we need to be careful with our trunks which are full of equipment that would have raised the ire of Homeland Security...in fact they'd have called in the Marines.

Chapter Twenty-Nine

We have a short meeting in the guesthouse before we hit the hay. Sparks, back in California, will work all night and we should have a full dossier on the Cubans, if that's what they are, by early morning. Monique leaves for her own place, a condo overlooking Lake Mangonia, only a couple of miles away.

We also have an early breakfast meeting with two friends from Palm Beach, Marco and Orlando Fuentes, a couple of Jewish Cuban heritage amigos with whom we've worked before. Very, very tough guys, who know the Cuban community, who served in the Israeli army with distinction, before returning to Florida to take over their grandfather's bail bond office, Freedom Fuentes. They're bringing the lox and bagels here at seven a.m.

Cocoa has taken the bedroom with the king size bed, appropriate I suppose as he fills a queen to capacity. I take a bedroom with a queen size relegating T-Rex to one of two twins in the third bedroom. I've just turned off the light, when there's a light rap on my door. As is my habit, my automatic is on the bedside table, and before answering the knock, I slip it under the sheet.

"Yes."

The door opens and there stands Mrs. Stanton, clad in a thigh length robe, bare feet, nicely backlit by the hall light.

I'm beginning to wonder if my retainer might include additional service other than 'husband recovery' as it's a moment before she speaks, and as it seems she's more than a little interested in my exposed upper body. Then my anticipation is broken.

"They called."

"Give me a second," I ask, and she shuts the door. As I sleep in the raw, it takes me a second to pull on my khakis and a tec shirt. Shoeless, I join her in the guesthouse kitchen, where she's making a cup of tea. She offers it to me, but I decline.

"Sorry if I woke you. I figured you'd be in the master bedroom, but I could tell by the mountain in that bed that it wasn't you."

"Cocoa needs the extra room. So, what's the story?"

"They want the funds transferred to a Nassau bank, Chippingham International, no later than five p.m. tomorrow. I have the account number."

"Damn, I was hoping they wanted diamonds or something that we'd have to deliver. This makes things very, very tough. Let's hope we get a line on these guys quickly. We can buy a little time as twenty mil would be hard for anyone to put together."

"They said they'd kill Gren if the transfer wasn't made on time."

I give her what I hope passes for a knowing smile. "Would you kill the goose about to lay a golden egg. They know we'll want proof of life?"

She's silent for a moment, then asks quietly, "There's a chance the money can be ready. The president of Gren's company, Brendon Austin, wants to meet with us in the morning."

"I hope you haven't advised anyone else of what's going on?"

"No one else. But since he has to arrange for the money…. I asked Brendon not to tell anyone else."

"Of course we'll meet, but let's make it here if that's possible. We're setting up our control center right here in the guest house den, and I don't want to stray far away."

"I'll call him as soon as we're through here. He's in Miami, but can be here if necessary."

"Good, but Mrs. Stanton, you need to be ready to stall just in case we're not onto these guys. I must caution you there's a good chance you'll pay, and still not get your husband back. If he can identify these guys…." I pause until I surmise, by the look on her face, that she gets it. "The more time we have to find and extract him, the better."

"I understand. But don't we know who did this. The brother of the man killed in Los Angeles?"

"We know what we know. It's what we don't know that worries me. We'll know a lot more in the morning."

"I'm calling Brendon, then let's get some sleep."

"Good idea."

I wake T-Rex at five a.m. T-Rex reminds me of a gila monster when he's awakened anytime before noon. I remind him that I'm armed and he gumbles his way to the shower.

Cocoa, as usual, is three hundred and fifty pounds of smiles. We meet up in the small guest house kitchen, where I already have the pot perking. Before I'm halfway through the first cup, my cell phone rattles an unknown caller, and I pick up to Orlando Fuentes, who reports that he and his brother, Marco, are in the driveway, a half hour early. That's one of the many reasons I enjoy working with the Fuentes brothers.

I've got at least six inches in height on both the boys, but we weigh about the same. Were they military equipment, they'd be Abram's Battle Tanks. They look so much alike it would be hard to tell them apart, except Orlando has a white eye from getting poked with a kitchen fork by some irate wife when he was concentrating on the skip he was picking up, and mama got behind him.

As promised, they have two sacks in tow from a local Deli, and as soon as we hit the kitchen and they renew old acquaintances with T-Rex and Cocoa, they lay out a spread of lox, bagels, onions, capers, and to oblige the goys, sweet rolls and donuts.

Orlando also produces a ream of papers.

"Here's the poop," he says with a full mouth, "on this Henri Albrech cat you wasted in L.A. His bro, Enrico Albrech, is big time in the illegal prescription drug game, known as the king of OxyContin...but the word is he's controlled by the Bahamian mob. His mama, by the way, is a black Bahama mama, his daddy is Albanian or some damn thing, but they've been in

Nassau for four generations. They hang with Cuban and some Bahamian gangbangers here, who distribute all the way to the Carolinas and Louisiana. It's said they have a connection to Chicago."

"So, where to they hang their hat?" I ask.

"Albrech and his bunch have got a compound, a regular go-to-the-mattresses place with four houses on three well fenced acres, down below Hypoluxo…out near the Loxahatchee alligator pond…Actually the Loxahatchee National Wildlife Refuge."

"Sounds like a good place to get rid of a body."

"Oi vey. The best. Two hundred twenty square miles of stinkin' mosquito swamp at the north end of the everglades. Of course some think it's beautiful. I think it's a shit-hole."

"This compound…should we reconnoiter the place?"

"Ahead of you. I've got a pardner down that way, Mo Gilbert, and asked him to case the joint last night and hang until we get back to him this morning. He's already in the bush near the compound taking pics and watching the movement. I just talked to him before pulling in the drive way and he's still on the job. Last night a pizza delivery truck brought in about a half dozen large pizzas. Nothing else going on. I figured it was worth the three hundred he cost."

"No problem. More importantly, did you find us a legal reason to bust the Albrech place?"

He gives me a Cheshire cat grin. "You pay us and in addition we may get a big score. Henri Albrech himself has skipped on a Federal bond for racketeering, a million bucks, and Fuentes Freedom just got a ten percent contract in the mail from Jefferson Federal in Alexandria. This could be a nice score for us."

"What's our cut," I ask, knowing the answer.

"How about one over your eye requiring about sixteen stitches."

He's laughing, but I know he's half serious. Only half serious, so I press it. "So if you score are you gonna wave the five hun a day I'm paying each of you?"

"How about one over the other eye." He's still smiling.

"You don't A.S.K., you don't G.E.T.," I say, and shrug my shoulders.

To my surprise, both Monique and Mrs. Stanton hit the door to the guesthouse about the same time. Mrs. Stanton looks a little worse for the wear, nicely dressed in a baby blue pantsuit and medium heels, but bags under her eyes confirm the fact she slept badly, or not at all.

Monique, on the other hand, in black jeans and a tightly fitted white silk blouse, ankle high lizard pattern boots, and her auburn hair pulled tightly back, looks both as if she just stepped out of Vogue and as if she's ready for action. And she is, as she carried a small gym bag and I know it's got a change of clothes inside. Probably black hiking boots and a black long sleeve top. The lizard-leather butt pack she wears matches the high heeled black boots, and I know the butt pack carries more than her make up and wallet.

We make the introductions to Mrs. Stanton, who looks a little worried, so I offer her a little comfort.

"The Fuentes brothers are long time associates of mine, and ex-military from one of the toughest militaries in the world. They were members of the Winged

Snakes, an elite unit of the Israeli Special Forces. There's not a bad guy in Florida who doesn't fear them."

She smiles tightly, then offers. "Brendon Austin will be here by seven. He's bringing his financial officer."

"Mrs. Stanton, we need to keep this quiet, for your husband's sake."

"It's a C.Y.A., a cover-your-ass play on Brendon's part. He does nothing that he can't blame on someone else. To be truthful, I never liked the man, but Gren thinks he's wonderful. I had no choice but to inform him...."

"Let's hope this stays with only ~~Austin~~ *Brandon* and his man. It's getting out of hand."

"Nothing, as I said, that I could do about it."

I wolf down a sweet roll and take my coffee to the den and set up a pair of laptops on the desk there— as Mrs. Stanton said, there's everything in the way of office equipment we could possibly need—then recover a waiting email and print out what Sparks has come up with, including a picture of Chippingham International, which as it turns out, is a single office in a small office building in Nassau. As I feared, the place is only a transfer point for the money, which I'm sure will hit a dozen banks all over the world in short order, to try and keep anyone from tracing it to it's actual recipient. One thing dope dealers learn to be good at is laundering money.

We've got to hope that Grenwald Stanton is not in Nassau, or somewhere else in the Caribbean. Let's hope he's tucked away in the compound down below Hypoluxo.

But then again, that would be far too easy.

Chapter Thirty

S parks has sent me all he can find on a Google Earth aerial view of the Albrech compound and as I'm printing it, another email arrives from Sparks. It seems the Albrech's own a Beaver, a million dollar aircraft capable of landing on water. Theirs happens to be converted to turbo prop jet engines driving a propeller. Capable of flying all the way to Nassau from the Palm Beach County Glades Airport, known to the locals as Pahokee, where they keep it tied to a dock just over the Herbert Hoover Dyke from the paved airstrip, in Lake Okeechobee, it's something I hadn't counted upon.

And it was the aircraft listed on a filed flight plan, with four on board, to Nassau last night. That could be very bad news.

The guest room phone rings, and Mrs. Stanton picks up, says, "They're here," and leaves for a moment, then reappears with a tall, distinguished gray haired man accompanied by a short dark balding one, who's furrowed brows remain so.

I give her a frown, but she ignores me as she introduces Brendon Austin, CEO of Janus Electronics, and Forrest Rothstein, CFO.

By his condescending glance at the five of us, and his blatant admiring glance at Monique, I've already judged Mr. Austin to be a total asshole. Mr. Rothstein is non-descript little grease ball, other than looking like a frustrated anal accountant whose books won't balance.

"I don't need to spend a lot of time here," Austin begins. "I've called each of my board members and talked with our insurance company. Four million dollars is the total of our insurance coverage for an executive abduction, and the board is willing to risk another one million dollars—"

"What!" Mrs. Stanton snaps, "Gren controls sixty five percent of the stock of Janus, and I know your cash position is three times the twenty million. I insist—"

Austin coldly interrupts her. "Has no bearing on the fact I can't authorize any more than our insurance will cover and the board will authorize, and you personally have no authority—"

"Brendon, you are a weasel, you've always been a weasel, and I pray Gren gets out of this mess so he can rub your nose in it." She turns to the cubby little CFO, "And Forrest, is this your position as well?"

The accountant stammers with an "eh, eh, eh…. I have to back up—"

"Get out," she yells, "I can't stand the smell of pussy cowards. Get out!"

Both of them spin on their heels and head for the door. The accountant glancing back at least five times as if he's got a Rottweiler about to take a chunk out of his generous butt. Austin pauses at the door and looks back. "You have to involve the FBI, Mrs. Stanton. If you don't the insurance may be voided."

"Get out, Brendon."

He slams the door much harder than necessary.

I've gained a new respect for Mrs. Stanton. She turns her attention to me. "I can scrape together a million or maybe a million five out of our various accounts. I'll get on the phone to the board members and get five million ready to transfer when you say go. I'll personally guarantee they get it back if the insurance company doesn't pay up. I'm worth twice what Gren is, which may be the reason he married me…but mine's in a trust and it'll take a month to get it freed up."

And I thought she was a trophy wife. Shows how wrong you can be. "Let's hope the five mil doesn't have to happen. We've got some planning to do, so if you'll excuse us."

"I can't sit in on this?"

"I'd prefer you don't. The less you know, the less you'll be able to testify to, should it not go smoothly. It's for your protection and ours."

"Fine, I'll go make my phone calls."

"While you're out, cut us a check for two hundred thou. I'll let the rest ride until you have your husband back."

She nods, and walks out.

The instant she leaves I get some sound and video equipment out of the trunks, brief T-Rex, and in minutes he's loaded up in Monique's SUV and is on his way to meet up with Fuente's man, Mo Gilbert, who Orlando immediately calls so he's on the lookout for our guy.

The rest of us gather around the breakfast table and begin planning a visit to the Albrech compound, which Mo has reported has a seven-foot cyclone fence surrounding all but the waterside, an electronically activated driveway gate, and video surveillance. On closer study, we figure that two of the four buildings are four car garages, as the driveways end there. One of them must also have a shop or a small apartment attach as a walk way goes from driveway to a step. The other two buildings are residences of some sort. Orlando calls his man, Mo, and we find the pizzas were delivered to the larger of the two residences, and no one has moved between the two. Whoever is there must be in the larger residence, I figure it to be about six thousand square feet, when we're advised it's one story. That's good news and bad news, as it's large with lots of rooms, but one story so we won't have stairs or two story balconies to breech.

Like much of south-central Florida, there's a red mangrove lined waterway at the rear of the property that, if Google Earth is right, ties into the Wildlife Reserve. There's a small dock, although, according to Mo, the only boat is a small outboard. There's not another house for a quarter mile in any direction, so the road to the gate to the place is long and lonely, and its easy to spot any approaching vehicle. But there's lots of undergrowth along the road, the waterway to the rear, and the surrounding terrain. Good cover for someone on foot. So we need to be prepared for night work, rough terrain, and a water approach if necessary.

Packed in the trunks are five bug-out bags each with Kevlar vests; 9mm hand guns with rails, LED lights, and laser sights; a Leatherman tool; aerosol mace grenades; throw-away lightweight eye, nose, and mouth covering gas masks to combat aerosol; flash and stun grenades; hand-held stun guns; tactical belt with spare magazines for the weapons and fittings for the rest of the gear; black tactical shirts, hoods, and reversible knit caps which are black on one side and hunter orange on the other should we want to be identified; Max-Cuff disposable restraints for hand and ankle cuffs; a Ka-Bar folding knife; a small personal first aid kit; night vision equipment; and water and energy bars. In addition we have one tactical backpack with bolt cutters; a Kel-Tec KSG 15 round tactical shotgun loaded for door breeching and other close work; twenty feet of explosive cord; and various small tools.

The Fuentes brothers have brought along some supplemental equipment, including a Blackhawk CQB ram for battering doors, and their own array of firearms, including the Uzis they still prefer. They also have re-breathing gear, knowing we'll be working near water.

Another trunk contains my new favorite sniper rifle, a Savage 10 FLCP-K in 308 Winchester with a variable scope up to 24 power; and the heart of any special weapons team, five MP-5 9mm Heckler Koch machine guns, HK's, with ambidextrous trigger configuration…the same firearm used by many swat teams, including Los Angeles. I have a Bureau of Tobacco and Firearms automatic weapon ownership license, however it's illegal no matter the license for a private person to own automatic weapons manufactured after 1986. And in some states, automatic weapon ownership is illegal no matter the federal license. The HK's are illegal for me to own and I'm taking a risk, but better that risk than risk not having enough firepower. But if there's any state that will cut me some slack, it's Florida.

Still, should it be necessary to utilize the automatic weapons, we'll handle the problem in a way that should keep us out of the slammer, and in addition deny their use, saying all that fire was from our 9mm side arms. It won't be believed, but nonetheless, that will be our story and we're sticking to it.

Mrs. Stanton has a Ford Expedition as a back up vehicle—more practical than the Mercedes SLS she normally drives. The Ford has a trailer hitch, and we borrow it and load up in both it and the Fuentes GMC three quarter ton pickup truck, with Marco driving. We've got to find a boat to rent, and Marco says he knows just the place, which he figures is no more than a mile from the compound, on the Wildlife Reserve. He's not sure about the route through the waterways, but I've downloaded a Google Earth aerial and we figure we can work it out. I've sent Orlando on another mission, as he has a buddy in the restaurant biz in Boynton Beach, who owes him big time.

We have no idea if we're on the right trail, but so far, it's our only trail.

Chapter Thirty-One

We head south on Highway 7 to Lee Road, then west to a public boat launch, where we're being met by the rental guy with a twenty foot fifty horsepower outboard fishing boat and rods and reels. We're only a mile or so from the Albrech compound. There will be no attempt to breech the house while it's still light. With our night goggles and gear, that will give us some advantage, presuming we find a way to kill the power, which is normally no problem.

Orlando has completed his task with his friend in the restaurant biz, and a Ricky's Cuban Home Delivery truck is parked in the boat launch parking area.

T-Rex, who we've called to meet us, and Orlando putt-putt out in the boat and have their phones, which work here only three or four miles west of Boynton Beach, as well as hand-held radios. Mo Gilbert is still on post watching the compound from binocular distance away, which is no easy task as the land is flat as a billiard table and covered with undergrowth and a few trees. T-Rex and Orlando will have an easy task for the next few hours…they will be fishing only a couple of hundred yards from the Albrech boat dock until we give them a yell.

Monique, Marco, Cocoa, and I head out to meet up with Mo Gilbert, only a couple of hundred yards from the Albrech compound, leaving the pizza truck in the boat ramp parking, so it's well out of sight of the compound.

Mo's instructed us to follow a trail west into the underbrush, near a sign cautioning against littering, and look for an old shed, which is the only place he could find to get some elevation to spy on the compound.

As we start into the brush, Monique gives a low squeal. "Damn, the mosquitoes. Anybody bring any bug spray?"

"There are only two mosquitoes in Santa Barbara, and they've been spayed." I say, but a little sheepishly.

"Yeah, and there are only a couple here in Florida. Of course, they are a couple, with millions of children and uncles and aunts and cousins."

"Very funny. This is your bailiwick. Where's your bug spray?"

"I can mace them." She says, and laughs as sheepishly as I've spoken.

"Let's check this out, then we'll hightail it back to the car."

Thank God it's only in the low eighties, without Florida's occasional devastating humidity, or it could really be miserable.

We wander through some low slash pine and palmettos until the shack comes into view, as well as the guy in camouflage with only half his head and binocs peering over the ridge of the roof. It's a tarpaper ten by twenty foot shack with a composition roof, windows and doors blown out, and looks as the last time it was used was during the Truman administration.

He doesn't hear us until we're six feet from the shack, and almost jumps out of his skin. "Damn, damn, I almost slipped." He works his way to the eave and drops to the ground, not bothering with the step ladder placed there, then sticks out a narrow hand. He's a little guy, not over one forty soaking wet, with features that look as if someone has squashed them together. Less than a normal distance between his mouth and eyes, with a button nose. I'll bet the Mo is a nickname for another nickname, Mouse.

I shake with him and introduce him around, as he reports.

"Other than the pizza delivery guy only one car...actually a pickup truck...has come and gone, and he returned with groceries, at least a half dozen grocery sacks. I slipped up to within forty yards of the place, the edge of the undergrowth, and set up the hyperbolic mike and recorder Rex brought, aiming it what I surmise is a living room window. I'll retrieve it when it gets dark. I've got to head in and chow down, if one of you can take over a while?"

I eyeball Cocoa and the roof, doubting if it will hold him, then turn to Marco, "Cocoa will crush the place, Monique will get a run in her nylons, and as you Fuentes boys pointed out, you're getting paid for the work no matter how much you make off the contract, so get your ass up there."

He eyes me coldly. "And you?"

"I'm what's known as the boss...you know, the guy with the checkbook."

He climbs to the top of the stepladder, then instructs, "Give me a boost," to his credit, and in moments is in place just below the ridge line. Even as cool as it is for Florida, it's got to be hot on that roof. I throw him up a bottle of water and tell him we'll bring him a sandwich.

As we head back to the car, Monique informs me, "I no longer wear nylons. Smooth well tanned legs need no accouterments."

"I noticed that myself, thanks. Particularly under jeans do they need no accouterments. It was a figure of speech trying to make it clear to Marco that you're a helpless female."

"The way he's been checking me out, I think he has that figured."

When we get back to the Ford Expedition, I give T-Rex a call. "How's the fishing?"

"Forgot the damn bait. But the casting and reeling in is fine. Caught three sticks and some moss…and saw an eight-foot gator. Ain't gonna be doin' no swimming."

"Don't worry about the gators…the coral snakes and Burmese pythons will probably get you first. Why don't you make a couple of passes by the compound and see what you can see. We're going into town to pick up some chow and will meet you back at the boat ramp at…." I glance at my phone to get the time.… "At three thirty."

"Ten four."

We hit a local drive through then start back, when Monique, who is sitting beside me in the front seat, surprises me with, "I want to go in first."

"Bullshit," I say. "I'm going in first. I'll pull up in the food truck and check the place out when they come to the door, maybe I'll get inside."

"And you don't think the fact they didn't order any food, and the fact a six foot two guy who looks like he eats nails will put them on edge?"

"Forget it. Remember the time I dressed as a priest and—"

"Don't tell me to forget it. Florida is my side of the world. You guys had all the fun at the Hollywood Bowl—"

"Ducking automatic weapons with ricochets splattering all around and broken glass peppering me while I'm trying to stay on the grassy side of the turf is not my idea of fun."

"You guys got all the action at the Hollywood Bowl, and now it's my turn. You know as well as I do if a woman answers the door she'll let her guard down if it's another woman, if a man answers...well, he'll be checking me out, and not for a piece of pizza."

I'm sighing deeply. Not because I don't think she can do the job, but because these are a bunch of real bad boys. Cocoa is in the seat behind, and leans forward.

"Hey, I can take the door, or we can get T-Rex to beach the boat. He's only five foot eleven, and he'll give them his stupid grin."

Monique is not backing down. "He's got a stupid grin, that's for damn sure, and a two inch scar through an eyebrow and the other eye is still half-black from that shit kicking he took at Jo Jo Bling's place. And Cocoa, you would scare a SWAT team. Besides, if it's one of the guys who got away from the fiasco in

L.A. who's in the place, they might recognize either one of you. I'm the only one who has a chance of getting in the door without a stick of dynamite. I want to do this, Brad."

"You're being a hard-head, Monique."

"Oh, yeah, and you're being soft-headed, but you know I'm right."

I again sigh deeply, then relent. "Okay, but you're wearing a wire and the mini-video cam, and a vest under your shirt, and you've got to agree that if anything looks off, you'll beat a trail back to the truck."

"The vest squishes my boobs down and will screw up the look."

"You're wearing the vest or you're not going in."

"Okay, okay, I'll wear the vest, but if I don't mesmerize the dork answering the door with my well-defined nips, it's your fault."

"I'll take the blame," I say, and can't help but glance at her well-defined nips. They are mesmerizing.

She laughs, then adds, "I'll take the bra up a couple of notches and the cleavage will do the trick."

"No doubt. I've never been good at hooking one back up a notch or two, only unhooking," I answer, not able to keep the smart-ass smile off my face, but this time containing my glance and keeping my eyes on the road.

She continues. "That's more than I need to know, bulldog, as if I didn't know. I'll check the place out, get what I can, deliver the pizza and chicken, and be back in the truck in a heartbeat. Then you hot dogs can charge the ramparts from the front and T-Rex and Orlando from the back if you think it's a go."

"We've got no choice unless they give you a tour of the place including looking in every closet. And I don't want you beyond the main room."

"Then when you go in, I'll cover the doors and windows from the front, as per the plan."

"Okay, it's your skin."

"And I plan to keep it unmarred."

"From your lips to God's ears, girl."

Chapter Thirty-Two

Mo's car is back at the boat ramp parking lot when we return, and he's leaning on the front fender smoking a Cuban cigar almost as big as he is. I stop and pick him up, and since it's not quite three thirty I go ahead and radio T-Rex and Orlando to come back and pick up some chow.

As we wait, I advise Mo. "I want to go in with you and pick up the recorder before it get's dark, and take a close look at the compound."

"No sweat."

In minutes, the boat grounds near the boat ramp and I take the boys out the sandwiches and soft drinks.

"How goes it?" I ask as I pass them over.

T-Rex yawns before he replies. "It's boring as hell, except for the broad in the string bikini."

"Where?"

"In the backyard. They've got a hot tub, a BBQ and a patio cover out back. And this blonde bombshell with legs from the ground to heaven walks out to their dock and gives us a wave and a smile as big as one of these alligator's as we idle by. Hard not to stop."

"You'll get a closer view come dark. I'll radio a go about a half hour after the sun goes down. When the lights go out, we go in. And don't be too trigger happy as the three of us will be coming in from the front."

"Can't wait." He takes a bite of the grilled ham and cheese I brought him. "You know I hate mustard."

"You're welcome. Stand by, a half hour after the top of the sun disappears."

"You got it."

We return to the shack and give Marco some chow, who eats while Mo and I make our way through the palmettos and slash pine to the spot where he's placed the small hyperbolic microphone and recorder. He belly crawls up through some low palmetto to the edge of the brush and retrieves the recorder, leaving the mike in place as he doesn't want to shake the palmetto where it's hidden, as it's in clear view of the house.

I do find a place where I can clearly see what I'm looking for, and that's the power lines coming into the main house, and the breaker box for the house. I also use my binocs to carefully check for video security cameras. They are either not there, or, more than likely, well concealed.

There are two large bald cypress in the front yard, a couple on each side of the main house, and a half-dozen in the rear of the place, the rest of the grounds are clean of all vegetation. The cypress will offer some cover, although if all goes as planned, the whole yard will be dark as the inside of one of those pythons now happily growing to obscene size in the everglades.

If everything goes as planned, which it seldom does.

These operations normally personify Murphy's Law, as the Hollywood Bowl again proved.

You've got to be ready for anything.

We spend the next hour listening to the recording of muted voices coming and going—the hyperbolic mike did a great job of picking up sounds—between bouts of Bob Marley drowning out most of the conversation with blaring Reggae music. I don't learn a hell of a lot, except they occasionally refer to "the asshole," and occasionally the "fat prick" whom I presume is Grenwald G. Stanton. It seems we agree on something. The bad news is they don't say "take him a drink of water," or "let him go to the john," or anything that might verify his presence.

Looks like we'll have to establish that for ourselves.

Just as the sun touches the horizon over the wildlife preserve, Cocoa, Marco and I climb in the back of the small delivery truck, and Monique, as agreed, drives up to the automatic gate, two hundred yards from the buildings.

She hits the button on the bottom of a box which she could have reached from the truck window, but doesn't, and climbs out to be in full view of the video camera which glowers down from a position high on one of the gate supports.

"What?" A female voice rattles over a speaker in the box.

"Got your food here?" Monique replies in her most innocuous voice, giving the camera an innocent grin.

"Nobody ordered any food." Then you can hear the voice lower as she turns away from whatever mike is in the house. "Did one of you dip shits order food. You know I'm cooking tonight?"

Then a male voice rings over the speaker. "Nobody ordered no damn food."

Monique reads from a paper in her hand. "I got *Pavo relleno con moros, pollo de la plancha, bistec empanizado*, ten *croquetas*, rice and black beans, *arroz con coco*, one fifth of Nassau Royale Banana Rum, two fifths of Don Lorenzo Dark Reserve Rum, and two quarts of fresh pineapple juice." She hesitates a moment as there's nothing but silence on the other end. Then adds, "Hey, I don't give a damn if you take this or not. This is pre-paid. Somebody ordered it and gave us a credit card. But I sure as hell can't eat it all myself."

Still there's no answer, but the gate begins to swing aside.

We stay well out of sight as she pulls up with the rear of the truck facing away from the front door of the house, rounds the truck and we hand her the three sacks of food, two that have been in a portable heater for the last few hours, and one from a cooler.

She has her arms full. She wears a Ricky's uniform hat that's a small version of a Carmen Miranda, with faux bananas, a half pineapple which conceals the camera, and flowers; and a bright green shirt with a Ricky's logo—two bright colored parrots and some printing—on both the shirt pocket and the back. It's her Ricky's Cuban costume, and the hat nicely conceals the tiny portable video camera which is remotely transmitting to the six-inch monitor we watch in the rear of the truck, and the shirt conceals her Kevlar vest. She also wears her butt pack.

The blonde who answers the door must be the same one T-Rex saw sunbathing out in the back. Even via the little video, she's a knockout.

She doesn't bother with hello and is frowning. "Who's credit card bought this stuff?"

"Sorry, I don't have that information," Monique answers.

"These assholes hate my cooking."

"Sorry, may I come in…this stuff is heavy?"

The blonde steps aside. Monique slowly scans the place, giving us as good a look as possible.

We can hear the blonde laugh, then say, "Nice chapeau. I don't imagine you want to sell that fruit bowl. I could use it for the next costume party."

Monique returns the laugh, then adds, "Nope, can't sell it, it belongs to my boss."

She crosses the room and we can see the sacks being rested upon a table. "I'm beat up," Monique's voice rings over the little speaker in the monitor. "I don't imagine you have a glass of water?"

"Sure, honey." The camera pans up to a very large black man who's entered her line of sight. He's eying Monique up and down with obvious appreciation.

"You a classy broad to be deliverin' crap," he says, his accent heavy Bahamian.

"Thanks. Lost my job at the accounting office and been on unemployment for two years…but it ran out. Had to take something."

"Yeah, it be a shitty time. I hear you say you beat up. You run an' play too hard last night, lil' mama? You want a little pick me up?"

There's silence for a moment, then Monique says, "The lady went to get me a glass of water."

"You don't know Maxine. She no lady."

"Whatever," Monique says, then adds, "what did you have in mind?"

"Maybe a line or two help you make it through de night."

Monique laughs again. "I got lots of deliveries to make."

"Just a lil' taste?"

"Sure, a half a line, maybe?

The big guy laughs a deep rumble, and we see a tiny one-gram jar shaking out a line of white powder onto the counter. The hat is coming off. Monique is taking a bit of a risk as she sits it on the counter, near a wall, where it gets the widest possible view of the room.

The big man pulls his wallet from his rear pants pocket and fishes out a hundred dollar bill, rolls it up, and hands it to Monique. She sticks it in a nostril, bends, and inhales half the line.

"You can haf' it all, baby doll," the big man says.

Another tall lanky guy enters the room. "What's happenin', mon?" he asks.

"Givin' this lady a little taste."

"Don't be fuckin' up," the thin one says.

"She be solid," the first one answers.

"Wow," Monique says, wiping her nose. "That's good stuff."

"Half coke, half OxyCottin. You be flyin' high. You make lots of deliveries ever' night, mama?"

"About twenty, sometimes more."

"Maybe you wanna go into biz wif us?" the thin one asks.

Monique laughs. "I'm a coward, man. A little taste is one thing, twenty years is another altogether." She hands the hundred dollar bill back to the big man, who grabs her hand and holds on a moment too long, making my adrenalin begin to flow…then gives her a wink and lets her go.

The blonde is back with the water and hands it to Monique, who takes a deep draw, then says, "I got to go. Thanks for the hospitality."

"You sure you don't wanna make some big bucks?" the tall one asks again.

"Out of my league, big boy. But thanks for the hit. That'll do for a tip."

"Shit, no way," the big one says and hands Monique back the hundred dollar bill.

"Wow, thanks, big guy," Monique says, then turns to the blonde. "Hey, keep the hat. I'll tell the boss someone hooked it out of the truck."

"Cool," the blonde says, and walks over and we see the view from her P.O.V. as she tries the hat on, and we see Monique for the first time inside the house.

"My pleasure," Monique says, and heads for the door.

"Hey," one of the guys yells at her as the hat disappears into another room, then we see the reflection of the blonde adjusting the hat in a mirror and the voices disappear. She's smiling and giggling. Unfortunately, she places the hat at a bad angle on the bathroom counter and leaves the room, closing the door behind herself.

I hold my breath until Monique climbs back into the truck.

"You do like I say, mama," one of the guy's voices rings through the window of the truck. And we duck lower. Obviously he's followed her out.

"You bet, count on it," Monique says as she backs the truck up and spins the wheel.

"Everything okay?" I ask her, from low behind the driver's seat, as she heads for the gate.

"It's cool, except I'm flying about a foot off the ground and burning up…that's bad stuff they're pushing. He wanted to make sure I kept my mouth shut about his offer to put me in the dope biz."

"Nice try with the hat," I say.

"Try?"

"Yeah, the blonde left it in the bathroom."

"Nice *try* is right. I hoped she'd leave it in the living room. At least she didn't dig around in the fruit. Maybe you boys will get a thrill watching her shower."

"It'll have to be soon, as we're going back in…" I glance at my phone and the time, "in forty minutes or so."

Chapter Thirty-Three

I wish we could wait until four in the morning, when everyone would likely be deep in slumber, but Grenwald Stanton may not have the time.

Exactly twenty five minutes after the top of the sun touches the horizon, then disappears, I use the bolt cutters to slice open a small space in the cyclone fence and do a military crawl, my HK and the bolt cutters cradled in my arms, to the side of the house and the power source. There are spotlights at the corners of the house, but, luckily, where the breaker box is positioned they are at their dimmest. I pause behind the wide trunk of a bald cypress and listen before doing the lizard the last twenty feet to the house, then, checking my watch to see we're exactly twenty-nine minutes past sundown, get prepared to rise and cut the pipe carrying the power lines down the wall to the breaker box, then, hopefully, all goes black.

Mo is out of this as I know little about him and don't risk the lives of my people on an unknown. He's to stay out in the road, outside the compound, with instructions that if he doesn't hear from us within thirty minutes of when the lights go out, he's to phone the local cops and tell them he's heard gunfire and screaming from the compound. If I'm able to get the gate to open, he's to jam it. I'm going in a bedroom window; the plan is for Cocoa and Marco to breech the front door with the ram—even if it's unlocked—making all the noise they can, but then step back out of the line of fire and hold their position; and for T-Rex and Orlando to come in the back, as quietly as possible. Monique will stay outside using the truck as cover to make sure no one makes a break for it out of any other doors or windows. She has the shotgun, and I wouldn't want to try and get past her.

All of us wear fold-down night vision goggles, which should give us great advantage.

Hopefully, anyone on the inside will have their attention, and firepower, trained on the front door.

All of us hope we can accomplish this with no gunfire, using mace and stun guns if possible…but with this bunch I doubt it possible.

They will think they're defending their stash of dope, probably from another gang, as cops would be well-marked and yelling police and sending dogs in ahead.

My phone clicks over to exactly thirty minutes from sundown, and I rise and the big bolt cutters do their work, sparks fly but my hands are protected with the heavy insulation on the grips of the cutters.

At exactly thirty minutes past sundown, I push the transmit button my hand held and say, "Go, go, go."

And as I go for the window, right on time I hear the loud crunch of the heavy Blackhawk ram striking the front door.

The window is locked, so I have to use the butt of the machine gun to bust and clean the glass out and lay across the sill for my vault through, only then folding the night vision goggles down. I have mace in my left hand and the HK in my right.

I go for the door, which I imagine leads out into a hallway, and throw it aside, and am suddenly totally blinded by the lights coming back on, at the same time as I hear gunfire so close it almost shatters my ear drums, and see the flash of a weapon. Falling back into the bedroom, I throw the night vision goggles off, but my vision is still flashing lights and flares and no definition. Hearing the noise of footfalls in front of me, I take a chance and spray the mace in an arc.

A woman screams and a man grunts as I back up and trip, backwards, onto a bed. I throw myself back over the bed and go to the floor on the far side, and hear heavy footfalls running away. I'm still unable to see, but splatter the ceiling with a burst from the machine gun, discouraging anyone from entering the room.

What a cluster fuck.

Finally, my vision begins to recover. I take a deep breath and risk looking over the side of the bed. The tall blonde is on her knees near a far wall, writhing, weeping, sobbing, and rubbing her eyes, trying to get rid of the mace. No one else is in the room.

I should have counted on a battery backup or emergency generator bringing the lights back on. I hope it didn't cost my buddies their lives.

Ducking out and quickly back in, I check the hallway. No one. I charge out and head the ten feet to where I can see into the living room. The front door is standing open, but no one's in sight. I reverse my direction and head back down the hall when more sporadic gunfire rings out from somewhere beyond the living room. I kick open another door leading from the hallway into a bedroom, but get nothing but blackness. Reaching in, I flick on the overhead light and see no one, so go on to the next door, as more gunfire comes from somewhere in the rear of the house.

The next door is a bathroom, where the Carmen Miranda hat still rests on the Formica top near the lav. But no one there either, although the small bathroom window is open and the curtains blow with the gentle breeze beginning to rise over the wildlife reserve. I worry that one of them is heading Monique's way?

The last door off the hallway is ajar, and it's dark inside. I flick on the combat light below the muzzle of the HK and give the door a hard kick and roll into the room, as all hell breaks loose. Muzzle blasts from across the room light things up even more than my LED combat light, and I, flat on the floor, raise the HK high enough to clear a bed and return fire, making a sweep with a burst.

"Goddamn, goddamn, goddamn," I hear. "No more," rings out. I'm prone on the floor and still cannot see a damn thing as a big four poster bed is blocking my view at the direction from which the gunfire came.

"Throw down your weapon," I shout, panning the other side of the room with my light.

"Here it come," the voice says, and a semi-automatic pistol sails out from behind the bed, landing with a thump in the middle of the room.

"Both hands, way up," I instruct.

"Hey, mon, you done shot me in one han', and in bof' my legs."

"Tough shit, raise your hands so I can see them, or I'll shoot the rest of you full of holes."

Two ham-size hands raise up from behind the bed, one of them bleeding profusely.

"I'm coming that way, and unless you want the rest of this thirty shot clip in your gut, you'll leave your hands up."

"I ain't going nowhere. I can't go nowhere."

I rise and cross the room, HK ready, and flip on an overhead light. It's the big man, black and wide-eyed, and he's bleeding from his hand and both legs, one of them pumping blood as his femoral must be hit.

"You've got about two minutes before you're a dead man, we don't get a tourniquet on that leg."

"Can I do it?"

He starts pulling his belt off and I let him. He puts his own tourniquet on the leg, and tightens it hard enough that the spurting stops. I'd use my cable tie cuffs on him, but then he couldn't keep the tourniquet tight. It's a quandary.

"You may live, you keep that real tight. You got any other weapons?" I ask.

"Nope, not here."

"I've got to step out of the room for a minute. It's up to you if I chuck a grenade back in here before I come back in and blow you into hamburger."

"I ain't doing nothing but trying to quit bleedin'."

"Don't do nothing or you're a dead man."

I check out the master bathroom to make sure Stanton's not tied up in the tub, give the big man one more instruction on my way out, "Don't make me kill you," then run back down the hall and into the room I'd originally entered. The blonde is still on her knees. I jerk her to her feet. "Your big buddy is in the master bedroom and he's bleeding bad. Get down there and get a compress on him. Use towels from the bathroom. Don't put a weapon in your hand or you'll be the one bleeding to death. Help him out."

"I can't see."

"Do like I say or you'll be bleeding bad!"

Her eyes, even tearing as they are, widen, and she hurries out and down the hall, sobbing as she goes.

"Coming in," I yell, and enter the living room the same time as Cocoa and Marco come through the front door. Near the door, mounted on the wall, is an audio box with a button. I press it and hope the car gate is opening so Mo can jam it.

All of us head to the rear of the house, through a dinning room and into a kitchen. Orlando and T-Rex have a tall thin guy on the floor, and he's gasping for breath, his hands secure behind him with Max-Cuff restraints, his ankles bound tightly as well.

T-Rex looks up and gives me a smile. "He don't like the stun gun on the back of his skinny neck," he says. "He's a piss poor shot or you'd be trying on my wardrobe."

"I hate your wardrobe, so stay alive."

I instruct Cocoa to go help the blonde, but to be careful as they've been alone in the room and to make sure he sees empty hands before exposing himself, him being a very large target.

I give the guy on the floor the toe of my boot in his ribs, hard enough that he grunts loudly.

"Mutherfucker," he manages with a gasp.

"Where's Stanton?" I ask.

"Who…" he says, then laughs under his breath.

This time the toe of my boot buries a couple of inches into his side.

He gasps, then gasps again, then manages. "You prick…."

"You have no idea what a prick I can be, and you might lose yours, you don't tell me where Stanton is."

"Don't know…know no Stanton." He doesn't laugh this time.

"What's your name? I need to know what to put on your headstone besides dick-less asshole?"

"Fuck you."

I bear down hard; boot on his neck.

"Fredo," he gasps.

"Okay, Fredo, I'll get back to you."

I turn my attention back to Rex, Marco, and Orlando. "I checked out the rest of the house best I could. No Stanton to be found. Orlando, you keep Fredo on the floor while Rex and I sweep the rest of the buildings."

"You got it. This dumb fuck emptied his clip at us, and missed every time. Can I just shoot him?"

"Not yet."

I free my handheld radio from my belt and give Monique a call. "You okay out there."

"Ten four," she reports.

"We've got things under control in here. Come in and you and Marco give the house a good search for Stanton, every closet, under every bed, then help Cocoa with the blonde and the big guy, who's got a few holes in him. We need your Florence Nightingale act. Rex and I are making a sweep through the outbuildings."

I again put my boot on the back on the thin guys neck. "And if I don't find him, I'll be back to ask you again. You be thinking about living the rest of your life with a stub where your dick used to be, Stubo."

"Fuck you, pig," he says, but he's sounding less tough all the time. He thinks we're cops, which is fine by me for the moment. When he finds out we're not, he may be more willing to talk as he'll know I'm more willing to make a steer out of who he thought was a bull.

We leave Orlando watching Fredo, with the last admonition, "Zap this asshole again if he gives you any lip."

None of the other buildings have had any lights on, so Mo has reported, other than outside floodlights, but that doesn't mean that Stanton is not imprisoned in one of them.

They have to be checked.

We head for the smaller house first, and coming along side I realize that the windows are false, and there's a wall behind them. They're merely plant-ons. We move to the front door and I realize it's heavy metal, and it's locked on the outside with a heavy padlock. Someone doesn't want visitors, and wants this place to look like a house, not like whatever it really is.

Rex and I look at each other and shrug. "What do you think," I ask.

"I think we need a Sherman tank to get inside."

"Come on," I say, and lead the way back to the house.

As I walk back into the kitchen, an intercom recessed into the kitchen wall crackles, "What's going on out there?" It's a voice from the great beyond.

Fredo is still flat on the floor. I poke him in the ribs with the toe of my boot. "If you don't want a few broken ribs, tell me who's on the intercom?"

"Okay, okay. It's a couple of lab guys who we got working."

"Lab?"

"Meth, out in the building what looks like a house. It ain't no house."

"They armed?"

"They not only ain't armed, they locked in. They a couple of cats from Dade Medical college, working off a dope bill, whose mama probably wants to know where they be."

I walk over to the intercom and push the button. "You guys okay out there. I'm an officer who's going to let you out."

"Thank God," the voice says.

I turn back to Fredo, "Where's the key to the padlock?"

"Key board on the porch, just outside the door, hanging over the washing machine."

As he said there's a key ring, and in moments T-Rex and I have the door open and two very appreciative young men rush out and take a deep breath of fresh air. The lab looks like something out of a Frankenstein movie, and smells worse.

"Anyone else in there," I ask the two.

"No, sir. You a cop?"

"Close enough. You're free. Go sit under that tree and wait, there's more cops coming."

"Can I call my mom?" one of them asks.

I smile and hand him my phone.

The fact I use the HK to wave them over seems enough encouragement for them to move, and they hurry away.

We search the two garage buildings and other than finding a row of five large gun safes, the six foot high three foot wide variety, there's nothing else of interest. I'd bet a dime to a donut that the safes are full of meth, OxyContin, and other items of interest to the DEA, but my interest is in a very wealthy old boy whose wife wants him back.

I retrieve my phone and caution the two college boys to stay put until the troops arrive, and I'm sure there will be a full platoon.

I just hope Stanton's not in far off Bahama, or his body isn't hidden in one of the safes or on the bottom of the swamp, sunk in a pile of gator crap.

If so, we're sunk as well.

Chapter Thirty-Four

I've left a radio with Mo outside the compound, and call him. "Is the gate taken care of?"

"You bet, jammed good."

"Call 911 now for an ambulance, tell them it's a heart attack so there's no cops involved. Give us another fifteen minutes, then give 911 another call and tell them we're bail enforcement, here with a valid contract, but that there's been a shooting and we need the locals on the scene."

"You got it," he says.

"Then you shag into the weeds out of sight. You don't need any grief. But standby in case I need you."

I don't want a bunch of cowboy local cops to come it shooting, but need emergency medical, and the odds are much less of the boys in blue coming in waving weapons if they have a heads up. Still, we need medical attention for the boy full of holes so I'm walking a fine line. But I have to have time to get some information out of the boys before even the EMT's arrive. I'm playing a close game, a high-risk game, but it's imperative we know where Grenwald Stanton is being held if we don't find him here.

As I'm heading for the guesthouse, my phone vibrates. I grab it up and answer, as silence is no longer necessary. It's Mrs. Stanton. "Brad, the FBI is here."

"Tell them you can't talk without your attorney present and call him and tell him don't hurry."

"I got it."

As soon as she's off the line, my phone vibrates again. It's Officer Annie, which makes me smile for the first time today. "Hey, Brad old buddy, you owe me a drink. I'm heading for Café del Sol—"

"Love to, but I'm still in Florida."

"Enjoying the bathing beauties in Palm Beach?"

"Enjoying the alligators in a stinkin' swamp at the moment. I'll call you tomorrow…or in a day or two."

"The brush off?"

"Hardly. In the middle of a gunfight. Rain check." I hang up. Hopefully, she'll understand.

By the time Rex and I have searched the lab and the garages, I can hear a siren. I hustle back to the house and again put a boot on the neck of the tall skinny Hispanic. "You've got about five minutes, son, before I make a capon out of you?"

"What the fuck's a capon?"

"A nutless chicken. Turn him over, Orlando."

Orlando and T-Rex roll the guy over and I pull my K-bar out. There's a bunch of bananas on the counter, and as Rex is jerking the guy's pants down, none to gently. I let him see me testing the knife on a banana. It slips through in a whisper. I hold it so half of it falls on his face.

"Prick," he yells at me.

"Maybe, but you're about to be prick-less." I give him my most crazy grin, and can see he's beginning to weaken.

"No fucking cop is gonna cut my dick off."

I grab a couple of paper towels off a roll on the counter then kneel at his side as T-Rex holds his legs and Orlando his arms. I grab the guy's dick—he's got a big dick and I can see why he'd want to keep it—and give it a stretch, and while he screams, ask, "What makes you think I'm a cop?"

Just as I lay the razor sharp blade against the base of his cock, he screams loud enough to rattle the windows, "He's out on a house boat with Enrico, the boss, and a couple of—"

"Enrico Albrech?"

"Yeah, yeah."

"Where, exactly?"

"In the middle of the reserve. He's supposed to call in a few minutes to see if the transfer has been made, then he's gonna feed Stanton to the gators. I've got the link up on the computer in the other room...."

I bear down a little harder with the cold back edge of the knife, and he gives an audible squeak. He has no way of knowing it's the back of the blade.

"Even if she pays?" I ask.

His voice is two octaves high. "He don't give a shit. Stanton got his little bro killed. Man, don't cut my dick!"

"You know the way out there?" I ask.

"I been out there fishin' a million times."

I instruct Orlando, "Put this asshole in the boat. I'll get Marco and the three of us will go out there. Where's your re-breathers?"

"Back in the truck at the boat launch."

I yell at Monique and meet her in the hall. "If the phone rings it's the guy who's got Stanton, in a houseboat out in the center of the reserve. We're headed out there—"

Both Cocoa and T-Rex appear in the master bedroom door. "We're going—"

"No, the Fuentes' and I are going, taking the other guy to show us the way. They got the re-breathers and know them well. The boat's too small for anymore, and I need you here when the cops show up…the FBI is not far behind us. Take care of the HK's asap."

"We got them both hooked up in here. Monique can handle—"

"No way, there's not room. She's never broken down an HK. Keep the Fibbies talking while we make this end."

They look disappointed, but shrug, "We'll handle the HK's," and turn back to the bedroom.

I turn back to Monique. "If he calls, try and make him think you're the blonde, and keep him talking. The longer he's distracted, the more chance we have to get Stanton before he becomes gator crap."

In moments the four of us are pushing the little fishing boat as fast as it will go back down the canal to the boat launch, have the gear loaded, then are picking our way down a tight, winding waterway, deep into the wildlife reserve, every time we pause to check directions, we're listening to the deep resounding bellow of bull alligators.

At times the boat can do no more than idle through the thick mangroves and tules. Fredo motions to slow down and we move quietly, the only sound the hum of the outboard and the occasional slap as we whack at the bugs who land on face or arms.

"Stop here a second," Fredo instructs and Marco, who's driving, slips it into neutral. "See the light out there."

"Yep," I answer.

"That should be them."

There's a large lake opening up in the foreground, and somewhere in the distance—hard to judge at night—maybe a half mile, is a half dozen lighted windows.

"How big is this houseboat?" I ask Fredo.

"Over fifty feet. She sleeps eight."

"Ladder at the rear?"

"Yeah. And at the front for swimmers. And anchor lines both front and rear."

"How   much   freeboard?"

"What's that mean?"

"Distance from the water to the deck?"

"No more than a foot...or maybe a foot and a half."

"What's the plan?" Marco asks.

"I'm thinking we drop you guys off with the re-breathers, and you pop up front and back, hopefully unseen. I'm going to hit them head on, and pull up next to the rail, distracting them from you guys with happy bull shit and hoping you get the drop on them."

"Pretty simple plan," Orlando says. "At least for those of you who don't have to swim with the gators."

"Gators don't do kosher. Besides, stick on of those Uzi's down their throat and they'll be discouraged."

"Ha ha," he says, but doesn't sound very convinced.

So I continue, "Sometimes simple is the best. I've got some helpful toys here."

Pulling my two flash grenades off my belt, I hand each of them one.

"The first time I use Stanton's name, if I don't get shot just pulling up to the rail, drop these babies on them. Remember, Enrico's worth a bunch of dough to you two. I won't grease him if you don't shoot my pay day."

"We wouldn't be here if Albrech wasn't worth a ton to us," Marco says with a snarl, and aims the bow for the houseboat.

I'm worried about them hearing us approach, then realize a little generator on board the houseboat would keep them from hearing a helicopter hovering overhead. I take the helm while they get into the re-breathers and we make a circle around the houseboat, dropping Marco off a hundred yards from the stern and Orlando a hundred yards from the bow.

"You're gonna get me killed," Fredo says as we complete the circle.

"Maybe, unless you keep us both alive, talking to Albrech like you've got a reason to be out here. He doesn't know me from Adam's off ox."

"Who the fuck is Adam's ox."

"Never mind. You talk to him and keep him interested and I won't have to shoot your dumb ass full of holes. Get it?"

"I get it."

"You screw up and I shoot you right after I shoot your boss."

"I get it, I get it. I don't give a shit about Albrech or anyone else. I'm just hired help. You gonna let me go if we get out of this?"

"You got a deal. You help out and you get a headstart. We'll drop you off at the boat launch."

"I'd shake, but you got me all tied up."

"And you're gonna stayed tied up."

We've arrived back opposite the side-rail and I turn toward the houseboat, wait until I figure both Orlando and Marco are in position at the bow and stern, then give the outboard enough power so I can cut it when fifty yards out and drift in.

The ka ka is about to hit the fan.

Chapter Thirty-Five

I can see four heads in the main salon of the houseboat as we drift forward, and all turn toward us as the bow of the small boat bumps into the side of the larger one. I yell out, "Hey, aboard the boat." An outside overhead light comes on.

Two no-neck gunnies, each palming a handgun, emerge first, onto the open aft deck.

"Who the fuck are you?" one of them asks, then shades his eyes from the glare of the overhead. Then he asks, "That you, Fredo?"

As I answer, a very large man emerges, with at least a fifty inch girth. He's not carrying, and wears Bermuda shorts and an un-tucked Hawaiian shirt big enough to be a sail for this houseboat. He's not what you'd call attractive, in fact he gives Jubba the Hut a run for ugly.

"Talk," I say to Fredo.

"Hey, boss. It's Fredo."

"What the fuck are you doing out here," the big man asks.

"Didn't you call? Somebody called. Maxine said to come on out."

The big man looks at his two gunnies. "One of you guys….?"

"We didn't call nobody."

We've got them all close together, and I've pressed my luck far enough, when the big man asks, "Who the hell are you, skipper?"

"I'm a friend of Mr. Stanton's," I say, and in a half a heart beat, a grenade rolls on board the aft open deck of the houseboat, at almost the same instant, a grenade smashes through a window on the front of the main salon, where the fourth head has not moved. A head I presume, I pray, that belongs to Grenwald Stanton.

All three of them are following the path of the grenade with their vision as it rolls across the deck. I cover my eyes as the flash grenade explodes with a blinding roar, then as quickly mount the railing and am over, as Marco mounts the ladder at the stern and Orlando at the bow, all of us facing away as the second grenade explodes with a roar inside the salon, and the sticky foul water odor of the swamp now reeks of gunpowder.

One of the gunnies is knocked flat on the deck, then raises to an elbow and with little regard as to who gets hit is firing his semi-automatic, panning the rear deck. He gets off four shots as we're diving flat on the fiberglass, before Marco rolls and kicks the weapon out of his hand and brings his Uzi across the guy's head. The shooter goes down flat like a flounder flopping on the deck and I spring up and bust into the second gunnie like a linebacker, knocking him and his weapon flying over the rail into the slimy drink.

I turn my attention to Albrech, but he's grasping his chest, heart center, and blood is billowing around his hand. He's taken one from his own man. He gasps and flops to his knees.

Knowing there's nothing I can do for the big man, I move.

Breaking past him, I charge into the salon, and there, withering on the floor is Grenwald Stanton, holding his thigh with both hands as he's wearing a shiny pair of handcuffs, blood seeping between his fingers.

"Jesus and Mary, I'm shot. God, help me, I'm shot, and I'm blind," he's yelling.

"You're shot in the leg, G.G. You'll be fine. The blindness is temporary from the flash grenade."

I jerk his belt off and apply it to his upper right thigh. He cries out like a scalded cat as I tighten it, but I ignore him and jerk it even tighter. "You need to make sure we loosen that every few minutes."

Through wide bloodshot and weeping eyes, he glares at me. "You're that Braddock asshole," he says, and his tone is not admiring.

"I'm that Braddock asshole, and you're on your way home." I dig a cuff key out of my watch pocket, never without one when I'm working, and get the cuffs off him.

"Call a fucking helicopter and get me to a hospital. You got me shot and tried to blow me all to hell."

I take a deep breath before I speak. "That's a flesh wound. It's on the outside of the thigh. You won't bleed out and it'll take longer for a chopper to get here, find us, and winch you up than it will to get you back to the boat launch ramp. Stop whining and you'll be home for a late supper."

Digging my phone out, I call Mrs. Stanton. She answers on the first ring.

"He's safe," I tell her. I don't mention he's a total asshole.

She gasps, then asks to speak to her husband. I hand him the phone and return to the rear deck, where the Fuentes have the unconscious gunman in plastic cuffs. I can hear Stanton behind me, saying what fuck ups we are getting him shot and trying to blow him all to hell.

I shake my head, thinking that if I feed him to the gators I probably won't collect the rest of what's coming to us.

We sweep the lake with the houseboat spotlight, looking for the other shooter—while Stanton threatens us with lawsuits and bodily harm—but the other bad guy's nowhere to be seen, so we say to hell with him and wish him luck with the gators.

I call and arrange for a life flight to pick up Stanton at the boat ramp, then call Mrs. Stanton and suggest she meet him at his destination, Bethesda Memorial in Boynton Beach. Then I call Monique and find she's deep into conversation with both the local cops and the FBI.

Enrico Albrech has no pulse, so we leave him where he's fallen.

We begin to load up, and Marco says, "I'm staying. I don't want something eating this fat bastard before we get him checked into the morgue and get a claim on the bounty."

"You got it. If you can get the boat back to the marina, fine, otherwise I'll send someone out."

"I'll get it back."

"I'd leave your brother with you, but we got a prisoner and need both a guard and driver."

"I'll get it back."

We keep the throttle wide open on the return trip, cutting in and out of the mangroves. I drive the first few minutes, then turn the boat over to Orlando while I work on the HK. Stanton crouches in the bow of the boat and I have a foot on the gunman while I work. He's regained consciousness, but is still groggy and moaning and laying on his gut in the bottom of the boat. I have the HK stripped down in moments, even bouncing along in the darkness among the mangroves. Each of our bug-out bags has parts to convert the machine guns back to semi-automatic, making them legal. I drop the original bolt and a couple of parts overboard.

It takes us less than twenty minutes to get back to the boat launch ramp and as we're driving the bow up onto the ramp, an emergency medical chopper is landing.

Stanton is still bitching and moaning as he's loaded into the chopper. I walk over and say, "You're welcome," but he doesn't stop complaining long enough to even acknowledge my presence.

Fredo is eyeing the brush like he'd like to make a break for it. I walk over and tell him to turn around, and cut away the cable-tie cuffs.

"I'm not gonna lie for you, but you got your head-start."

He nods appreciatively, and jogs out into the darkness.

Now I've got more important business, and Orlando and I head back to the compound. As Ricky Ricardo would say to Lucy, "I've got some splain' to do."

On the way, I call Monique.

"You're missing the party," she says.

"Oh, yeah."

"Yeah, there's already more acronyms here than in the Pentagon. Local sheriffs, FBI, DEA, ATF, and believe it or not, USFW."

"Who's the last one?"

"United States Fish and Wildlife Service."

"Did we forget to get a license for Bahamian assholes?" I ask.

She laughs. "Speaking of acronyms, just get here before they put out an APB and you get a picture on the post office wall."

"We're almost to the gate."

Before I turn into the compound, I call Mo on my cell, and he promptly appears out of the underbrush.

"Hey, I can't give you a ride as I've got a command performance, but if you want to hoof it back to your car you can get the hell out of here. We'll touch bases in the morning and get you paid. Good job."

He strikes out back down the road toward the boat ramp.

Chapter Thirty-Six

Clete Patterson is the FBI Agent in Charge of the Miami Division, and even in starched white shirt, carefully knotted tie, and razor creased trousers is not as anal as many I've met. In fact, he seems almost giddy as we've helped him make a major bust, and actually smiles when I tell him one of his Florida most-wanted is getting cold and stiff in the bottom of a houseboat not five or six miles from where we stand. He's getting a warrant to get into the gun safes, wanting to be double safe with the legalities, but already has enough dope from the lab to put all of them away for a good long while.

When I arrived I noticed, besides a half dozen cars, two vans, and a black helicopter with no markings, that those who were participants in the recent excitement were and are nicely separated. The two boys from the lab are still perched under the tree, now in cuffs and guarded and being questioned by two plainclothes guys. Cocoa and Monique, badge holders and brass hanging out of their shirt pockets, are seated in lawn chairs, twenty feet apart, but grouped, each with a plainclothesman behind. A pair of CSI guys are swabbing their hands, I presume for gun powder residue. They, to Patterson's credit, are not cuffed. Orlando walks over to join them, and is promptly assigned his own lawn chair. The DEA has crime tape all over the building that turned out to be a meth lab. And in a vehicle, locked in the rear, is Maxine, the blonde. T-Rex and the big black guy I'd swept with the HK are missing.

"One of my guys isn't here?" I ask Patterson before he starts grilling me.

"He's at the Bethesda emergency with the guy who took a few...both legs and a hand. We've got people there. They'll give your guy a ride back after they get a local cop as a guard on Jackson." He smiles. "Do you know who the big guy is?"

"No idea."

"Hogart Jackson, known as Hog in the trade. He's wanted in Nassau for bank robbery and murder. They can have him in about forty years, when we're through with him. He's a very bad boy."

"Well, then he's my gift to you."

"He's a little worse for wear at the moment."

"Had to be done," I say. "Him or me."

"Hog runs with a partner, a tall skinny guy. You seen him?"

I shrug unknowingly.

He moves away and waves to me to come on. "Let's go inside. Howard Osteen, the lead guy with the Miami office of ATF wants a word with you. He's not real high on some of the gun shot patterns and the obvious rapid fire from you guys. You know your people gave us nothing...said you were the guy to talk to."

I give him a tight smile. "Your people would say the same if they were being questioned."

"You got a point there."

Osteen is a brick of a guy, equally wide in the hips, waist, shoulders, and damn near the neck, which flares out from his ears, making his shoulders look sloped. They aren't. He's the proverbial brick shit house, and appears to be as solid.

He shakes hands without speaking, one of those guys with whom you want to sink the shake deep so he doesn't bust your fingers, then waves me into the bedroom where I'd entered the house via the busted window and points up at the gunshot pattern on the ceiling, where I'd sprayed a fourth of a clip. A half dozen holes are suspiciously evenly spaced.

"That's automatic weapon fire," he says, accusingly.

"Oh, yeah?"

"Yeah. But your people say the HK's you've got are all semi-auto conversions. I didn't know you could convert an HK."

"Now you know. I'll loan you one to take to the range and check out. It fires single on the single setting, single on the three shot setting, and single on full auto. One trigger pull, one shot."

"Don't worry about loaning me one. They are all going to my firearm forensics guys to be checked out."

I give him a little too wide a smile. "So, when do I get them back?"

"Four or five months, if they check out, and if our guys are not too busy."

I'm still smiling. "You paying rent on them?"

"You won't be laughing if they don't check out."

I ignore him and turn back to Patterson who has a bit of a smug self-satisfied smile, and ask him, "So, are my people and I free to go?"

"There was something about a bail bond contract, which if memory serves me, makes a good deal of what you're doing here legal...or not."

"It's in the glove compartment of the truck. That's Orlando Fuentes who came back with me, and his brother Marco is on the houseboat with what remains of your 'most wanted.' The contract is in their name, Fuentes Freedom Bonds. We're working for them, and are all Bond Enforcement Agents. And, of course, all licensed to carry in thirty two states including Florida." I give him Marco's cell number and he jots it down, calls over another agent, tells him to get on it, then turns back to me.

"Right, and the Grenwald Stanton kidnapping just happened to be going on at the same time?"

"If you say so. No matter, you got your man, Enrico Albrech, and you guys got Mr. Stanton freed. And you solved the case of two missing Dade Medical students. The press will give you a pat on the back for your fast efficient action and we'll give you all the credit, which of course you deserve. I'll be surprised if the next time I see you you're not a Deputy Director."

He smiles knowingly. "Aren't you the generous fellow? What medical students?"

"You'll figure it out as your guy is interviewing them now. I'm here to serve and glad to be of help. Good citizen and all that."

"Let me check out the contract and you all promise to be in my office in Miami first thing in the morning and you can go...try and not spend a lot of time getting your stories together. You can go...after the crime scene guys swab your hands." He hands me a card.

"Hey, I've already fessed up to firing my weapon."

"Ah, and suspects have never recanted?"

"Let's get it done, and forget that suspect crap." I yawn and stretch then add, "I'm ready for some sack time. By the way, the two kids I mentioned before, the med students...who were working the lab, who you guys have hooked up under that tree over there, were said to be kidnapped from Dade Medical...that was told to me by one of the perps, and the kids are here under duress. The first thing they did when I released them from their lab-prison was call mama. Go easy on them."

He nods and I give him my best Marine salute but he doesn't smile, or return it. However, I know he's a happy camper.

I do not mention Fredo to him, the tall skinny guy; after all, a deal's a deal. He'll get that out of us tomorrow as an "Oh, by the way." If Fredo's smart he's already half way back to the Bahamas, and if the guy I knocked off the houseboat is really lucky, he's not giving some twelve foot gator indigestion.

My first piece of business now is to get my three hundred thousand dollar check out of Mrs. Stanton, before Mr. Stanton wants to deduct his medical bills from our proceeds...or worse. Probably worse. I'm not insane as the definition of insanity is doing the same thing over and over expecting a different result, and I don't. I expect him to try and stiff us, but I have a plan.

Now, to see if we can pay our bills this month and for a few months to come.

Chapter Thirty-Seven

I call T-Rex and find he's still at Bethesda Medical, and tell him to sit tight as we're on our way.

By the time we get there there's a sheriff's deputy on duty outside Hogart Jackson's room, listening to T-Rex regale him with tales of bounty hunting. Hog is temporarily repaired and sedated, and about ready to go into surgery for both his hand and his femoral artery. He is, of course, securely cuffed to his bed.

I get no pleasure from filling anybody full of holes, but the remorse is much less when it's a truly bad guy. Believing you make your own choices in life, I spend little time worrying about a guy's background— did his daddy molest him?—or about his motivations to become a bad guy in the first instance. My simple theory: it is what it is. And that keeps me sane…although there's some disagreement on that fact. Still, I spend my time worrying about the next bad guy, not what happened to the last bad guy.

Cocoa, Monique, and I gather Rex up and we head to another floor, where our employer…or I should say, our employer's husband, is ensconced for the night.

We encounter two old friends in the hallway outside his room. The Stanton twins, Britney and

Bobby, now clean and sober, run up and throw arms, alternatively, around both T-Rex and I, then together hug Cocoa as it requires two their size. Monique is left out of the hugging, but thanked profusely.

"Thank you, thank you, thank you all, for saving daddy," they say, almost in unison, as twins are apt to do.

I eye them both up and down. They looked good, even high on whatever Jo Jo had them high on, but look even better now, as if they'd just stepped out of Vogue.

"How's daddy getting along?" I ask.

"Fine. He doesn't want visitors, he even asked us to leave the room...but fine."

"And your mother?"

"She's in with daddy," the one I think is Bobby says. "You want me to get her?"

I nod, and she disappears into the room.

As the door opens and Bobby and Mrs. Stanton slip out, I can't help but hear Grenwald shouting, "Bullshit. It's not going to happen."

The door closes behind them, and Mrs. Stanton looks a little sheepish. Not a good sign.

"Are you all okay," she asks.

"Hunky dory, and very lucky," I say, then wait for her to continue as I can see she has more to say.

"He won't pay. He says you got him shot, or shot him, and almost got him blown to pieces."

I can see her surprise at my afore-planned reply. "He didn't employ us, you did." She made the mistake of mentioning the fact she had more money than Grenwald.

"You think I should pay?" she asks, looking a little astounded and agast.

"To be truthful, I don't care who pays, but I want a check for three hundred thousand as that was the agreement, and albeit it was an oral one, it was in front of all these folks. We delivered, now it's your turn."

"Give me a moment." She again disappears into the room, and I can hear the muffled noise of two people shouting at each other.

I turn to the girls. It's speech time. "Ladies, we risked our lives, as you might remember, to get you girls out of that trash heap you got yourself into, we again risked our lives to recover your daddy, who was about to become a snack for the alligators out in the wildlife preserve. Your daddy got himself into this mess by hiring a bunch of amateurs against my explicit admonition, one of whom was the brother of a very, very bad guy. And that guy and those amateurs precipitated a lot of gunfire that almost got the two of you scarred up from bullet holes and could have gotten anyone of us killed, and even though it got your daddy nicked, he's alive and full of piss and vinegar as is obvious. And he'll be home tomorrow.

"You girls would not be so beautiful with puckered scars all over your bodies, or if you were rotting in a grave."

I pause to give them time to create a mental picture of the walking dead. "Three times in the last couple of weeks, we've had lots of mean people trying to fill us full of bullet holes…each time to protect Stantons. Don't you think we should be paid?"

The good news is I get a nod from both of them. Then, with all sincerity I ask, "Do you want us to be at your beck and call if you have trouble again?"

They nod again, this time more enthusiastically.

"Well?" Monique asks, when they hesitate.

"Well?" T-Rex adds.

"My feelings are hurt," Cocoa says, and looks as if he's about to pucker up and bawl.

There's dead silence for a moment, except for the shouting resonating through the hospital room door...then both girls spin on their very high heels and push inside.

I give my crew a smile and a compliment. "You three deserve Oscars."

The level of the shouting rises several octaves, and I can see that Grenwald is being out-shouted, overwhelmed, and inundated in female wrath. I think the ladies are winning, partially because he's flat on his back in a hospital bed and too weak to launch an adequate counter attack.

Suddenly there's silence. The door opens again, and Mrs. Stanton reappears. "The girls are staying here with their father. If you'll follow me back to the house, I'll cut you a check. Gren has kindly agreed to repay me."

I don't choke on her 'kindly.'

"Yes, ma'am," I say, and don't add, 'it will be a pleasure,' but it will, as I expected the process of prying a check out of the Stantons to be much tougher. You don't get a couple of billion stashed away by being easy.

Of course the deals never done until the check clears.

Chapter Thirty-Eight

I'm at First Manhattan in Miami at eight when the doors open, and leave smiling as I've converted the check to the cashier's variety.

We've put away a cool six hundred fifty grand, minus less than a hundred in expenses, in fewer than thirty days. All is going very, very well, which makes me very, very nervous. Murphy's Law is still lurking out there in the weeds. Rex is circling the block, and sees the smile on my face as he slows to pick me up.

"So, went well?" he asks.

"Yep. Let's fulfill our promised appearance and interrogation, then head for the office and I'll write a few bonus checks, then we'll take everyone to a fat steak and a few cocktails...we should celebrate, maybe the Chesterfield or Taboo in Palm Beach."

"Works for me," he says.

It's off to the District office of the FBI, and Agent in Charge Clete Patterson and minions, where we're meeting up with the Fuentes boys, Monique, and Cocoa, who should already be there keeping the anal types at bay.

As expected, there are a bevy of fibbies awaiting, and we're separated into a half dozen interview rooms and our statements are recorded and video taped, to be compared later for inconsistencies. Like Espinoza and

Laukenbach did, we're admonished not to leave the state, and like them, it's a suggestion, not a court order. So I smile and nod, like a puppy dog happy to have a treat. And, as I did with my boys in Santa Barbara, I plan to do exactly what and when is in Quiet Ops' best interest.

By three in the afternoon, ahead of the traffic, we're out of there and on our way back to West Palm Beach and the office, and with any luck, getting our work done so we can celebrate our new-found fortune at my favorite East Coast watering hole.

As we head north I find an oldies station—not hard to do in Florida—and tune in to Frank Sinatra doing it his way.

"Must you?" Rex asks.

"You can live with it for a half hour. Remember, I'm the guy about to write bonus checks." He shakes his head, wishing he had some ear plugs.

Our East Coast Quiet Ops office is on the eighth floor of a sparkling white building overlooking the inland waterway. We have a great view of Trump's hundred thirty million dollar pad, and, as soon as we light, Rex heads for the telescope we keep there for killing-time-entertainment, and checks to see if the Donald has any bathing beauties out near the pool, while I write checks.

He emits a low whistle a couple of times, so the Donald must be doing fine.

I don't have the first check written before my phone jingles with a call from General McClanahan.

"Yes, sir," I answer appropriately.

"You doing okay, young man?" he asks.

"Yes, sir, should be heading your way in a week or so."

"No hurry, there's been two process servers here trying to lay some papers on you."

I think 'fuck' but don't say it. "I'll give Harrison a call and ask him to accept service. Advise them to go to his office, should they show up again."

"And that cop buddy of yours and his yap dog have been by a couple of times. Said you weren't supposed to leave town."

"I took that as advice, not an order. You mean the big dude, Espinoza, and Laukenbach?"

"That's them."

"I'll head back tomorrow, much as I hate to."

"I'll be playing golf."

"I should have stayed in the Corps so I could become a gentleman of leisure."

"You'd have never made general, not that there's ever been a Marine who should have made general...except for Chesty, of course. You're a lousy politician, don't play golf or tennis, and talk way too straight."

I chuckle, even with the lousy process service news. The general's a good judge of character. "See you soon."

I make a mental note to call my attorney, Harrison Bull, who's properly named as his horns have skewered all who've thought they could use the courts to pick my pocket, or get even with me for perceived wrongs...and who's kept me semi-liquid and more than semi out of jail. I knew, however, things were going far to well. At least I've had an hour to revel in it. The bad news, Harrison isn't inexpensive; the good, I've got some dough to use to try and hang onto some dough.

Hanging up I realize I'd turned my phone off when entering the hospital last night, and not turned it back on until this morning, and haven't checked my voice mail, so I do.

Three calls from Espinoza with a tart "Call me." Two more from Officer Annie, which makes me smile and get a twitch as I haven't satisfied my manly urges in a month—about three and a half weeks beyond the norm—and have high hopes for this particular lady as she's head and shoulders, and other great parts, ahead of any other candidate. Two other calls from bondsmen sound promising for the bank account, and one from someone I'd never in my life expected to hear from, Kenny MacMann, my favorite musician, who left me a message and said "Yes, I'm that Kenny MacMann." Kenny's an expatriate hippy sax player who made it double-good with album after album of instrumentals and is nationally renowned. Seems somebody hooked his favorite sax and he wants it back as he feels crippled and inadequate without Sam the sax. I wonder about guys who give names to inanimate objects, however, he's got deep pockets. He's a neighbor of General McClanahan's, only a few houses away, so he can afford the very best...and that's Quiet Ops.

I take the time to return the MacMann call, but get voice mail and leave a message that I'll be back in the state tomorrow, and will call again.

Before I can pick up my pen and get back to check writing, my phone rings with a call from Espinoza, his ring being the theme from Dragnet.

"I was just dialing you," I lie.

"Bullshit." He knows me too well. "I got word you're in Florida."

"Somebody got it right."

"I guess you didn't hear our suggestion not to leave town?"

"I did, and took it as a suggestion."

"When are you coming back? I need a bail enforcement agent, and there's a rumor you passed the test."

I laugh. "No test, except under fire. I did go to the Burton school of Bail Bond enforcement." He makes no comment so I continue. "So, they finally caught up with you? I only chase skips...I don't do bail. What did they charge you with, donut destruction?"

"Ha ha. I need you to go into a residence...a job for which we have only strong suspicions, no grounds to get a warrant...I've tried."

"So, how can I get in there without you having grounds to arrest me? Or is this another 'do nothing but peek in the window,' with a wink?"

"Nope, there's the likelihood of a skip hiding on the premises, a gentleman who's wanted badly by Apex Bonds in San Diego, and I've already contacted the bondsman and you should have a contract waiting in your fax. Apex owed me a favor."

I sigh deeply, then buck up. "Big bail I hope?"

"Nope, a hundred grand and I said you'd take it for a nickel as it's a gimme."

"By nickel, I presume you mean five grand?"

"No, a nickel." Now he laughs. "Yes, five grand. You owe me for not holding you as a material witness."

"Damn it. I was gonna take advantage of a couple of my favorite W.P.B. watering holes for a week or so."

"You want to solve the Poindexter thing, right? You want to find Ronnell, right?"

"You bet, both are thorns in my craw."

"Then get back here. This won't wait, and we don't have the manpower to keep a man on stakeout at the house waiting for Chaco to move, and if he moves we'll never see him again. You'll love this job, this guy's a stone-cold-killer with a half-dozen jail house tear tats."

"Chaco Rodriquez, the print you found on the knife. Oh, boy, can't wait. I'll get a ticket for early tomorrow. I don't imagine you can pick me up at LAX?"

"I can pick you up at Santa Barbara, or meet the Airport bus and give you a ride home."

"Don't bust your ass, old buddy. I thought you were in a hurry?"

"See you when you get here."

Let's see, it seems I've made another great deal. Five grand to pick up a stone-cold-killer who would slice me open from Adam's apple to a-hole without a blink, and it'll cost me two grand for the late reservation ticket, if I leave Cocoa and T-Rex behind. If I schedule them to go with me, I'll be a grand in the hole.

I think I should go back to night school and take negotiation 1A.

But then, what are friends for?

Chapter Thirty-Nine

The house Chaco is rumored to be holed up in is on Bregante Lane, in what passes for a squalid area in Santa Barbara, which is a laugh as with even run down shacks on fifty foot wide lots selling for the better part of a million, and with the Sear's Craftsman kit-house circa 1920 California bungalows on both sides currently being remodeled, the area is anything but a slum, however, like many slums, cars are parked on front lawns, and a couple of driveways sport older cars on blocks.

Being highly populated with fuzzy liberal trust fund babies, Santa Barbara has no ordinance to keep five families from living in the same house, which is why it has some areas that are less desirable than others, but none cheap.

And there are lots of folks, all Hispanic, coming and going from the subject house. At least three families must be occupying same.

It's mid-afternoon before I'm parked, in my oat colored Chevy, a couple of houses away, observing the comings and goings. I could be more comfortable as I'm geared up pretty well, and sweating, sticky, and itchy.

As is normal when on a job, I have a sidearm, a 9mm Beretta, in this instance in the center of my back covered by my untucked Hawaiian shirt. Not so normal is an ankle gun, a .38 Colt police special revolver; and because I think Chaco special—stone cold killer special—and I'm alone, being too cheap to buy short-term tickets for Cocoa and T-Rex, an abnormal tiny five shot .22 mag Wasp is strapped on my thigh in it's nylon holster, up high in the crotch. I'm also wearing a Kevlar vest under the shirt.

As promised the bail contract was in the basket below my fax. That was the good news upon arriving at my office, which is still smelling of fresh paint. The bad news is my decorator, Lance LeRoy, caught me there, and seemed to have forgotten that I'd saved him from a couple of homophobes a while back, and that he said he'd redecorate the office in appreciation. He presented me with a bill for six thousand dollars for the art work and upholstering. It's not that I'm unappreciative, but he seemed to think so when I advised him to remove same if it wasn't gratis, as promised.

He left in a prissy huff. And he'd earlier thought me so attractive.

I can see another lawsuit in the making.

I'm reading a not-so-good book, killing time while on this stake out, when I look up to see a shapely young lady, her gleaming black hair mostly covered with a scarf, her eyes behind sunglasses with lens's larger around than a Coke can, her legs appearing longer in five inch heels, exit the house and cross the Bermuda grass lawn to a old Dodge pickup that's been pimped out to fit into the neighborhood. Lowered, freshly painted in a forest green with yellow striping, a yellow and green tonneau cover over the bed, windows too dark to be legal, radical sixteen inch wheels; it looks right at home on this particular street. I can hear it fire up from two houses away, and know it's not only not stock, but has little in the way of mufflers. It rumbles past and I wait until she turns toward town then start the Chevy, pull into a driveway across the street, and back out and follow, careful to keep more than a block behind.

I'd probably be better served watching the house for a while, but I'm bored with both the stakeout and the book.

She only goes a couple of blocks after turning, and pulls up in front of a little market, *mercado* in this instance as the signs are mostly in Spanish, and jumps out and runs inside. I park four car lengths behind and climb out and walk up to follow her in, and what a surprise I have. Ronnell, a great ass that sunglasses can't hide, sans blonde hair—now I'm wondering if it's a wig—buying a case of Coors. She's pulled the sunglasses off which is the only reason I make her, and glances over with those striking blue eyes, catching me with a surprised look on my face which melts away almost instantly, but seemingly not quickly enough. I can see her flush and those beautiful eyes flare—one of them with the yellow of a recovering black eye beneath—but I go back to picking out my favorite variety of Jerky, and pay her no attention as she pays and quickly leaves. I do not follow, hoping she thinks her disguise worked. In addition to the black eye, she looks as if she's recovering from a split lip. The lady was on the wrong end of a beating not too long ago.

When I casually return to the car she and the pickup are long gone. I dial Espinoza, who doesn't answer and the phone goes to voice mail. I advise him. "I haven't made Chaco yet, but guess what beautiful blonde, now with raven black hair, is in residence...Ronny baby. I'm heading back to the subject address in a half hour and will be in my Joe Jenkin's Plumbing and HVAC van. Can you go in with your crew as she's at least a material witness? Call me, and get your ass over here."

If she saw me drive up thinking I might be tailing her, I can't return to the stakeout in my Chevy.

I return to the office and trade for the van, still decorated with the plumbing, heating and ventilating signs.

I make the mistake of jumping back on the freeway, which obviously has some problem up ahead. It takes me forty-five minutes to get back in position on Bregante Lane. My prior parking place is taken, and all street parking will soon be gone, as it's approaching five and the working stiffs who jam all the houses nearby will be coming home. Espinoza is nowhere in sight and has not returned my call. I have to park four houses away.

It's warm so I have the windows down, which is no excuse as I should be watching the house intently, not reading, so I shouldn't be surprised when I hear, "Hey, fuckhead, you come to fix the swamp cooler," and look over to see a very bad-ass looking tattooed Hispanic gentleman—a Mexican version of Mike Tyson—holding an ugly Desert Eagle semi-auto, with a caliber about the size of my thumb.

But I am.

I pride myself are being hard to sneak up on.

Or at least I used to.

Chapter Forty

I'm feeling pretty stupid at the moment, and am wondering if I'm faster than this ugly fuck's trigger finger.

Not likely.

As Chaco, who I recognize from his booking photos, cocks the exposed hammer on the mondo semi-auto, I'm wondering if I'll I have to take the chance to even think more about reaching for any one of the many weapons that decorate my body.

He's about to kill me, but will kill me reach or not.

"I'm getting in," he says, which solves my quandary for a moment and gives me some relief as I'm already planning my funeral. He opens the door and climbs into the bucket seat. "Drive over and pull in our driveway." He's a big guy, fatter than his booking photos look, but he slips in easily. Maybe it's not fat.

I give him a stupid grin, as hard as it is to muster, "I don't have time to stay for a visit. I got to get back to work. I just stopped here in the shade to read a while."

"Fuck you. Do it."

I fire it up and comply, not feeling like arguing with what looks to be a .50 caliber, which would likely blow me in half. The green pickup is parked on the front lawn, probably to leave room for others in the driveway. They'll be angry to find my big van hogging the spot. When I pull up in the tight driveway and stop, so close to the hedge on the driver's side that my door won't open, he demands, "Two finger the *pistola* out."

"What *pistola*?"

"You keep fuckin' with me and I'll blow your ass away right here in front of *mi tia's*."

"It's on my back. I gotta reach behind me. So, is your aunt home?"

"Reach, asshole, but reach easy. *Muy despacio*."

I think about reaching back with my left hand and trying a tricky-dick shot with my hand behind my back, but even if I center punch him with the 9mm he's likely to react with a trigger pull that puts my spine in splinters and the splinters will punch through the van door and land out in the flower bed.

So I reach with my right, work the Beretta loose, and hand it over, hanging from thumb and index finger. He shoves it in his belt.

"Now, let's see your skinny ankles," he says, eyeing me as if he's got one over on me, and he does.

"Hey, *gordo*, my ankles aren't skinny."

"Reach, *flaco*."

I work up a smile as I say, "I'll two finger that one also." I work the pants leg up and hand him the revolver, which he shoves in the pocket of his oversize cargo pants, which are only half-calf long. I'd call them shorts, but they're longer than shorts and shorter than pants, and ugly as hell.

"Be very careful, *amigo*," he says, his smile as tight as a snake's, and I comply. "You must be reading

Guns and Ammo," he says, with a small grin, actually showing yellow teeth.

He looks over his shoulder, studying the rear of the van, making sure there's nothing there that I could use as a weapon. "Climb to the back of the van," he orders, at the same time opening his own door and stepping out, giving me room to swing between the seats yet staying both in sight and out of my reach. "Then go to the back, quick, *muy pronto*, and I'll let you out."

I'm thinking about the Wasp on my thigh, but by the time I fish it out through my fly he'll be at the back door and have it open, and even if I can palm it, I don't relish a shoot out with a .22, even a .22 mag, against a .50. I could hit him three times before he knew he was hit, unless I hit him in the head. Bad odds.

He opens the doors but stands far enough back so I have no chance of going for him as I exit.

There's a side door into the house off the driveway, and he waves me on. I climb two steps and enter a kitchen, with him close behind. Ronnell is sitting at a two-person chrome-legged Formica topped table, her legs folded under her, an open can of Coors in hand. There are two small ½ pint Mason jars on the table, holes punched in top for salt and pepper. A tiny pot with a plastic daisy and a very small Mexican flag on an eight inch dowel separate the contrived salt and pepper shakers.

She gives me a stunning smile, and asks, "You wanna beer, Bulldog?"

"Have we met?" I ask with as charming a smile as I can work up.

"Don't think so, and I'd remember," she says, and I think there's a compliment in there somewhere. She adds, "But I've seen you around."

"So, how do you know my nickname?"

"Allen told me to watch out for you. Showed me a picture. And pointed you out one day when you were riding by."

I play stupid. "Allen...Allen who?"

"Poindexter. You know, the guy who you tried to blackmail."

"Hey, I'm one of the good guys. I go after the blackmailers."

Chaco growls, "Enough old times bullshit. Sit," he commands, pointing at the other kitchen chair.

I do. He turns to Ronny. "Come over here, baby, and hold this gun on this asshole while I tie him up."

"I'm afraid of that big gun," she says, nervously.

"Hold the fucking gun," he snaps.

She moves over and takes the Desert Eagle, having to hold it in both hands. It bobs up and down with her trying to control the weight. Chaco still has my Beretta in his belt.

"Be careful with that thing," I ask, then advise, "It goes off, it's likely to break both your wrists and blow a hole in me the size of this table."

"Shut the fuck up," Chaco says, as he grabs a kitchen butcher knife out of a wooden block with several and cuts the cord off the toaster.

"Your auntie is gonna be pissed about that," I say, but he pays little attention.

"Hands behind," he snaps, and I wrap them behind the chair while he works at wrapping and tying my wrists with the cord. He gives up and slides the tie up to my elbows, and somewhat painfully for me, sucks them up together. It's not my wrists, but it's effective as I'm all but hamstrung.

Chaco takes the firearm back from Ronny and shoves it in his belt.

"You're not gonna kill him, are you Chaco?" Ronny asks.

"Probably, *sustantivo*, but not yet. Get your stuff together. We gonna head for Mexico as soon as we get packed. We're made here. No telling who else knows."

"I told you I don't wanna go to Mexico," she says, her voice pleading.

He checks the load, then hands her the Beretta. "Watch him. Just point and pull if he gives you shit. I've got to go to the garage for some stuff to throw in the back of my beautiful little Chiquita."

"Chiquita?" I ask.

"My baby Dodge," he says.

I've always wondered about guys who name inanimate objects. This guy probably has an endearment for his dick. It's seems Ronny may also, to my astonishment.

He heads out the kitchen door, and Ronny leans against a counter and holds the Beretta casually, it's muzzle pointed at the floor, the beer in her other hand.

"So, how'd you get tied up with this dope dealing scumbag?" I ask.

She glances at the door nervously, and to my surprise, before she can answer, a five year old *muchacha,* eyes like flashing black obsidians, hair to the middle of her back, runs into the room. "Can I have a cookie, Aunt Ronny?" the little girl asks, then sees me and pulls up shyly.

"Sure, Maria," Ronny says and sits the Beretta down on the counter and removes the top of a fat Aunt Jemima cookie jar and hands the kid one. "*Leche*…milk, please?" the kid asks. Then she notices my arms strapped behind my back and the chair. "What are you playing, Aunt Ronny?"

Ronny ignores the question. "I forgot to get any milk, honey. Uncle Chaco will get you some later."

"In Mexico?" I ask.

"I ain't going to Mexico," Ronny says, as the kid skips out of the room.

"Chaco says you are. You'll like it there. Hot, bugs, nobody speaks English. No doctors. No drug stores or beauty shops." It's a lie, but it seems to be working.

So I add the coup d' grace. "Besides, they love blondes and it won't be long before Chaco is passing you around to his fat sweaty friends." Then I notice something.

"Where's the rock Poindexter gave you."

"Chaco traded it for a few kilos."

"And gave you the money, right?"

"No."

"Ronny, when are you gonna stop being a doormat for men?"

"I ain't no doormat. I handle my men just fine."

"Sure you do. Where's your ring, and how'd you get that black eye and split lip."

"None of your business."

"He's going to kill you or sell you when he tires of you, you know that don't you. You're not a stupid blonde are you? They sell blondes in Mexico."

I can see a flash of fear in her eyes, then she merely shrugs.

So I add, "The cops are on their way here. They find you with a gun on me and they'll hold you as an accessory to kidnapping."

"You ain't kidnapped."

"Oh, yeah. Holding someone against their will is kidnapping, and kidnapping's a capital crime. Kidnap and get the needle." She looks as if she doesn't believe me, then answers my first question.

"When Chaco and his buddy followed me because they couldn't find my old man, Barney, they came into Allen's house. Allen stood up to them and they stuck him in the tummy and shoved him over the cliff. Allen was a good guy...for a dork. He didn't even scream."

"So, you trotted out of there with them?" I'm a little incredulous.

"Chaco liked my looks, said that's the only reason I didn't go over the cliff with Allen...and said Barney owed him for a kilo. He said I had to go with him and twisted my arm when I wouldn't tell them where Barney was...so I told him Barney was due back at the house in an hour. I didn't want my arm broken." She pouts a lip out far enough for a buzzard to land thereon, then continues, "Barney came home and didn't have the money or the dope...and I guess you know what they did to Barney."

"And you didn't want that to happen to you?"

"No, it made me cry to watch."

"I should hope so," I say, again a little incredulous.

"And, doormat, Chaco gave you that black eye and split lip?"

"I ain't no doormat. But, yeah, Chaco did it. I wouldn't let him backdoor me...but he did anyway...you don't think this split lip will affect my looks do you?"

"Not this time, next time he beats you up it probably will."

"I didn't have anywhere else to go, and Chaco said I should go with him so he didn't have to kill me." She shrugs. "Easy choice for me."

"Well, you got another easy choice."

Chapter Forty-One

If I'm going to get out of here without being in a body bag, I've got to talk fast. I say again. "You've got another choice, you know. It's time you stopped being a doormat."

"What choice?" Ronny asks, almost innocently.

"Cut me loose and you'll be a hero to the cops. Hold that gun on me until Chaco gets back, and you'll do time at best, and maybe get a lethal injection as they'll figure you were in on your old man's murder and for sure on Poindexter's. After all, it was common knowledge you were dicking Poindexter—"

"I was not, he thought we had to wait until we were married, Barney told me not to do him as it would make him crazy to marry me…and besides, all that was Barney's idea."

Jesus, Poindexter died for this broad without getting a taste.

I don't let her catch a breath, "And what they did to Barney…some of those prison dike sluts will do worse to you, while you're waiting for the needle. You don't like being backdoored? You won't have an orifice that won't be reamed out, and they may cut you some new ones just to watch you squirm."

I'm getting to her as her eyes are filling with tears.

"I don't hear no sirens," she says, still a little adamant.

"You think they'll come after a stone cold killer like Chaco and let him know they're coming. SWAT is probably circling the place right now with those big ugly shotguns, and they'll shoot anything that moves."

About that time, propitiously, a helicopter flies low enough over the house that you can almost feel the beat of the rotors.

"See," I say, glancing up. "There's the cops now."

"Jeeze," she says, glancing up, as a couple of tears track her cheeks, then she eyes me fearfully. "I can't untie that cord."

"Then grab a butcher knife and cut it, quick." As much as I dislike Laukenbach, and as much as I'm lying about the cops circling the house, I'm hoping to see his ugly face crashing through the front door, but Espinoza still has not returned my call.

She's sawing away with one hand, the Beretta hanging loosely in the other, when Chaco hits the steps at a run, and bursts into the house.

"Get out…." he starts to say, "the cops" but only mouths it as he realizes what Ronny is doing. "You bitch," he says, and comes for her at the same time he's reaching for the big automatic shoved in his belt with one hand, and reaching back with an open hand as if he's going to slap her into next week with the other.

"No, Chaco. No," she screams. The Beretta snaps up and fires and Chaco's eyes widen as he gets to her, stumbles, then brings both big hands to her throat, but her semi-automatic keeps firing as quickly as she can pull the trigger, some hitting the big man, some smashing into cabinets and ricocheting around the little kitchen, even as Chaco loosens his grip and sinks to his knees, blood flowing from his open mouth, then he hits the floor.

She's firing, I'm ducking as best I can, feeling one ricochet tear across my side, and fighting the cord and it's loosening, and finally falls away just as Chaco flops to his back. But he's got the Desert Eagle in hand, trying to raise it.

I hear the Beretta click, having shot the last of the clip.

She screams as he manages to level the cannon on her, then the .50 cal roars, spitting flame half way across the room, and Ronny flies out through the door the child had exited from, blown off her feet, crashing to her back, into what appears to be the living room.

The Desert Eagle slips out of Chaco's hand just as I gain my freedom and leap up and kick it away, but unnecessarily, as the big man's eyes are glazing over. She's hit him three times in the chest and once in the belly, but the gushing blood is stopping from wounds and mouth as his heart has ceased pumping.

It's suddenly deadly silent, with dust motes floating around the kitchen, wafting slowly, catching the reflection of the late sun through the kitchen window—a window now with a spider web hole from a stray 9mm.

I check my side which is stinging like hell, and see that a shot has torn my shirt and creased the Kevlar before burying itself harmlessly in a lower kitchen cabinet, it's a malformed ricochet and I can pluck it out with my fingers, which I do, shoving it in a pocket. I turn to the doorway in the sudden silence.

The Sear's Craftsman has stopped reverberating from the dozen reports of gunfire, and the silence is deafening until I finally hear the tiny voice of little girl in the other room. The sweet sound of the little girl is almost surreal after the shocking trip-hammer of gunfire and stench of powder.

"Aunt Ronny, you've got a big oowey. ...Aunt Ronny?"

But Aunt Ronny doesn't answer.

I hear more footsteps on the porch outside the kitchen door, and am about to go for the Desert Eagle, when I see Espinoza glance in the window, then duck back.

"Come on in," I yell. "Fun's over."

He slowly opens the door, then steps in, his Glock in hand, but hanging loosely at his side. "Damn if the stone cold killer ain't stone cold killed."

"You're late," I say.

"And it looks like we'll be late to the Café del Sol as we got a mess to clean up here." He's smiling widely.

"What's that we? This time I didn't fire a shot."

"You gettin' slow in your old age?" he asks.

I don't bother to reply to that.

Laukenbach appears on the back porch, peeks in, then opens the door and wanders in.

"Hell, Braddock, for a minute there I thought maybe you were shot."

"Hell, Harold, sorry to disappoint."

"Didn't mean it that way. ...I'm buying tonight."

"Check the rest of the house," Espinoza instructs his partner.

"Works for me," I say, as Laukenbach disappears into the living room, then down a hallway, but I'm not smiling. I honest to God think he was hoping the body on the floor was mine. I stretch and yawn, trying to throw off the lingering adrenalin. "But I've got a few things to do first."

Walking to the door separating kitchen from living room, I see that the little girl, hands behind her as if she's in parade rest, standing quietly. She's staring down, wide eyed and without understanding, at the young woman who she's come to know as Aunt Ronny. Aunt Ronny is staring back, but not blinking or twitching, and the relatively small hole in the center of her chest belies the gore blown over much of the floor around her from what must be a fist sized exit wound.

Walking over slowly as to not startle the child, I extend my arms and she almost leaps into them. With her cradled in my left arm, I open the front door and exit to the porch, where there's a canvas covered swinging love seat. I snuggle into the cushion and begin to swing gently, the squeek of springs keeping time...she immediately shoves a thumb in her mouth.

"What's your name, sweetheart?"

"Emolina," she says without looking up.

"Where's your mama, Emolina?"

"I like Emmy better."

"So, Emmy, where's mommy?"

"Mommy and my two aunties and my uncles are working. Mommy will be home when it gets dark. My brothers and cousins and grandma will too. Grammy will bring me an ice cream to have after supper." She looks up at me for the first time. "I saw Uncle Chaco and he had lots of bleeds. Grandma told him he should be working or something bad would happen."

"Yes, he does have lots of bleeds. Grandmas are really smart and you should listen to them. Your mama or grandma will explain all of it to you when they get home. Is it okay if I rock you for awhile?"

"I like it."

"Me too, it's peaceful," I say, and I'm not lying. I could go to sleep in a heartbeat, and speaking of heartbeats, I'm thrilled mine is still pounding away.

Chapter Forty-Two

It wasn't two but three lawsuits, as I'm served with another a week after the big shoot out at Chaco's aunt's house. I take a little teasing from around town as Laukenbach has reported that some hundred pound blonde had me tied up and that he and Espinoza had to save me…whatever.

I finally get around to calling Harrison Bull and make an appointment to come in. Jo Jo Bling has sued me and the company for a cool million on some trumped up B.S. that it was my fault, and Quiet Op's fault, that he got shot. Harrison assures me that we will prevail, and in fact will get it dismissed with some kind of motion…shouldn't be more than ten grand in fees. Which, coincidentally, is the amount of my deductible on my major liability policy, which has even more exclusions than my health insurance. Why I pay for any of it is beyond comprehension.

My office neighbor in the suite below has sued me for business interruption and water damage due to the fire. He's a guy I've bought two dozen drinks for over the last couple of years—and, of course, the last damn drink he'll ever see from me—as he, too, hangs at Café del Sol. He says he has to do the dirty deed and that it's not his fault, it's his insurance company insisting. I don't know how I could have had the fire in my office and gotten away with twenty grand in repairs, and he and his insurance company claim seventy-five thousand. Harrison actually laughs this one off as it turns out both the insurance agent and I are insured by the same company. He says they'll love negotiating with themselves, but the right hand doesn't know what the left hand is doing.

The third lawsuit is for ten grand, the max in small claims court. I guess my decorator, Lance LeRoy, is no longer enamored with my Greek god bod. I hope another pair of homophobes want to slap him around so I can applaud...not really, but I will make him sign a liability waiver before I kick their butts, and it's likely that he'll catch an elbow in the subsequent melee. The decorator needs his nose redecorated.

By the time T-Rex gets back to town, I've made a firm appointment with Kenny MacMann and gotten two more contracts for skips, so we've got plenty to do.

I'm surprised when Cocoa walks into the office, wearing the only size eight and a quarter pork pie hat in existence, close behind Rex. Which means Cocoa must have paid for his own flight, as I didn't. An ominous beginning.

"Got to talk to you," Cocoa says.

"Shoot."

"I got a job offer and I'm gonna take it. It ain't cause I don't love you guys."

I'm disappointed, but I extend my hand and shake with him. "I'm never one to tell a guy he shouldn't move onward and upward."

"Jo Jo Bling. He say it's the least we can do since we got all his bodyguards shot up."

"And I don't guess Chandra had anything to do with this decision?"

Cocoa smiles, as only a big black Somoan can smile, and nods. "You got me. Chandra...and a hundred grand a year."

"You sure you wanna get involved with how he makes his money?"

"He's sworn off the side deals. Says he is on the straight and narrow and into nothing but music."

"I hope so, for your sake and his. And for the world's."

"And Chandra's. He promised Chandra, and she promised me."

"You know you're always welcome at our fire, should you get slimed by Jo Jo, which is likely. You know I don't think much of the boy."

"He's changed...but thanks. I'll remember."

"Do me one favor?"

"You know it."

"Tell him he owes me twenty large for the fire. I won't forget it. In fact it may be ninety five large, should I lose the lawsuit filed by our neighbors below."

"I'll do it."

I take both Rex and Cocoa to supper at Café del Sol, and guess who walks in, looking like a million bucks. She eyes me and strides over.

"You were going to call me back. It's been over a week."

"I was waiting to save up enough money to take you to the The Stonehouse at San Ysidro Ranch for supper. High class ladies deserve the very best."

"Date five, or are you all talk?"

"Do I look like a guy who's been busting his butt so hard for a month that he hasn't had time to get...to romance a lady...and is all talk?" I don't tell her that I've been waking up every morning with one so hard the cat can't scratch it. I'm afraid to pull it down because if I lose my grip it'll hit me so hard in the belly it'll knock my breath out.

"Nope," she says, and gives me a knowing smile. "You don't look like that guy. If you haven't saved enough I'll stake you to a few bucks until next payday."

"Actually, my ship just came in"

"Your car or mine, sailor?"

I turn to Cocoa and Rex. "Sorry boys, you're on your own."

Afterward

It seems we're getting into the big leagues.

Special Agent in Charge Clete Robertson made the biggest dope bust in Florida in the last year, as it seems the gun safes were only a small part of the haul. There was a basement below the lab with several hundred kilos of blow, Mexican brown, and a million OxyContin pills—probably counterfeit, but that's illegal as well. He called me, chewed my ass for leaving the state, then said he would buy dinner if he ever got in our neck of the woods. Shortly thereafter, Special Agent in Charge in Santa Barbara, Sam Sanchez, called at Robertson's suggestion, and wants to sit with us...and is maybe willing to shove a little biz our way. I will have to return to Florida for Hog's trial, unless he pleads out which is likely in today's trade away courts.

They never did catch up with Fredo, the skinny Hispanic who guided us to the houseboat, or the other Albrech employee who took his leave from the boat thanks to my quick linebacker move...he may well be gator munchies. But he's probably sipping a mojica in the Bahamas with Fredo.

All police agencies either love or hate, but are envious of, the Supreme Court's 1873 *Taylor v. Taintor* decision, and many are getting as smart as Espinoza. The case established the legality of a bounty hunter entering, even on Sunday, the abode of a skip for any re-arrest, without a search warrant; a step far beyond normal police power. Power pays...as well as corrupts.

Chaco, too, had a substantial stash of dope, and was major bust for Espinoza and Laukenbach and for Santa Barbara, not to speak of the donut duo solving a very prominent murder.

The good news is we've gained some law enforcement friends. Always important in our business.

I do get a smile, as I get to see Jo Jo Bling again...but that isn't the motivation for the smile. I've received a wedding invitation to see Cocoa and Chandra get hitched at Duke's in Malibu, entertainment by Jo Jo Bling and the Homey's. Wow...T-Rex will love it. Not the shortest engagement on record, but a fast merging of the mountains. I have high hopes for them.

The bad news, Chaco's gang, the Mission Hombres, have put out a contract on me.

So, somebody wants to kill me.

So...what the fuck's new?

Look for other exciting bounty hunter
books from

Bob Burton

&

L. J. Martin

Crimson Hit
Bullet Blues

Both available on Amazon
& other fine booksellers